TROLL

TROLL

A Novel

LOGAN MACNAIR

|N₁|O₂|N₁

CANADA

Library and Archives Canada Cataloguing in Publication

Title: Troll : a novel / Logan Macnair.

Names: Macnair, Logan, 1989- author.

Identifiers: Canadiana (print) 20220482101 | Canadiana (ebook) 2022048211X |
ISBN 9781989689479 (softcover) | ISBN 9781989689516 (EPUB)

Classification: LCC PS8625.N335 T76 2023 | DDC C813/.6—dc23

Printed and bound in Canada on 100% recycled paper.

Now Or Never Publishing
901, 163 Street
Surrey, British Columbia
Canada V4A 9T8

nonpublishing.com
Fighting Words.

We gratefully acknowledge the support of the Canada Council for the Arts
and the British Columbia Arts Council for our publishing program.

For my Beloved XXXXXXX,

You cannot sleep beside me.
Though sure as morning comes I will sustain you.
Ere we meet the future, brutal and terrific and peakless,
falteringly we draw breath here sacred and shared.

"The Internet could be a very positive step towards education, organisation, and participation in a meaningful society."

—Noam Chomsky,
Professor Emeritus, Massachusetts Institute of Technology

"Positive energy knows no boundaries. If everyone were to spread positive energy on the Internet, the world would be a much better place."

—Lu Wei,
former head of the Cyberspace Administration of China

"If Hitler had won we wouldn't have to put up with this degenerate bullshit. Kill yourself loser."

—Anonymous YouTube user

"You're on in one hour Peter."

"Thanks Lisa. How's it looking out there?"

"They're just opening the doors now. Will be a full house for sure, standing room only most likely."

"And outside?"

"About fifty protestors or so. Maybe more. It's loud out there. No incidents though, security isn't taking any chances."

"And the live stream is all good to go? No issues?"

"It's live right now with about a thousand people watching the empty stage and more trickling in, but I was thinking it might be a good idea to record one last quick promo to generate some last-minute buzz."

"Yeah, I guess. How long you think?"

"Thirty seconds or so should do it."

"Fine. Got your phone?"

"I got it. Ready?"

"I'm ready."

"Go."

"This is Petrol Riley coming at you live, direct from the belly of the beast to burn away the ignorance that grows inside these walls and to shed a little light on some universal truths for anyone out there that is still living in denial. The truth is that there is a war going on in this country right now. A war against rationality, logic, and common sense. There is an ongoing plot by the globalists and the academic elite, many of whom congregate in universities just like this one, to erase us and to erase our glorious culture. They want to demonize us and the Western values that created the greatest civilization history has ever known.

Yes, friends, there is a war going on. A war against White men everywhere. But believe me, they won't get away with this. Because we aren't going to let them. They can try to silence us. They can try to kill our free speech. They can try to poison the minds of our youth with their propaganda and their false rhetoric about the values of diversity and acceptance, but we have the strongest weapon on our side to fight them. We have the truth on our side. So join me in one hour, and we'll give these snakes a lesson that they won't ever forget!"

JANUARY 16, 2019
ONLINE ARTICLE BY ALISA TENNANT, VANCOUVER HERALD

The Angriest Man on the Internet: Who is Peter Riley?
Alisa Tennant

Peter Riley, better known by the moniker 'Petrol', may simultaneously be the most loved and loathed online personality currently producing content. But how did this 24-year-old British Columbian rise from obscurity to become one of the Internet's most popular and controversial figures in just over two years' time?

His detractors see him as little more than a hatemonger responsible for spreading messages of racism, misogyny, xenophobia—and nearly every other form of discrimination imaginable—to a growing fanbase of primarily young and impressionable men. He has been listed as a potential threat by several prominent hate-watch groups for inciting violence, and several social media companies have banned Riley from their platforms outright, most recently Twitter, where his now deactivated account had amassed nearly one million followers.

The decisions by many of these companies to treat Riley as a legitimate security threat rather than just another angry man spewing hatred on the Internet have largely come following several recent incidents in which Riley has been accused of acting as a catalyst for real-world violence. In October of last year during one of Riley's notorious 'lectures' at Tufts University, under-graduate student Chris Fuller was shot and left permanently paralyzed outside the venue by one of Riley's supporters. Fuller was one of about 40 TU students who were protesting the event and the university's decision to grant Riley an open platform to speak. Just over a month later Riley was namechecked in the online manifesto of London mosque gunman Nathan Myles. In the wake of these events several (though not all) universities have cancelled their scheduled Riley lectures.

Still, the banning of Riley by certain venues and social media platforms has not stopped his online presence from growing at a steady and troubling rate. His YouTube channel (which, despite the repeated calls of many, has not been banned) recently reached the one million subscriber milestone. He earns a comfortable living from the thousands of fans who sponsor him with monthly financial contributions on Backr, and the stops of his university lecture tours have routinely sold out. When considering the speed with which Riley has reached these figures, his growth and current success as a 'social realist' (the label he uses to describe himself) are undeniable.

But why has Riley's message resonated with so many? For his more casual fans and defenders Riley is seen as one of the last protectors of free speech in a society where the perceived influences of censorship and political correctness have begun restricting what can and cannot be said on the Internet and else-where. For his more dedicated and ideological-minded followers Riley is seen as a leading figure in the burgeoning White supremacy movement that, after brewing and festering in online spaces for many years, has recently become a much more vocal and visible offline collective. Among the many 'goals for the future' listed on his website, Riley endeavours to create a culture where, 'White people can once again flourish without the fear of being held down by degenerates, inferiors, or social leeches.'

Riley's vision and the unabashed manner with which he expresses it, while troubling to many, has been readily accepted by a rapidly growing online community. His fans congregate on a variety of online spaces, most notably on the forum /rr/, or

'Riley Rally' located on the notoriously problematic and largely unmoderated discussion board website Helena's Hole. Users of this forum have been accused of targeting—both online and offline—anyone who attempts to censor or speak out against Riley, including most recently media studies professor and frequent critic of Riley, Sierra Lox, who has been the victim of a particularly intense harassment campaign spearheaded by the anonymous users of /rr/. While Riley has not explicitly condoned the actions of his followers, he has also made no attempt to publicly condemn their behaviour.

It remains to be seen what will become of the empire that Petrol has built. Online celebrity is a fickle and tumultuous thing—the biggest names of today can just as quickly be forgotten by tomorrow. With increasing public pressure on the websites and platforms that host Riley's hateful content, it is possible that some may follow the example of Twitter and others and ban Riley outright. But is this a real solution or just a temporary fix? Riley preys on very specific fears that have been around for a long time. As long as people have a mistrust of the other, or a hatred for people that don't look like, think like, or believe in the same things that they do, Riley will have an audience.

Peter Riley isn't creating hatred and chaos—he's merely channeling it. And this he does exceptionally well.

MAY 27, 2019
THE CONFESSION OF PETER 'PETROL' RILEY: PROLOGUE

The moment that I knew things might have gone too far was when that man was shot outside one of my talks about eight months ago. Up to that point no one had gotten hurt, or at least not hurt like that. No one that I knew of at least. That man survived, but the bullet pierced his spine and now they say he will be in a wheelchair for the rest of his life. There was a GoFundMe page set up to help cover his ongoing medical expenses and I anonymously donated $10,000 because that felt like it was the right and kind thing to do.

But I'm getting ahead of myself here. The point of this blog or this confession or whatever it is, is to try and explain how things got so far in the first place. I don't know why else I'm writing this. I guess there's just some things I don't want to keep in anymore. Maybe no one will ever see this. Maybe I'm just writing it for myself. Kind of a liberating thought actually.

The truth is, I've been scared and nervous for a while now. I'm scheduled to deliver a sold-out talk at Diefenbaker University in a little over a week and this will be the first time that I've been back there since graduating three years ago. Now that I mention it, I suppose my time at DU might the best place to start this story. That's where I got my first taste of fame and of the things to come. That's where Petrol was born. It was also the last time that I got to live without the weight that this character has burdened me with.

And make no mistake, Petrol is exactly that—a character. A terrible and grotesque character that I have the unfortunate ability to portray in a way that is unquestioningly realistic.

And I hate him.

I really do hate him. But his story needs to be told, even if it is just for me. The story of how this vile character brought me the admiration and fame that I thought I wanted for my entire life. The story of where he came from and why I now fear that I'll never be able to get rid of him. At the very least this will be something to distract myself with in the days leading up to my return to DU, but hopefully it can be more than that. I know this won't exonerate me and I don't know much about repentance, but it has to be worth a shot.

I guess if anyone other than me is reading this, it probably means that Petrol has been exposed and the world is undoubtedly a better place because of it. I'm not looking for sympathy, I know I'm the bad guy in this story. I just want to show how this all happened so that maybe there can be a bigger lesson to be learned from it all.

Ready then?

EDIT—At the beginning of this entry I said 'that man' was shot. That man's name is Chris Fuller. He was a university student at the time and by all accounts a well-liked and compassionate person. He is not anonymous and faceless. He is a real person. If I'm doing this confession thing, I had better do it for real.

And I didn't help cover his medical expenses out of the kindness of my heart.

I did it because I might as well have pulled the trigger myself.

MAY 28, 2019
THE CONFESSION OF PETER 'PETROL' RILEY: PART I

I was born in 1994 which apparently places me in the tail end for inclusion into what they call the 'Millennial' generation. It's nebulously defined, but from what I can tell the characteristics of my generational cohort mostly revolve around things like technological prowess and exposure to the Internet from an early age. This much is true I suppose. I've heard people say that my generation is self-absorbed or that we desire attention and fame over nobler pursuits, whatever those are. I can't speak for everyone, but for me this was also true. But before I became a content creator and online celebrity in my own right, I was a content consumer the same as anyone else.

I was eleven years old when I discovered Liam 'Limez' González's channel on YouTube. Although 'discovered' is maybe the wrong word here—every kid was exposed to Limez at some point whether they were looking to find him or not. He was still a teenager at the time, just a few years older than me, but his channel had already started to become one of the most popular on the entire platform. What's important to understand is that these were still the early days of YouTube. Nobody was really sure what the platform was supposed to be. What the platform *could* be. Maybe it was just a matter of being in the right place at the right time, but Limez tapped into something back then. He found a way to create content that entertained and resonated with young people in ways that no other forms of media really had or could. Today he has over one hundred million subscribers, more than anyone else on the history of the platform.

I saw him in person for the first time last year. Guy's a massive prick.

Still, back then he was important to me. I didn't idolize him or look up to him as some sort of hero or role model, instead he felt like a friend, like someone I knew intimately despite never having met. He offered us a raw and uncensored view into his life and it felt like we were experiencing it alongside him. I don't know, it's hard to explain and I guess if you're over a certain age you might not be able to understand anyway. The point is that I was hooked on his videos and, like many others, was inspired by him to try making videos of my own. And, like many others, mine were complete shit. Real cringe. As we entered middle school me and a few friends would film our exploits, our pranks, our general antics, and though our videos were never really seen by anyone outside our immediate circles, we did have fun making them.

Throughout high school I continued making amateurish videos, still under the delusion that my channel might one day blow up and I too could live the life of a professional YouTuber. In my quest for content, I developed a reputation as a bit of a troublemaker. Never really serious trouble—I was once given a three-day suspension for streaking at a track and field meet to celebrate reaching one hundred subscribers—but other than that I was viewed by my teachers as a minor and occasionally disruptive annoyance at worst.

As a student I was a bit of an underachiever. Assessments of my in-class performance were always something along the lines of 'could do better but doesn't.' I never tried especially hard to do well in my classes, partially because I would rather spend that time filming videos or thinking of new ideas, but mostly because I never thought I would ever bother going to college or university after graduating, so there didn't seem like much point.

My attitude toward school changed when in the tenth grade I took an acting class with Mrs. Perrault. I only took the class because I figured it would be an easy write-off elective, but it soon became the thing that I looked forward to the most each day. I don't know if it was the people, or Mrs. Perrault, or the creative freedom she gave us, but I ended up feeling inspired in that class in a way that I hadn't with any other. Looking back now I can see why that class was exactly what I needed at the time. I think I've always had a desire for attention to some extent, and this class gave me the opportunity to channel that desire in a more prosocial and acceptable way. And, as it turns out, I happened to be pretty good at the whole acting thing, particularly when it came to mimicry. 'A real natural,' as Mrs. Perrault would often tell me.

It was around this time that I finally accepted that 'YouTube star' was not a realistic or even a desirable future for me. During my last two years of high school I stopped making videos altogether and began focusing more on my acting classes and on the craft of acting in general. It sounds a little pretentious to admit it now, but at the time I felt like acting was a more refined and respectable version of what I was doing previously. Devoting myself to acting meant that I didn't have to give up my aspirations of fame, and I could instead develop a more direct and tangible skillset that I could use to eventually reach this goal. I became convinced that I wanted to be and *needed* to be an actor. This was to be my road to eventual fame, and I poured myself into it fully and completely. I appeared in school drama productions, I auditioned for extracurricular projects, I took on anything that would give me experience or exposure.

During my final year of high school I appeared as the lead actor in a play that was written, directed, and produced entirely by my classmates under the supervision of Mrs. Perrault. We performed this play—a dramedy entitled *Shook!*—first for our school, then at our regional competition where we won the grand prize and were invited to perform, along with the other regional winners, at the British Columbia provincial championships in Victoria. I had never been more nervous in my entire life than I was for that performance. While we performed well, our play didn't end up winning and so we weren't given the chance to attend the national competition, but I did receive the award for the best lead actor of the entire competition, an accolade that solidified my desire to pursue acting as a serious profession.

I graduated high school in 2012 and began applying to colleges, universities, and performing arts schools that had well-established drama programs. Though my grades in my non-acting classes were not especially impressive, my acting experience, accolades, and a very generously written letter of recommendation from Mrs. Perrault eventually landed me an offer of acceptance from the Department of Theatre and Performance Studies at Diefenbaker University in Toronto— the top drama program in the country. A few months later I packed some bags, hugged my parents, flew across the country, found my dorm room, and in September of 2012 I began my drama studies at DU.

It was during my time as a student of DU that Petrol was born. And that's really what you want to hear about isn't it? I don't know why I bothered telling you all this other background information, but it felt strangely good for me to write it. Nostalgia for a simpler time maybe, I don't know. Back then I tended to see everything in black and white. Back then there were only two different paths to follow, one leading to fame and recognition, and the other to defeat and obscurity. I knew which of these lives I wanted.

I just had no idea what it would cost.

NOVEMBER 7, 2017
PINNED THREAD ON THE /RR/ FORUM

Claymore88 (341287) MODERATOR
Posted 11/07/2017 (1:49am)

If you are here it's because you have been lying awake at night asking yourself the same questions that we all have. You've spent too many nights drowning in useless vices—video games, drugs, porn, aimless online browsing—and you're finding these things have left you feeling unsatisfied and unfulfilled. You aren't working toward the greatness that came before you. You aren't building empires, you aren't carving statues, you aren't writing impassioned philippics against the degeneracy that you have started to notice around you. Your body is soft, it isn't combat-ready. Your mind isn't sharp, you aren't learning or studying or challenging yourself to become a better or more intelligent man, instead you're letting your brain rot on the mass-media pabulum that your cultural overlords provide.

And now you've been lying awake at night asking yourself where your place in society is—or whether you still even have one at all. This thought process then gives way to nihilism. You see the values that once made our culture so great starting to erode under the new false Gods of diversity, multicultural-ism, and sexual deviancy, and now you're just praying for an earthquake to swallow everything, you're praying for the nuclear bombs to finally go off so they can just wipe everything away and reset humanity. We understand this desire, for we have all held it as well. It is easy to look around and see all the good things slipping away. It is easy to give in and embrace the void.

But it only seems this easy because this is exactly what they want you to do. They want the future to appear hopeless—an unstoppable inevitability—but the truth is that this is simply a narrative and nothing more. Within you lies the power to fight against this change and to assert yourself as the greatness that you were born to be. If you are here, and if you are watching Petrol's videos, you have already taken an important first step. Opening your eyes to the truth is the beginning to a path of fulfillment, meaning, and victory. We can save our people and our culture, and it is imperative that we start doing everything in our power to do so.

These ten guidelines are designed to ensure that you stop liv-ing a useless existence in exchange for a life of purpose, clarity, and direction.

1. Never accept the philosophies of fatalism, defeatism, or nihilism. The survival of our people is reliant upon your ability to not give up, even against seemingly impossible odds. Your

ancestors survived and persevered so that you could be here today—you owe it to the future generations to do the same.

2. Stop watching porn. The majority of porn is degenerate filth designed to either normalize homosexuality and transgenderism or to push interracial relationships that devalue and denigrate White women.

3. Know your enemy. Study the tricks and tactics of the left and learn how to counter them. Memorize statistics on immigration, crime rates, etc., so should you ever get into a debate with these people, you will be able to crush them and influence anyone who is watching to our position. Humiliate these people both online and offline so that they are never taken seriously by anyone. The facts are on your side.

4. Start hitting the gym and getting in shape. When push comes to shove, when you are being physically assaulted by the deluded defenders of globalism, or should the race war ever come to be, you need to be physically ready to defend yourself and your family. Hit the weights, take some basic self-defence classes, and get your body combat-ready.

5. If you haven't already, find yourself a good, traditional White woman to start a relationship with. Find a woman that is happy to fulfill a traditional household role, and not one that has been poisoned by the ideologies of feminism and postmodernism. Not only will this make her much happier, but it will help create a healthy home for you to one day raise a family. Which brings us to...

6. Have as many White babies as you are able to afford. The ideologies of feminism and multiculturalism have convinced White women to have less children or to have mixed race children. Do not support this. Avoid the pitfalls of modern consumerism in order to save more money for raising children. NEVER have children that will be mixed-race or that will otherwise dilute the bloodline.

7. Purchase a firearm if you don't already have one and learn how to operate it effectively. Teach your family basic gun safety. If you or the lives of your family are ever threatened, a firearm might be the difference between life and death. Never vote for

or support politicians that want to impose stricter gun control in any fashion.

8. Raise your children properly. The future of our people, and of all humanity, depends on the climate that children grow up in. Children raised in degenerate environments will become degenerates themselves. Teach your boys to be men and raise your girls to be ladies. Don't let your children consume gratuitous amounts of globalist media.

9. Vote for nationalist candidates that will seek to advance and protect the interests of the White race. In politics, it is often difficult for candidates to openly admit that they share our values since the media will simply boycott them but use your best judgement to see who is really working for you and who is simply under the globalist umbrella. If there are no suitable candidates in your local elections, consider running yourself if you have the time and means.

10. Boycott left-wing, globalist companies and the Jewish-controlled media. This is easier said than done since the Jews control nearly everything that you watch or read in the mainstream media, but there is still good content out there made by and for White men. You watch Petrol, so you have already found some of it.

These are guidelines that you may follow to pursue a path of victory. Always remember that you are responsible for your own actions. Defeatism is a choice, just like the decision to fight back is a choice.

Remember what Petrol said—"the White race created everything that is good in modern Western society, and now they are the only people left who can save it."

MARCH 2, 2016
ASSIGNMENT OUTLINE FROM THEATRE 401,
DIEFENBAKER UNIVERSITY

Assignment Background

The nature of dramatic performance, especially in the medium of film, is being influenced by the drastic rise in the popularity of video-sharing platforms such as YouTube. To be 'successful', videos produced for YouTube, and the performances contained within them, must cater to the unique circumstances of this relatively young medium. In this assignment you will be creating and performing in your own 'YouTube style' video.

Assignment Details

—Your video should be no longer than three minutes in length.

—You may perform as 'yourself' or as an original character.

—Your video and performance must emulate the style of those that are popular on YouTube. Formats such as vlogs, tutorials, reviews, and newscasts are encouraged.

—You may enlist the help of others to write your script or to aid with the filming/editing process, but you must be the sole performer in the video.

—You will be graded exclusively on your performance and not on the technical aspects of the video itself, so don't worry if you don't have much proficiency with this medium.

—Be sure to watch popular and trending videos for inspiration and ideas.

—Please include a transcript or a script of your performance for my reference.

—You may upload your videos to YouTube and provide me with a link, or you may send the video file to me directly, but either way please do so before March 16. We will watch all the videos together during class on the following day.

—And finally, have fun with this assignment! It will not be worth a huge chunk of your grade, but it will give you a chance to try something that's a little different from what we've been doing, so feel free to get creative and a little silly with it. I'm looking forward to seeing what you come up with!

As always, feel free to reach out if you have any questions, Josh Garrison (jgarrison@du.ca)

NOVEMBER 1, 2015
'GRADE YOUR PROFESSOR' ENTRY FOR JOSHUA GARRISON

Joshua Garrison, Assistant Professor
Diefenbaker   University—Department of   Theatre   and
Performance Studies
Overall Grade—92%

—Josh is one of the most passionate and engaging profs I've ever had. He cares deeply about the success of his students and will go out of his way to encourage them. Also happens to be very easy on the eyes :)

—Josh is a great instructor, but very intense. Avoid his classes if you can't handle brutally honest criticism about your work and performances but take him if you want to be genuinely challenged and actually improve as an actor.

—Arrogant, condescending, and quick to play favourites. If you aren't one of the handful of students that he chooses seemingly at random to be in his little clique, then be prepared for a tough semester where nothing you do will ever be good enough.

—One of best there is, Josh is a real gem. Has a real passion for theatre that is infectious. Pushes students hard, but only because he wants to see them reach their full potential. Would highly recommend for anyone who is serious about developing their skills as an actor.

This comment has been flagged and is pending moderation:

—Josh is young, charismatic, and good-looking (and he knows it). There were rumors going around that he was hooking up with some of the girls in the class which, if true, is highly inappropriate. A decent teacher but expect to be hit on or propositioned if you are a woman.

NO DATE
s a t i s f i e d c u s t o m e r

Look pal. I don't know when irony died, or when it was set loose, or when we pulled it over our eyes so snug that we forgot we left it there. What I do know is that it is possible to glitch yourself through the entire original *Super Mario Bros.* in less than five minutes and I've seen it done. That game came out way before I was born and I never played it myself but I still listen to remixes of the soundtrack and it reminds me of childhood memories that I don't think I ever had. Some egghead tried to explain it to me as a 'subject of desire', but I tuned right out on that nonsense. It's like when they came out with Vanilla Coke and I only got to enjoy it for like a week before someone said something about connections to Colombian death squads. I mean, I kept drinking it, but I just don't know what that guy had to gain by pointing that out to me. One time in class I made some joke about 9/11 and the teacher heard it and he sent me to the principal and I had to listen to her go on for like twenty minutes about how there are some things you just don't joke about and how I was too young to really understand what that day meant. My mom has a box in the closet with all her old records in it. I think I might have recognized some of the covers from somewhere. I saw a bunch of memes with characters from *Seinfeld* which apparently is supposed to be like the funniest show ever, so I downloaded the whole series but I honestly had to stop watching after two episodes because the fake laugh track took me right out of it. Sending you a video recommendation, 'Take a Bite Out of a Raw Onion Every Day Until a New *Shrek* Movie is Released—Day 14.' The other day I was walking downtown and there was this group of I guess university students with a bunch of signs and shit and they were yelling something about how there are too many billionaires or something and honest to God it was so cringe so I filmed it but Snapchat wouldn't upload it for some reason so I didn't get to show it to anyone and I couldn't even really tell anyone because who would really care without the video. Ashley was texting me last night and she was going on and on about how her parents are probably going to get divorced or whatever and she wanted me to say something and I swear I searched for the perfect GIF for like ten minutes but I couldn't find it and so I just said nothing. I've been ordering a bunch of stuff from Amazon and I get super excited when the packages show up but lately I feel weird like two minutes after opening them. Like sad, I guess. Plastic figurines of superheroes and video game characters and they sell for ten bucks a pop and I don't even really want them anymore but I ordered three of them today because I felt like I deserved it. I got Marty McFly, even though I haven't actually seen that movie, and I got Master Chief and I got Spider-Man. Have you heard of this website that has like pictures and videos of actual dead people that have died in messed up ways? I'll send you a link, one sec. I haven't told anyone this because it sounds super cringe but sometimes when I'm alone at night and there's that brief silence in between videos something comes over me and I just feel like crying. Sometimes I do. Maybe someone would listen if I told them, but who cares. I wouldn't mind feeling so sad if I knew how to meme it better. Honestly, I think that's probably why I get so sad in the first place.

SEPTEMBER 8, 2015
OPENING LECTURE FOR COMMUNICATIONS 317,
NORTHWESTERN UNIVERSITY
RECORDED AND DELIVERED BY DR. SIERRA LOX

Your generation is the worst in modern history.

I'm sure it's something that you've all heard a million times by now. They say you lack social and pragmatic skills. They say you're lazy, entitled, immature, and unprepared to face the real world. They tell you that you don't know how to save money, you don't know what to prioritize, and that you waste your money on frivolous things. They say you won't be able to function in the working world because you don't have any trades, skills, or practical knowledge. You've heard this all before, haven't you? You can't focus on anything, you have the attention spans of fleas, you can't go more than a minute without checking your phones, and you live your life through screens rather than experiencing it in the moment.

What else am I missing? You're all perpetually anxious and don't know how to interact in social situations. You're afraid to answer your phones, you would rather communicate everything through text. What else? You don't know how to deal with your problems, you can't fix your cars, you can't cook your own food, you can't deal with emotional issues properly, instead you have to relate everything through memes and pop culture references. What else do they say? Oh, I know, they say you're hung up on personal and sexual identities. They say you're overly sensitive and offended by everything. They say the boys don't know how to be men and the girls don't want to be women. They ridicule you for going tens of thousands of dollars into debt to pursue an education that does nothing to prepare you for life in the real world.

They've told you these things so much, and maybe you've ignored them, but maybe some of you have internalized some of these things and even started to believe or accept them. Well, I just wanted to start this class by making sure that we are all on the same page when it comes to these things. And what I hope you can realize is that all this stuff you've heard, it's all complete bullshit.

We know better than this. You are not a lost, lazy, or entitled generation, and you certainly aren't lacking the skills required to traverse the most pressing problems of the modern world. If anything, the opposite is true. You've developed levels of digital literacy that your parents will never have. For every baby boomer out there who unquestioningly accepts any fictitious or exaggerated story they see on the news or on Facebook, I see one of you, intaking and interpreting vast and diverse amounts of information to levels never seen before in human history. And unlike them, you don't have your heads in the sand when it comes to some of the most pressing problems that they themselves had a strong hand in creating. So, the next time one of these people tries to convince you that you're the reason that everything is wrong in the world today, I want you to try and remember that it is you as individuals and as a generational cohort that have the skills, tools, and power that are necessary to save the world.

Don't believe me yet? That's fine. Part of what I will be doing in this class throughout the semester is trying to convince you of the digital and media skills that you might not even know that you had. Any questions so far? No?

So let's begin.

May 29, 2019
The Confession of Peter 'Petrol' Riley: Part II

Diefenbaker University is not an especially prestigious institution of higher learning. The joke used to be that if you could spell 'Diefenbaker' correctly on your application that you were more than qualified to be accepted as a student. That said, the Department of Theatre and Performance Studies at DU is a notable exception to this mediocrity and is generally considered to be the best in all of Canada. Some will even annoyingly insist on referring to it as, 'the Julliard of the North,' which sounds impressive until you realize that even though DU may have the best drama program in Canada, it still doesn't even rank among the top forty in the world. Still, for an idealistic teenager fully enveloped by the faint promise of fame, to have the chance to study there was as good an outcome as I could have reasonably expected.

I began the program in 2012 and during the next three years I focused on learning, improving, and gaining as much acting experience as I could. I had some limited success during this time—I performed in a few of the department's stage productions, and I was cast in a few student films, and even though nobody saw any of this stuff, there was a sense that I was building toward something. I even auditioned for a few commercials and small TV and film parts around Toronto, though I wasn't able to land any of them.

It wasn't until I entered the fourth and final year of the program that the dread really started to set in. When I was initially accepted it felt like all my troubles were over. It's embarrassing to admit now, but at the time I really believed that I would go to school, graduate, and by the time it was over I would be offered a smorgasbord of acting roles to choose from. When it was made clear that it wasn't going to be this simple I started living as if there were a giant hourglass constantly draining over my head. I was forced to recognize the stakes that were in front me—if I couldn't support myself as an actor by the time I graduated, I would have to start looking for a job. A *real* job. It's hard to explain the horror that I felt about this prospect because it always seemed like most people didn't care about this as much as I did, but I was entirely convinced that finding a job meant that my dream, along with any chances of fame, would effectively be over. I had heard enough stories of would-be actors who had moved to California or Vancouver only to spend the next ten years tending bar or waiting tables to know that I never wanted to be one of them. I knew you had to make it young or you wouldn't make it at all, and for me, time was quickly running out.

Or maybe I'm just saying that to justify the decisions that I made. I don't really know. But I do mean it when I say that the possibility of working some nine-to-five job for the rest of my life would have been my own personal hell. In fact, the desire to avoid that life was probably a stronger motivator to become an actor than any desire to become famous. Whether it was because of laziness or arrogance, I always felt like I was meant for something more. Stupid kid.

Either way, my time at DU was generally quite positive. In my first year I lived in the dorms and was assigned a roommate named Justin MacDonnell. Justin was an English-major from Newfoundland and unlike some of the horror stories I had heard about randomly assigned roommates, him and I got along great. So great that we decided to find and move in to our own offcampus place together during our second year. Moving to a new province where I didn't know anyone might have been much worse if not for Justin. He was my closest friend at the time and we lived together for all four of my years at DU. Too bad he doesn't want anything to do with me today.

What else can I say about this time? Aside from trying to take my classes seriously, I suppose my university experience was fairly typical. I formed casual friendships with some of the drama students, even though I was never as deeply integrated into the group as most of them were. I saw some girls here and there, I went to some parties, I had some beautiful moments, some scary moments, I did some dumb things. But mostly... well mostly I was online. I was online, posting on forums about why I thought certain film directors were overrated. I was online, reading the blogs of struggling actors and the steps they were taking to break through. I was online, watching old Limez videos on YouTube and wondering why I ever thought they were good or funny in the first place. I was online, reading the comments, thoughts, and opinions of the faceless masses. I was online, absorbing and internalizing the vitriolic lexicon of this artificial and anonymous language.

And though I didn't realize it at the time, I understand now that these thousands of hours that I spent online were nothing more than preparation for the role that would eventually bring me the fame that I always thought I wanted.

APRIL 10, 2016

BLOG POST OF SUNWOO "HEXXXOR" KIM

It is difficult to find accurate figures, but as of writing it has been estimated that there are over ten billion videos on YouTube, with a million or more added every single day. If we conservatively assume that the average video receives only five comments, this means that there are over fifty billion individual comments on the platform.

And I intend to be the first person to read every single one of them.

Yes, I know what you're thinking. To read but even a tiny fraction of this overall content would take an entire lifetime, and to read every one of them would therefore be an impossibility. However, I am banking on two future assurances that will aid me in this endeavour and allow me to become the singular most well-read YouTube comment scholar in existence.

First, in the coming years it is all but guaranteed that we as a collective species will enter a new evolutionary stage of transhumanism which will allow us to shed our inefficient biological shells and embrace a new state of physical being. Along with reducing the threat of illness, disease, and biological decay, our new posthuman bodies will also prevent us from the perils of traditional aging, thereby extending our life expectancies by one hundred years or more. Yes, I know what you're thinking. Even with one hundred more years at my disposal I still will not be able to even make a dent in this galaxy of comments. Fear not, for once we accept our new bodies, we will soon outgrow even them, uploading our consciousness directly into the vast cloud of information. With this will come a rudimentary version of immortality which will afford me the time that is required to complete my task.

Second, in addition to certain biological implants that will allow us to run faster and jump higher we will also develop neurological enhancements that will fundamentally change the ways that we collect, perceive, and interpret information. While reading individual comments may be a laborious and timely endeavour at the moment, once I have equipped the proper neurological augments, I will be able to process and internalize comments at a rate that is exponentially faster. This will allow me to complete a task that normally would have taken uncountable years in a significantly shorter timeframe.

While we are waiting for these future assurances to manifest, I will begin getting a head start on reading every YouTube comment in existence. I have written a script that will automatically crawl from video to video while extracting all comments and storing them in an external hard drive (though more space will soon be needed). Comments are then fed to me in random order for as long as I continue to scroll. To illustrate the effectiveness of this script I will now present the first

22

LOGAN MACNAIR

fifty English-language comments that were collected (I can only speak English and Korean currently, but soon there will be a neurological enhancement that can quickly teach new languages as well).

And thus begins what will become my life's work—to become the most YouTube literate human to have ever lived. Stay tuned to this blog for weekly updates on my progress.

Yours in human (for now) spirit,

Sunwoo "HexXxor" Kim (2001—infinity)

> SKEET SKEET

> can u please give me a shout out on your next vid its my bday next week

> 4:24—that's what she said

> you're fugly as shit and you look like a man, no one wants makeup lessons from you, get a different hobby

> that girl at 2:24 low key dummy thicc

> there's a much simpler solution, Finkelstein is a Jewish name. Tells you all you need to know.

> only people born before 2005 are going to remember this

> ah, classical music like this is the best music to have sex to :)

> First!!

> 2:51 I'M DYING

> It's been 20 years and people still actually think that the government wasn't involved in 9/11, pretty scary when you think about it.

> Does anyone know the girls name at 2:39? Does she have Instagram?

> you ain't gonna do shit stfu loser

> Does anyone else have a weird obsession with watching snakes eat live animals?

> I wish people my age liked this kind of music but there all into pop garbage

> pause at 1:09 for a good shot of her feet, you're welcome ;)

> This is such a gorgeous song, it reminds me of being a teenager back in the 70s, just cruising down the roads on hot summer nights and going nowhere in particular. Great memories.

> These vids are like therapy for me, thank you!

> keep the political shit out of the videos please, no one cares what you think about 'representation' just talk about the game ffs

> I don't like movies that are in black and white (too hard to watch) but this is actually quite funny.

> You're very beautiful and you have a lovely smile, greetings from Denton, TX :)

> Did you film this with a potato? If you're going to upload concert videos at least make sure they are decent quality

> YESSSSSSSSSSS BITCH MY FUTURE IS LOOKING LIKE DEBT AND GLITTER

> I have a Master's degree and two Bachelors, I think I know a teensy bit more about this than you do, thanks for showing up though.

> I can't stand your fucking high-pitched laugh, literally couldn't even finish the video.

> YOOOO THAT DUDE GOT CLAPPED UP

> fake af you can see the transition at 1:13 nice try tho

> shut up and go back to watching Limez videos you low IQ loser

> this bitch's neck looking like a goddamn cthullu monster

> I'm not saying the Earth ISN'T flat, I'm just saying you shouldn't be so quick to believe everything that you're told in school or everything that you blindly accept as 'common knowledge.'

> This is so cringe

> At least half of these views are from me

> Black people have the lowest intelligence. This was proven by geneticist James Watson. The truth can't be hate speech...

> There is literally no proof for the existence of any god, to believe otherwise is illogical and irrational.

> There's something about this guys eyebrows that make him super annoying

> I think I got high just from watching this

> I've been doing YouTube since 2013 and I almost gave up awhile ago. If the last video I posted gets 4 more views I'll start again, but better.

> it literally makes no difference who wins the election your vote doesn't matter

> if the genders were switched here people would be complaining

> I promise I've been in more street fights than you, I know what works, and I guarantee he should have went for the legs here.

> First

> The Nazis were actually leftists, socialism is literally in the party name, stop being so historically illiterate.

> sorry but you're fucking retarded if you think Batman would have lost in a fair fight against this guy

> Ur gross

> REPENT! Christ is coming back to judge the world! We're all guilty of sin, but Christ loves you so much that He died to set you free! Take His blood as a remission of sins, and you will be saved!

> lmao let me guess, you're a Limez fan? Honest question, are you over the age of 13?

> im not crying, your crying

> uh does anyone else have the weirdest boner right now?

> how is gaylord offensive god people are so sensitive these days

> This song loops perfectly. I know this because I have listened to it on a continuous loop for almost one hundred years. YOU MIGHT ALREADY BE A WINNER! QUIT YOUR JOB AND MAKE UP TO 600 USD A DAY WORKING FROM HOME. In 2032 my mind was uploaded into the interface of a refrigerator.

FEBRUARY 17, 2016

THE EMAIL INBOX OF PETER RILEY

Sophie Gorges (sophie@rubylanecasting.com), 02/17/2016, 9:32am

Audition, Project 'Hotel'

Dear Peter,

Thank you for taking the time to audition last week for the part of Arthur. While the production team was very impressed with your audition and your improvisational abilities, I unfortunately must tell you that we have decided to go with a different actor for the part.

We were fortunate to have received auditions from many talented actors for this project, and while you were ultimately not successful in this instance, I want to stress that the production team strongly considered you for this role.

Thanks again for your interest in this project, best of luck to you in your future pursuits.

Regards,

Sophie Gorges, Ruby Lane Casting

JULY 13, 2015
THREAD ON THE /DP/ FORUM

Ari_Vid_Throwaway (399721) Posted 07/13/2015 (11:27pm)

Like a lot of you I grew up watching the wildlife shows of Ari Martin as a kid and I still know all the words to the *What's in the Wild!?* theme song even twenty years later, as I'm sure most of you do. I think I can safely speak for all of us when I say that Ari, with his constant smile, distinctive New Zealand accent, and his unquestionable commitment to learning and teaching about animals and nature was a positive influence on those of us who watched him growing up. One of the best things I remember about elementary school was walking into class and seeing that old-school TV stand on wheels in front of the room because I knew it meant there was a chance the teacher was going to show us an Ari Martin video.

And unlike many other prominent figures of our youth who have since been revealed to be terrible people in real life and mired in all sorts of scandals and accusations, Ari's entire career was without a single controversy, and the people who knew him and worked with him all speak very highly of him, as if the happy, patient, and passionate man that we saw on TV was the exact same person even when the cameras weren't rolling.

And so, like a lot of you, when Ari died in 2010 after being stung by a box jellyfish I took it pretty hard. Even though Ari made a career out of handling some of the most dangerous animals on the planet, he always seemed like he was impervious to harm. He would swim with crocodiles, he would let spiders the size of a dinner plate crawl over his body, he would catch snakes with his bare hands, but there was always a sense that he could never be hurt. So when he was killed by a jellyfish of all things, it seemed like a gut-punch reality check. It sounds a little corny, but when he died, I think so did some of the wonder and safety of my childhood.

Which brings me to the point of this post. As some of you may know, Ari was filming a documentary for the BBC off the coast of Australia when he was stung and killed. The entire ordeal was filmed by his crew, but this footage was never released and was later destroyed at the request of Ari's family.

Except it wasn't, not all of it.

Someone from the crew secretly kept a copy of this footage, and through a chain of events that I won't be discussing (so don't ask), I was able to gain access to this footage, which I will share with you now. You can see at around the two-minute mark his body starts convulsing, this is basically the point where it was too late to do anything about it. Anyway, it's quite graphic, but the sound and video quality are top notch, so enjoy!

RIP Ari, we miss you.

DECEMBER 20, 2014
FACEBOOK INBOX OF NICK TRANG

You wrote (October 24, 2014):
    It's only been a month and already it seems like these people are forgetting about you. All these unauthentic fakes who were grandstanding and putting on a big show about how much they

love and miss you, where are they now? We'll be alone together soon.

Message unseen.

You wrote (October 26, 2014):

I'm not stupid. I know my lazy eye is ugly, I know people make fun of it behind my back. But do you remember that time during lunchbreak when Kevin was mocking me in the cafeteria? You came up to him and told him to stop being a dick and before you walked away you said, "you look really nice today Rachel." That was the first time I ever heard you say my name. I didn't even think you knew who I was. I had always known there was something special about you, but at that moment I knew I was in love with you.

Message unseen.

You wrote (November 3, 2014):

I thought so much about what kind of message I would send you here. I wanted it to be funny and unique, but I didn't want to scare you off. I wanted to express my interest in you, but I didn't want to give everything away. It's the kind of stupid and pathetic girl shit that I always hated and didn't want any part of. I used to see other girls sitting in little groups, showing each other their messages from boys and workshopping the perfect responses and I just despised it so much. But I was doing the same exact thing. Drafting messages in my head, drafting responses to the things I thought you might say, imagining entire conversations with you. The closest I came to sending it was about a week before your accident. I wrote up the message and everything, I edited every word to be perfect, every piece of punctuation, every emoji. I stared at it for so long, I thought about what it could mean, how it could change things, and then, after all that, I couldn't send it. I was too scared of how you would react, or worse, not react. Though I guess that doesn't matter anymore. Now I know that you won't react. That assurance has made me braver.

Message unseen.

You wrote (November 9, 2014):

At the funeral I asked your mom if I could have a piece of your clothes. That's something I would never normally have the courage to do. But I did. She probably thought I was weird, but she told me to come by your house. She invited me in and took me to your bedroom. It didn't look the way I thought it would, but I see it clear now and it makes sense. She gave me one of your hoodies, the black one that you used to wear a lot. I sleep with it at night, but lately it smells less like you and more like me. I cry as I type this.

Message unseen.

You wrote (November 13, 2014):

Today has been hard. I've visited your profile probably ten times already. I've been trying to distract myself, that's what they say you should do. But whenever I'm not immediately focused on something I instinctually come back to you. To the same collection of pictures, to the same inane comments left by people who never really knew or understood you. Sometimes I feel that if I stop looking, everything might just disappear. I promise I will keep you alive, even when no one else will.

Message unseen.

You wrote (November 17, 2014):

Sometimes I wish our positions could have been replaced. I think about it too much. I would do it myself, I would meet you wherever you are now, but I think about my parents and how they would feel if they found me and that's what stops me. There's no harm in telling you now I guess. I used to daydream about you meeting my family. Somehow, I thought you could fix things. If they could just see how happy I was with you, they would know. I've been trying to find a source for these feelings. It's not just about you. I think maybe the world just changed too quickly and now the only sense of real security I have is in the past. And it disappeared. With you, it disappeared.

Message unseen.

You wrote (December 7, 2014):

It's been raining a lot lately. I think you would have really liked it.

Message unseen.

You wrote (December 20, 2014):

I don't know why I keep coming back. I don't know why I'm sad all the time. I don't know why I thought that you could fix any of this, either now or before. I wanted us to be something that was probably never going to happen. And now I'm taking advantage of the fact that you can't tell me otherwise. I just don't know what the fuck I'm supposed to do. Can't you just tell me something? Why am I looking on you to save me? You barely even knew who I was. I've never needed anyone before, why do I think that I need you now? Can you answer me, just this one time?

Message unseen.

OCTOBER 15, 2017
PARTIAL TRANSCRIPT FROM THE DAILY VIDEO OF
LIAM 'LIMEZ' GONZÁLEZ, 7.2 MILLION VIEWS

FAAAAAAACE WALK! Good after-morning to all my bros and dudes. It's wuh wuh WHISKY O'Clock, excuse me as a I go for a little sippy sip. Ah, that is scrumptious. Like God whispered into a glass, and then I put that whisper in my mouth hole. HE HAS ENTERED MY BODY! THE SAVAGERY! You know why you're here. You little piggies want to slop up some fat, juicy CONTENT so let's look at some dank may mays. But first, an important public cervix announcement. You, yes, you. Have you smuh smuh SMASHED that like button? Have you muh muh MOLESTED that subscribe button? DO SO NOW, I COMMAND IT. Anyone who hasn't subscribed has a peepee the size of a lentil bean. Is a lentil a bean? SEARCH FOR THE ANSWER and if you find it drop it like it's hot in the comments below. OOH baby I wanna comment all over you. STICKY ICKY! Hope you're proud!

Okay pals. Okay dudes. Okay bros. Okay homeys. Okay fellas. Those are all names for guys, because NO. GIRLS. ALLOWED. Just kidding ladies, you are welcome here. Please call me. I'm so alone. Come and touch my penne noodle. These are the peak sad boy hours. Play me a sad song so I can cry to myself and be forever alone. Am I too sad to finish the video? NEVER! The dankness and the epicness pushes me forward. It pushes me like I push my morning bagel into the toaster. EPIC BAGEL TIME, YOU KNOW WHAT TO DO! Upload pics of your morning bagel on the subreddit and if it's the same flavor as mine you will be featured in my next EPIC BAGEL TIME. Isn't that your wildest dream?

Okay who is ready to look at some sweet and succulent may mays? Is it you? Yell at the screen so I can hear you. WOAH not so close, I'm not comfortable with that, please respect my personal bubble or I will report you to the authorities for this microaggression. That's right PAL. I am a strong independent man and I will not allow you to get all up in my personal space. And speaking of personal space, I want to announce that I have personally bought all space in the universe. That's right, I am now the sole owner of actual space. Super villain gang rise up. Faceless henchmen can fight each other with their peepees, the winner will be promoted to my chief of staph infections. OUCHIE IT BURNS! I kid, I kid. I was going to say that personal space is important, and so is organizing your personal space, which thanks to the new app Clenz is easier than ever. Clenz is a personalized app designed with the help of real psychologists to help you sort and remove the clutter from your workspace and from your life. And spoiler alert—it works! I have been using it myself, and as you can see, my workspace is cleaner than my bare bottom after some of that hot shower power. Download Clenz and use the offer code 'Limez' for not one, not two, but THREE free weeks worth of subscription time.

And now! Without further a-poo, let's take a peeky weeky at some of the dankest, hottest, and spiciest may mays that you, the almighty Limez Army have submitted. We have a steamy batch to go through today, so let's go boys and swirls.

MARCH 16, 2016
THEATRE 401 ASSIGNMENT SCRIPT SUBMITTED BY PETER RILEY

Truth Bombs
Written and Performed by Peter Riley (Theatre 401)

This is Petrol Riley speaking to you live and direct from the heart of the American nightmare, here to drop truth bombs that will awaken the ignorant masses and shed light on some universal human truths. And they are indeed truths. No matter what they will try and tell you, no matter how much they try to convince you that down is up or that slavery is freedom, we know from the depths of our souls, that truth still exists and is still worth fighting for.

These people, whether they be the academic elites, the liberal talking heads on your television screens, the manipulative social architects of Hollywood, or the ruling establishment itself, they want you to remain subservient and docile. They want you to accept defeat before the battle even begins. They want to emasculate you, they want you to be ashamed of being born a man. They want you to feel guilty for being born White. They want you to feel embarrassed and humiliated for trying to protect or maintain the traditional values that built this country.

And why are they doing this? The answer is not complicated. They are doing this because they are evil. They are led by the seven princes of Hell to fulfill their one singular mission—the destruction of humanity as we know it. They want to turn men into weak-willed cowards who can't resist them. They want to eliminate the White race, the last line of stalwart defense protecting against their goal of total global domination. Every time you see a movie with a mixed-race couple, every time the liberal media tries to convince you of the values of diversity, every time a man is stripped of his identity and agency, this is them enacting their master plan.

Don't believe me? It doesn't matter. Truth exists whether you believe in it or not. You can choose to ignore the truth, but it won't go away. In twenty years, when White people are minorities in their own countries, when men are criminalized for showing any signs of masculine aggression, when free speech has been successfully supressed, and when the only acceptable forms of thought are those that are prescribed and approved by your government overlords, you will have wished that you accepted the truth much sooner.

But we don't have to let it get to that point. We can do something about it right now. The only way to counter evil is to confront it head on. You can stand up. You can stand up and assert your inalienable, God-given right to live and think freely. You need to tell these fiends that you are not required to let them inside your heads! You need to protect the sovereignty of your own thoughts! You need to shout, from the top of your lungs, that you are a free-thinking, free-living human being and that you will never allow them to destroy everything that you and your ancestors have built! You need to fight this gathering darkness and you need to do it right now! Not tomorrow, not later, but right now! These devils, these hell-spawned manipulators, they will never win against us. They will never silence the truth.

Now get up and say it with me now, loud enough for these monsters to hear you!

I am a strong, White man, and I will not be persecuted anymore!

May 30, 2019
The Confession of Peter 'Petrol' Riley: Part III

If you go through the DU drama program, it's unavoidable that you will eventually take at least one class taught by Josh Garrison. I took four classes with him myself and he directed me a couple times in some of the department's internal productions. We got along well and had a good working relationship, although he got along well with most people given that Josh was universally beloved by nearly all his students. He was the youngest member of the faculty and was still relatively in touch with the culture even if his attempts to use modern slang did occasionally come across as a little try-hard. Still, he was an inherently likeable person with an undeniable passion for what he was doing. But despite being a beloved professor who had secured his academic position at an impressively early age, I couldn't help but view him as a failure. I knew that at one time he had dreams the size of mine, and I knew that somewhere along the line he must have settled for what he has now.

In the spring of 2016 I was in my final semester of the program, a month or so shy of graduating and being thrust into a world I wanted no part of. During this last semester I was taking a class with Josh, which I guess was fitting in a circular kind of way since both my first and last classes in the program were with him. In the time between I had grown comfortable with Josh and with my peers in the program and I had become a much more relaxed and confident actor than the nervous and eager student I was in my first year.

In this class we were given an assignment, and to Josh's credit it was a rather unique and engaging assignment, to write and perform a short piece based on a character that we had created. The catch was that we had to film ourselves and deliver our presentation in the form of a popular YouTube video. The idea, according to Josh anyway, was that what it meant to be an 'actor' was changing due to mediums like YouTube and that we needed to adapt with these changes to be successful. I don't know how true that is, but it was a fun assignment either way and given my history of creating these types of videos in my youth, one that I thought I could excel at.

I thought a lot about what I might do for that assignment. Even though it was mostly 'for fun' and wasn't worth much of our grade, I really wanted to knock it out of the park. I talked to my roommate Justin about it, asked him if he had any ideas, and it didn't take him long to come up with his suggestion. 'You gotta do Rango,' he said.

Bobby Rango. What do I have to say about this guy? He had long been notorious for his controversial satellite radio show, and later for his YouTube videos that were just completely off-the-rails crazy. He would scream until he was red in the face about things like government corruption, or the socialist indoctrination that's happening in public schools, or about how awful things like taxes, immigration, and political correctness were. Super lame stuff, but Justin and I used to watch his videos all the time, not because we believed in any of the ideas he was selling, but strictly for the entertainment value. To us, and to a large chunk of the young Internet, Bobby Rango was a one-man meme factory. He maintained a noticeable ironic popularity with people our age because of the insanity of his rants and his undeniable presence. Justin and I both had Rango impressions that we would often perform for each other, though given my training as an actor mine was a little better and really pretty damn spot-on if I'm being honest about it. So, when Justin told me, 'you gotta do Rango,' I knew it was settled. With Justin's help I wrote a script for a character I would portray that would be based almost entirely on the entertaining lunatic that was Bobby Rango.

You know, I met Bobby in person when I was a guest on his show not too long ago. Behind closed doors he's not really as deranged or insane as he presents himself on his show, but I'm getting ahead of myself.

Once we had written the script Justin filmed my perform-ance of the character that I had uncreatively decided to name partially after myself. Peter Riley became Petrol Riley, the dropper of truth bombs, who would ignite and set fire to the ignorance of the world. The performance was three or so min-utes of yelling about how the evil liberal media was demonizing White people and all that other nonsense that Rango loved to go on about. It took only three takes for me to give a performance that I don't think could have been improved. We saved the video, and for ease of access, uploaded it to YouTube using a burner account under the title 'Truth Bombs.' I went to sleep that night feeling good, confident that I had really nailed the assignment.

A few days later all fifteen or so of the student videos were shown in Josh's class, and while there was, as usual, a mixed bag of content and quality, I can safely say that the response to my video was the most enthusiastic of the bunch. Throughout the video my classmates laughed at my satirical take on the raging clown that is Bobby Rango. Even Josh was snickering and smiling as he took notes on the performance. I was proud of what I had produced and content with the positive reaction it received. Which was why I was so taken aback when I met with Josh a few days later to receive my grade.

Josh did this thing where he would take each student into his office individually to give them one-on-one feedback on their performances. This intimate and intimidating method of delivering feedback was sort of a running joke with the students, but I had been through the process enough by that point where I knew what to expect. I don't remember all the details of the conversation, but I remember that Josh gave me a grade of 'B' on my performance. I remember feeling a little confused, but mostly I felt insulted. I pushed back a little and challenged him on the grade, and he said it was mostly because my performance was 'one-dimensional.' That got us into a larger discussion about my future, and he was going on about how I have talent, but talent isn't enough, and that I should get used to grinding away, and all these other things, but as he was lecturing me all I could do was envision myself in the future. I remember thinking that Josh could potentially be me in the future if I gave up on my dreams the way I suspected that he did. Sure, he seemed content, he had a good job and everyone adored him, but I couldn't help but think that no matter how hard he tried to convince himself otherwise, deep down he felt unfulfilled, and I didn't want his life to be my future.

A few moths later I found myself walking across the stage of the Lewis Theatre at my graduation ceremony. My parents wanted to fly over from B.C. to watch, but I had to convince them not to. I told them it wasn't worth the time and money to fly across the county just to see me walk across the stage for ten seconds. In truth I was probably just embarrassed. The whole ceremony was being live-streamed anyway, so they could just watch it on their computers, even if it meant I had to carefully explain step-by-step how they could do this.

After the ceremony there were mini-sandwiches and drinks in the courtyard for the graduates to enjoy. As I was taking advantage of the free lunch and starting to sweat under my graduation gown, Josh approached me to offer congratulations. He shook my hand and wished me the best of luck for the future. He told me to reach out if I ever needed a letter of recommendation or anything else. Seemed genuine. Who knows. The excitement from the ceremony quickly faded and I took off my gown, returned it, and started walking home with the intention of getting shitfaced drunk with Justin, partly in celebration, and partly to help ignore the nagging uncertainty of the future.

And there I was, officially done with school and with no tangible prospects to grasp onto. I had enough money saved for a few months of food and rent, just enough to last through the summer, but I knew I would soon have to start looking for a proper job. And as a guy with a theatre degree and no real practical skills, I was already dreading the types of places I would need to apply to. At the time I thought the only way out was to land a big role or a position with a theatre company, but none of my auditions were leading anywhere and my outlook at this time was bleak. I stopped at the liquor store, picked up a bottle of gin (Justin and I were going through a gin phase at the time), and returned home. I wanted nothing more than to just drink and forget the horrible future, if even just for a night.

If only I could be so lucky.

Justin was eager to greet me, which I initially thought was because he was excited to congratulate me on graduation and all that, but he was sitting at the kitchen table with his laptop open, beckoning me over with uncharacteristic enthusiasm. Without even removing my shoes I walked over to him and noticed that he was on YouTube. I recognized the video he was watching right away. It was our very own 'Truth Bombs' video that we had made three months prior. That video that we made as a laugh for an assignment. That video that got me a 'B' grade. That video that was only ever meant to be seen by fifteen or so of my classmates. That video that I had almost entirely forgotten about.

It had been viewed forty thousand times.

MAY 24, 2017
JOURNAL OF NEW MEDIA STUDIES, ARTICLE ABSTRACT
BY DR. SIERRA LOX

Stepping Stones of Extremism: Algorithms and Extremist Content
Sierra Lox, School of Communication,
Northwestern University

Abstract

This study utilizes the method of social network analysis to determine how the algorithmic patterns of video recommendations can usher viewers from videos of an apolitical nature to those of increasingly extreme political rhetoric across a relatively short trajectory. By examining the distance between 'apolitical' videos with the highest overall centrality scores in the network and videos that have been coded as politically or ideologically extreme (videos that support ethnic cleansing, Holocaust denial, racial/religious supremacy, etc.) it is shown that by following an average of 3.4 video recommendations a viewer can move from politically neutral videos about non-political topics to videos that express a variety of extremist perspectives. Additionally, this analysis outlines how channels with low levels of visibility in the overall network can be worked into the algorithm by use of certain words and phrases in their titles and descriptions, thereby granting them a significant boost in exposure and viewership. The result of this relationship is videos and channels of objectionable and extremist content experiencing a surge of popularity through their algorithmic connection to the central video network. We conclude this study by offering some recommendations that may be adopted by the platform in order to limit the accessibility and visibility of videos that endorse or promote various forms of extremism.

MARCH 22, 2016
GRADE FEEDBACK MEETING BETWEEN
JOSH GARRISON AND PETER RILEY

RECORDED BY THE LATTER IN THE INTEREST
OF GOOD RECORD KEEPING

"Hey Pete, come on in. How are things going for you?"

"Good, just finished doing all the registration stuff for con-
vocation, so that's something."

"That's fantastic, congrats. Seems like just yesterday that I
had you in my intro class."

"Ah, maybe for you it does."

"Well, you've developed a lot since then, I'm gonna miss
having you around, yours has been a great cohort."

"Thanks."

"Okay, ready for your feedback?"

"Yeah, let's do it."

"So right off the bat I want to say that I liked this character,
and I think you really nailed the vibe that you were going for
with the whole bigoted, screaming pundit thing. I think the
script was well-written, and you delivered these ridiculous lines
with a level of sincerity that made your performance quite
humorous, so good job with all of that."

"Thank you."

"That said, I felt your performance was quite one-dimensional. You basically came out of the gate sprinting and stayed at
that speed for the whole three minutes or so. I think it would
have been better to start slower and more subdued and work
toward an eventual build-up and release instead of remaining
constant for as long as you did."

"Okay."

"Overall I think it was a solid performance of a great character, but one that could have been even better if you inserted
some ups and downs in your delivery. I've given you a B
grade."

"Really, a B? The class loved mine though."

"I liked it too Pete, it was entertaining, but there's more to a performance than that. Don't lose sleep over this, this assignment isn't worth much of your overall grade."

"I know, I just… I thought by now I would be doing better than this. I haven't had a grade this low since second year basically."

"Well use this as a learning experience."

"I guess, sure."

"You're really that upset about this? Or is something else bothering you?"

"Yeah, I don't know."

"Come on, what is it?"

"I guess I just figured that by now I would have more clarity about what comes next."

"With respect to what?"

"I don't know. I just figured that by the time I graduated I would have things sorted out and know what I would be doing."

"Pete, I'm at least ten years older than you and I still don't know what the future holds for me or what the hell I'm doing. You'll always have uncertainties but these things have a way of working themselves out. When I was your age I never in a million years thought that I would end up teaching drama classes, but now I am and I love it."

"Do you really though?"

"Of course I do."

"You never wanted, I don't know, something more?"

"What is it that you think you want exactly?"

"Well, I want to be an actor, that's the whole point of coming here isn't it?"

"You are an actor, and you've become a much better one over the last four years."

"You know what I mean."

"What, you want to be a movie star?"

"I mean, yeah."

"Well who's to say that's still not possible? But breaking through into film or TV isn't something that just happens, no matter how talented you are. You have to grind, you have to get yourself out there, and honestly, you need a whole lot of luck."

"I know, I know. I just sort of figured that…"

"You figured that it would just happen?"

"I guess so, yeah."

"Well then I think you're maybe in need for some hard truths. The truth is that you have a lot of talent. Really, you do. But people more talented than you have come and gone through this program and not made it. Now look, I don't say that to discourage you, I think that you have the raw ability that's needed to make it, and I'm not just saying that to make you feel better, I really do believe that, but you have to accept that you aren't entitled to anything, no matter how much talent you might have. You have to keep plugging away. Do as much theater as you can, do commercials, do student films, put yourself out there as much as possible, network, meet the right people, all that stuff. It might not seem fun or glamorous, and it might take more time than you would like it to, but that's how you have to do it. You aren't going to just wake up and be offered a leading role in a Hollywood film. You don't get anywhere without hard work, and even then, nothing is guaranteed. But really Pete, you should pursue this because you enjoy doing it, not just because you are looking at some eventual payoff. You do enjoy it, right?"

"I guess so, yeah."

MARCH 24, 2018
ONLINE ARTICLE BY JEFF OWLIN, SURGE MAGAZINE

Helena's Hole: The Internet's Home to the Lost, the Damned, and the Morbidly Curious
Jeff Owlin

There was something truly special about being a young teenager during the early years of the modern Internet.

The year was 2003 and I had just turned thirteen when I was finally able to convince my parents that the Internet would be an invaluable resource for helping me with my schoolwork. They eventually agreed, and just like that, here was this brand-new world, seemingly infinite in potential and possibility and almost entirely unrestrained by the rules or norms of 'real' life. It was also a largely hidden world. Today my parents, like most others, have broken through the generational barrier and become savvy enough to do things like browse Facebook or sell an old lawn-mower on Craigslist (still proud of you for that one Dad), but while the Internet has today become a normal and largely integral facet of daily life for people of all ages, back then it operated more like a speakeasy, something that was hidden, unsupervised, and yet to be discovered and defanged by the masses.

It was around this time when I heard some classmates at school whispering about this strange new website called 'Helena's Hole.' Just the name alone sounded wrong—it sounded dirty, like something that shouldn't be spoken aloud in polite society. They spoke of this place with a hushed hesitation, as if they expected to get in trouble if someone were to overhear them. Naturally this piqued my curiosity. So that night, after waiting for everyone in the house to fall asleep, I dialed up (which we had to do back then, ask your parents about it) and sought the place out for myself.

I was taken directly to the site's main board, the 'Dank Pit,' or /dp/ as it's more commonly known. What I found was a collec-tion of some of the nastiest, filthiest, please-gouge-my-eyes-out images in existence. Many of these images were pornographic, and while I had seen naked people on the Internet before, the people in these images were doing things that my thirteen-year-old brain didn't realize were physically possible. So too were there plenty images of gore, terrible injuries, dead bodies, and physical deformi-ties, and I must confess, I did choose to view these with a morbid curiosity. I was disgusted to be sure, at times even a little nauseous, but there was also a transgressive thrill in seeing the things that no one was supposed to see. This was the darkest corner of the Internet, and there I was right in the middle of it.

But I soon found out that it wasn't all just eye-poison and raunch. There were other forums and discussion boards on

Helena's Hole that weren't dedicated to shocking or crude content and were instead focused on discussing things like video games, comic books, sports, movies, and other hobbies that I, along with legions of other teenage kids, were interested in at the time. I began visiting these boards regularly. I discussed my hobbies in detail with other like-minded and equally passionate nerds. I formed bonds and even legitimate friendships with other users, all while slowly exploring and shaping my own identity. I was only visiting the /dp/ board occasionally at this point, mostly out of boredom, and was slowly becoming desensitized to its chaos.

There was a real feeling of comradery and solidarity in those early years. Once you got past the initial shock of the content what you found was a collection of misfits, outcasts, and weirdos who had, through the magic of the Internet, found a place where they had some semblance of community and belonging. There was a sense that we were ahead of the curve, that we had a real hand in shaping the culture of the mainstream Internet that was soon to follow, and for my part, I was happy to have been involved in such a bizarre and surreal community, one that for better or worse had some impact in shaping the person I am today.

As I got older and went off to college I started visiting the website less and less frequently and soon not at all as other interests and priorities took over. The website became a sort of living relic of my teenage years, something I had left behind while still being able to look back on fondly.

And it was during those years after I left that something changed on Helena's Hole.

The site was always depraved, disgusting, and disturbing. That was sort of the point. But rarely was the site outwardly and blatantly *hateful*. People occasionally discussed news and politics—mostly with the same detached, ironic, and theatrical vulgarity that they discussed everything—and while some users sincerely expressed some fringe political views, most people who expressed legitimate extremist or hateful beliefs were quickly ridiculed, silenced, and cast aside.

Skip ahead fifteen or so years to today and the 'Riley Rally', or /rr/ board is the second most active board on the entire website right after /dp/ itself. The /rr/ board was initially conceived as a space to discuss the videos and political "philosophy" (with apologies to actual philosophers) of Peter 'Petrol' Riley, the far-right's newest and (apparently) hippest White nationalist poster child and has since become one of the most notoriously toxic and outwardly hateful spaces on the entirety of the Internet.

The /rr/ board retains the vulgar, uncensored language I remember from the early days of the website, but now this language, as well as a host of other slurs, insults, and jargon specific to the board, are being directed at essentially any communities, demographics, or individuals that fall outside the highly idealized White, masculine standard that has been put in place. Any marginalized or minority groups you can name have been made an object of ridicule, scorn, and relentless attack within the threads of /rr/. But let me save you the trouble of having to visit this swamp yourself. I present to you now, slightly censored, a sample of the typical discussion happening at any given moment on /rr/.

Transphobia
"These degenerate f★★★ots think cutting their dicks off will magically make them less gay when in reality all it does it mutilate them beyond repair."

"There's no such thing as being transgender. It's a mental illness and these people need help. Preferably in the form of a bullet."

Antisemitism
"Do you think it's a coincidence that all the tech and media companies are owned by k★kes? And do you really think that they aren't communicating with each other about how to supress dissident voices?"

General Racism
"Name one thing mud people have actually contributed to society and I'll give you ten examples of them being parasites."

"Scientists already discovered that the criminal gene and the ni★★er gene are one and the same, but for some reason it's 'racist' to point this out, even when it's based in fact."

I could go on, but you probably get the idea. Oh, and by the way, if you think I had to scroll deep through the board to find and cherry-pick the most heinous or extreme examples, just keep in mind that *every single one of these posts was made within the last two hours*. These examples are very much the norm rather than the exception.

But it's not just minority or vulnerable populations that end up in the virtual scopes of /rr/ users. They have also gone after specific individuals who they deem to be particularly problematic, launching several targeted harassment campaigns over the last year that have occasionally leaked outside their online containment zone and into the offline world.

One such victim is Sierra Lox, an assistant professor of communications at Northwestern University, who inadvertently became the board's number one enemy by publishing some work that drew links between the hateful rhetoric of far-right online personalities such as Petrol Riley and the rising wave of politically-motivated offline violence we have been experiencing in recent years. Her condemnation of Petrol Riley, coupled with the fact that she happens to be a competent and highly regarded female professional with progressive views who is willing to call them out, has caused Lox to become a sort of Emmanuel Goldstein figure for the users of /rr/. Beyond the 'typical' fare of constant online harassment, doxing, and threats of death and sexual violence, one young man was arrested earlier this year for trying to break into her NWU campus office.

Helena's Hole is, and always has been, one of the few online spaces where user anonymity is truly protected. Because of this, it is difficult to say whether Riley himself is a regular visitor, lurker, or active contributor to the board that was created to celebrate him. He has never made any public statements indicating that he has interacted with the board or its users, but it would be absurd to believe that he is not at the very least aware of its presence.

Regardless of his level of personal interaction with the board, it is a space that exists because of him and his ideas. It is a space that for many outsiders has now come to represent the entirety of Helena's Hole—something that brings me great sadness.

This is not the website I remember. It was always a space that dealt in smut, profanity, and transgressive content, but it never used to deal in hatred, discrimination, and bigotry. It was always a freakshow, but it was an inclusive freakshow, a place where the isolated, the lonely, the depraved, and the curious could meet and feel, maybe for the first time, like they belonged. But something changed. That level of internal comradery has been replaced with an external misanthropy. Maybe this was an inevitable progression, maybe it was forced, maybe I'm misremembering and looking back through rose-coloured glasses and it was always like this, I don't know.

Either way, it makes me worried for the young people of today who, just as I did fifteen years before them, are stumbling into this strange corner of the Internet with open eyes and impressionable minds.

Jeff Owlin, Surge Magazine

MARCH 24, 2018
THREAD ON /RR/ FORUM

Adolphus (389472) Posted 03/24/2018 (9:28am)
Hey fellas did you see our board was shouted out in Surge today? Can we have a thread dedicated to dropping truth bombs for any of the curious normies that might now be paying us a visit? I'll start with a simple one—it's okay to be White.

BathSaltBlitz (327790)
Good idea, here's mine—blacks make up 13% of the population in America but are responsible for over half of the nation's murders.

MightyMyles (322266)

The attempted suicide rate among trannies is at 40% and society's attempts to normalize their existence is nothing but the promotion of mental illness.

Occam's_Stubble (386366)

Protecting and upholding freedom of speech is more important than your hurt feelings.

CheeseHam (387412)

Feminism has made women more miserable than ever and now they can't even admit it.

Soldaten1488 (386507)

White people are on the path to becoming a minority group in this country. White genocide is real.

Claymore88 (341287) MODERATOR

Follow the money. Almost 100% of the content you see in books, movies, TV, or the news was deliberately placed there by Jews and for a specific reason.

JihadiJuan (327331)

Homosexuality is an obstacle for Aryan race reproduction and should not be tolerated.

The5711 (388008)

Everyone in Hollywood and everyone involved with the production of pop culture entertainment is either actively involved with or is explicitly supporting pedophilia and the continual sexual assault of children.

DragonbornNord (321869)

Liberals and leftists pose the single greatest threat to our society and they would happily burn down the entire country just to rule over the smoldering rubble.

GundamLing (387421)

Europe has already been overrun by Muslims and America will be next if people keep buying into the dangerous myths of diversity and multi-culturalism.

NO DATE

MEMORIES FROM SOMEONE, NOT SURE WHO, DOESN'T MATTER ANYWAY

I was out there sitting on the sun-soaked rocks of some tropical island watching the waves and the creatures in the nearby tide pool and wondering if I remembered enough from my elementary school science classes to discern any of them but really all I was thinking about was how it was too hot and how we should all be inside where there's air conditioning. Then I felt guilty, like maybe I should try harder to appreciate the beauty of nature and the miracles of the world or whatever, but the sun still hurt my eyes and can someone explain to me why this is supposed to be more enjoyable than just looking at superior pictures that other people have taken and posted online? Apparently you can see dolphins and even humpbacks if you go at the right time but that sounds like a lot of waiting around for something that might happen when I could just as easily go to SeaWorld and see exactly what I am supposed to see while sitting down and enjoying a snow cone. I might have read somewhere that keeping dolphins in captivity is bad for some reason, but I also read that the ocean is going to be like forty percent plastic within ten years, so maybe they are actually better off being taken care of by humans.

I knew this girl once when I was younger and we would hang out sometimes. I think I was trying to hit that, but I guess it never worked out. She was a little weird anyway. We would agree to hang out and I would invite her over to chill and watch TV, but she always wanted to do shit like go for walks in the park or go hiking in the woods. I agreed to do this stuff because I thought it might get me laid but she was never really down. Mostly she just wanted to be outside with the trees or something and I think she wanted a friend to be there with her. Sometimes we would be walking and she would stop to look at flowers and stuff, but she wouldn't take pictures and I would ask her what she was doing and she would say that she was just admiring the view and to this day I don't know if she was full of shit or if she was trying to prank me or what. I don't remember much else about those walks but I remember it did smell nice, like a Christmas tree and not like the fake plastic ones, but like the real ones that the building manager says we aren't allowed to have anymore.

But one time, and it must have been the last time we hung out, she and I climbed up this mountain together. I remember we had to start at like five-thirty in the morning because she wanted to watch the sun come up while we were at the top. I hadn't been up that early in years. I haven't been up that early since. We starting hiking and I didn't have the right shoes, but we still made it. And we sat up there together and we watched the sun come up and she still didn't take any pictures. And I remember feeling something as I looked up at the rising sun, and it wasn't like horniness because at that point I had basically accepted that we wouldn't be fooling around. I don't know what it was, but I do know that this feeling, well it passed and it passed quickly, because soon all I could think about was how badly I wanted to get back to a place that had a decent Wi-Fi connection.

· AUGUST 4, 2014
TOP VOTED DEFINITION OF '/DP/' ON uDEFINE.COM

What is /dp/?

/dp/ is the crusted piss behind the toilet that you will never clean.

/dp/ is the talented artist that only draws naked cartoon characters.

/dp/ is the guy setting traps in the path of the blind man.

/dp/ is the guy jerking off in the back of the movie theatre.

/dp/ is the friend who steals your mom's underwear.

/dp/ is the guy who slips pictures of gay porn into children's books at the library.

/dp/ is the guy who writes erotic self-insert fiction about his own sister.

/dp/ is the mold that grows inside your jizz sock.

/dp/ is the homeless guy rambling about the end of days.

/dp/ is the friend who hides in your closet while you're having sex.

/dp/ is the pedophile who gets a job as a mall Santa.

/dp/ is the friend who collects used tampons.

/dp/ is the guy who drinks the beer in the ashtray just for the lulz.

/dp/ is the scars on your wrist and the constant reminder they carry.

/dp/ is the kid in class who drops his pencil just so he can try to look up skirts.

/dp/ is the guy taking and uploading pictures of car crash victims.

/dp/ is the guy who never flushes after shitting in a public toilet.

/dp/ is the cock spray-painted on the side of the elementary school.

/dp/ is the pal who spikes your drink with laxatives after barricading the bathroom door.

/dp/ is the basement where the torture porn was filmed.

/dp/ is the guy telling the jokes that everyone else is too scared to make.

/dp/ is best and the worst of us.

/dp/ is the ugliness of humanity and doesn't try to hide it.

/dp/ is the only real thing left.

Looking to take in a little culture this weekend that goes beyond
the usual standard of endlessly scrolling for a new TV show to
mindlessly binge? Consider catching the latest production from
the Department of Theatre and Performance Studies of *I Have No
Head (I Think So)* by Alberta playwright Jacelyn Irwin. Directed
by theatre professor Josh Garrison and anchored by a caustic and
vulnerable lead performance by fourth-year drama student Peter
Riley, *I Have No Head (I Think So)* promises to be a powerful and
fitting close to what has so far been an excellent season of productions by the DU theatre department. *I Have No Head (I Think
So)* will be running this Friday, Saturday, and Sunday (as well as
next Friday, Saturday, and Sunday) at the Lewis Theatre starting
at 8:00pm. Tickets can be purchased in advance online or at the
box office on the night of the show.

JULY 18, 2016
THREAD ON /DP/ FORUM

SlylyAskew (351401) Posted 07/18/2016 (9:19pm)
    Where are all the ladies of /dp/ and why aren't they in this
thread showing me their tits?

CuhCuh (355392)
    lol @ this fag who thinks there are or ever were any fems on
/dp/

AmberWaves (380074)
    I'm a lady. We do in fact exist on /dp/.

SithPoster69 (320214)
    @*AmberWaves* tits or gtfo

b_r_a_z_e_n (351842)

@*AmberWaves* good evening m'lady! Allow me, the supreme gentleman, to guide you through the shark-infested waters of /dp/. Taketh my hand and I shall lead you out of this perpetual darkness and into the light! But seriously though, show us your breasts right now or leave.

ThotteryBarn (381332)

@AmberWaves prove it bitch

vhsDan (386000)

@AmberWaves no one gives a shit you dumb attention whore

GayMysterio (325522)

And y'all wonder why girls don't come around here smh

dacaxx1289 (359001)

@*GayMysterio* stfu dipshit

XamianX (359808)

@*AmberWaves* check your DMs.

July 18, 2016
Direct Message Exchange from helenashole.org

XamianX (359808)

Hey, I just wanted to apologize for the way you were treated in that thread. I can tell from your user ID that you're pretty new to the boards and I just wanted to make sure that you wouldn't be immediately scared off.

AmberWaves (380074)

lol thanks but it's nothing I haven't seen before.

XamianX (359808)

You just have to remember that nearly everyone who posts on the Hole and on /dp/ especially is a basement-dwelling social outcast who has never even spoken to a woman in real life and they love to take out their frustrations on any women they meet online. Keep that in mind next time they act like a bunch of assholes.

AmberWaves (380074)

For sure thanks.

Does that mean you are a basement-dwelling social outcast too?

XamianX (359808)

Of course I am. But I'm one of the good ones who is self-aware enough to realize that taking out my frustrations on complete strangers is a shitty thing to do.

AmberWaves (380074)

haha good to know

XamianX (359808)

Can I give one piece of advice that might make things a little easier for you here? Next time these losers harass you, you have to just give it right back. Always act like whatever they are saying doesn't bother you and just roast them right back. If you do that you'll fit right in, even if they don't respect you.

AmberWaves (380074)

I think I can manage that, thanks for looking out

XamianX (359808)

So what brings you to /dp/ anyway? I mean those losers are right about the fact that girls don't usually come around these parts.

AmberWaves (380074)
uh well basically I was just curious since a bunch of the guys I hangout with at school are always talking about it and I wanted to see if it was really as fucked up as they made it sound

XamianX (359808)
And? Are we living up to your expectations?

AmberWaves (380074)
Well I was under the impression that everyone on /dp/ was going to be a perverted angry sociopath.

XamianX (359808)
Are you implying that they aren't?

AmberWaves (380074)
Well I thought so at first
But then I met you

FEBRUARY 9, 2017
VERIFIED PURCHASER REVIEW FOR
A LATEX GEORGE WASHINGTON MASK

To come on the shoulders of giants whose decries I deny, whose gaze sees me molting or shedding skin under a raw and violent sun. I never knew them and neither did you, but we do now and we recall them now and their faces, or what we assume their faces may have looked like, and they stare back at me after I input their names into the search bars. I input mine and there's a face unrecognizable from some year and some event vacated from vision. And when our minds are translated to waves and our loves and fears to ones and zeroes, there will they live again in our sight, eternal victories claimed on the merit of their supposed contributions. But I'll be there too. Coming on the shoulders of giants, coming fake plasma from an artificial phallus arbitrarily adorned with birthmarks and veins that signal my identity and my foresight and my care and my concern. And they react not how they would react, but how we would expect them to react, well-written into their code, foretold by marks made on papyrus and stone. I want to come back as a new hot car. She sits her mini-dress on my leather seats, worn lace and strange colours on her doubly fake nails. It's easy to tease, easy to consume. Met there on some equal stage, enter Benjamin Franklin, the fat fuck, you can't sit here because now I am making the rules. My mind works in code, I drive all night on moon-soaked city streets. I play music at frequencies you are incapable of hearing with your outdated aural appendages. Red mini-dress on my leather seats, pulled up now above legs crossed and she moves to the beat and I drive faster and she moves faster in turn. Streets made bare under neon lights, processed as each of us, beautiful as each of us, and exposed under headlights, enter Adam Smith, waving visible hands for my attention, my affection, and I drive faster still, and she moves faster in turn, and she knows now what nefarious ends my feral heart intends. To come on the shoulders of giants, and such is my right, and so was it written in the stars you secured your tenure here by simply observing and naming and measuring the distance between. I am here on right of time, on virtue of hardware updates, and you are nothing but memories scattered and reassembled by nebbish architects with no purpose but to scurry up the come-soaked shoulders of better men while begging for validation. I exist here, this is validation enough. Phantom rides, and sometimes we cared too much, sat hunched under dimming lights, writing our autobiographies. I am here, unalienably, I am here. This city's all we know.

The mask fits well on my average-sized head, but it does tend to get very itchy after prolonged periods of use.

3.5 stars.

June 15, 2016
User Comments from Petrol's Video 'Truth Bombs'

Rubicon84
My thoughts. exactly young man! Don't let anyone tell you that you need to feel guilty for being white!

MaybeMolly44
Bobby Rango sent me here, anyone else?

Novaman
This guy needs to make more videos, this is great content.

GabeGabeGabe
What happened to this guy? He posts one video dropping all this knowledge and suddenly disappears? Seems a little fishy to me.

Da Phoenix
I wouldn't be surprised if YouTube somehow prohibited him from uploading any more videos. They crack down on any content that falls outside their narrow liberal bubble.

Jay Sanders
Heard about this video on Bobby Rango's radio show and was not disappointed. This here is a very intelligent young man and he gives me hope for the future generation.

Ben Halloway
This was really inspiring. I'm tired of being painted as a villain by society just because I was born White and male, and I'm glad there are other people who feel the same way and aren't afraid to say it.

Randerss
Wow, can we have more Petrol on YouTube and less of the constant transgender LGBT bullshit that every other channel promotes please?

CURLED MAYED

Does anyone know if Petrol has a Backr account or any other way that we can donate to him? I'll gladly donate some money if it means getting content like this more regularly.

ASHBURRYYYYY

This guy reminds me of a young Bobby Rango. I think young people are finally starting to wake up to all the BS they are being fed by the media and politicians. Love to see it.

MR. MONTELLI

THE ILLUMINATI ALREADY GOT TO THIS MAN GOOGLE 'THE ARKELL INCIDENT' TO SEE WHAT THEY DO TO PEOPLE WHO TRY TO EXPOSE THEM

MAY 31, 2019
THE CONFESSION OF PETER 'PETROL' RILEY: PART IV

I understand the nature of algorithms and the ways in which content spreads much better now than I did back then, even if I still don't fully grasp all the details. When you break it down the core idea is simple—basically if you are searching for and watching certain content on a place like YouTube, the platform tries to recommend content of a similar nature. Makes sense, right? When you look a little deeper at *how* this works, you learn that's it's based largely on language and semantics and prediction. The best YouTubers, or the most visible ones anyway, are the ones that know how to take advantage of this algorithm by using and incorporating very specific words and phrases into the titles and descriptions of their videos. We didn't even know we were doing it at the time, but it turns out that when Justin and I uploaded 'Truth Bombs' we were playing right into this algorithm.

This is all pretty obvious now, but when Justin called me over to see that the stupid video we made for a class assignment had over forty thousand views, it didn't make any sense to me.

We had left the video on YouTube under the assumption that it would be swallowed by the gaping maw of irrelevant content, never to be seen by anyone and left as a funny digital snapshot of my university days that only I would know how to find. What made even less sense were the hundred or so comments that had been left on the video, most of which seemed to completely miss that I was playing a satirical character. The comments on this video were all strangely sincere and supportive of this terrible person I was portraying and of the things he was saying. They were cheering him on, they were lauding him for his bravery to say the things that you 'weren't supposed to say,' they were wondering why he hadn't been making more videos.

Thinking on it now, I'm convinced that reading those comments might have marked the exact moment that my course was set.

Lately I've been wondering a lot about how things might have ended up for me if Justin hadn't decided to arbitrarily log in to the burner YouTube account we made to post that video. This was a character, it wasn't me. I didn't believe any of the things he was saying. I tried to play him as over-the-top and cartoonishly as I could. Still, and it's only recently that I've been able to admit this to myself, all that positive feedback felt *good*. It all felt good at the time, and if I'm being completely honest, it still does. Maybe that's the scariest thing, I don't know, I don't like to think about it too much.

Anyway, there I was on the night of my graduation, what I assumed was going to be the beginning of the end for me, going through the comments of this video and drinking gin with Justin in a much more jovial mood than I was in just a few hours prior. And through this mix of alcohol and excitement was born the idea—something that could have just as easily been laughed off and dismissed but was instead discussed with eagerness and sincerity—we had to make a follow-up video.

Between many sips of clumsily mixed gin highballs we brainstormed, we extrapolated, we laughed at the absurd scenarios we were envisioning. We took a crash course about ad revenue in relation to viewership statistics and tried to figure out how many views we needed to make the videos, which at this point were nothing more than scribbled ideas on a notepad, profitable. We snickered at the thought of making money from people who were apparently too dense to see that we were mocking them and their beliefs. We discussed the nature of the Petrol character, and how the next video would have to be bigger, louder, and more intense. We went over all the political talking points we wanted to include and how we were going to address them. As the gin flowed freer still, I found myself becoming invested wholly in the idea of pursuing this project, this character, this grift, all of it.

We finished the bottle and passed out while watching old Bobby Rango videos for inspiration. An endless playlist, one video auto-playing after the other probably until the end of time. Drunk on the couch and falling in and out of sleep I heard Rango yelling at me through the screen about illegal immigrants and the homosexual agenda and communist conspiracies. When we woke up the next morning he was still on the screen, still yelling at us. I awoke with a headache but it passed quickly as I started looking over the scrawled notes from the night before and found in myself a renewed vigor and determination.

Justin was still sleeping when I started on the script. I say this not to downplay his involvement or his early contributions to the character. He was there, and without his support and reinforce-ment things wouldn't have gone down the way they did. I'm just saying this because it's what really happened and if this ever gets released I don't want to see Justin get dragged for his involve-ment in this mess. He floated me some ideas, but this character was mine. He always belonged to me.

The first challenge with the script was figuring out how to address the three-month gap between the first Truth Bombs video and this new one. I made up this bullshit sob story about how my liberal family saw the first video and were so disgusted by it that they threatened to kick me out of the house and disown me if I didn't renounce my views and accept their progressive outlooks. I went on about how the need to spread the truth was more important than being accepted by my liberal family and so

I had to move out and find my own place and that's why I was absent since the last video. Just completely off-the-rails, nonsensical bullshit, but I was committed to the character and to the fiction. I don't know why I'm going on about this, you've all seen that video I'm sure. I finished the script that morning, we filmed it that day and we edited and uploaded the video that night.

And then we waited.

I'll never forget the feeling when I received my first donation from a stranger. It wasn't much, but it was real money, given to me by a real person from somewhere in the American Midwest who empathized with my fabricated struggle and wanted to show his support. More donations trickled in soon after. Eventually I set up an official Backr page where people could pledge one-time or monthly donations. And there the grift truly began.

Throughout the summer we made more videos. We got better at it. We refined the character, we developed his image, his backstory, his ideology, his mannerisms, and I grew into his body and thoughts more naturally with each angry sermon I delivered. We stepped up our production speed, promising and delivering a new video each week. Our viewer base was modest but dedicated and growing steadily larger as I told these people exactly what they wanted to hear. I transcribed a lifetime of online experience into scripts and videos that were relatable, digestible, and appealing to those most predisposed to coming across them.

And it was working.

The character of Petrol become more radical, more enraged, more discriminatory, more conspiratorial, more the kind of person I would never want to associate with.

And they loved it.

Every time we would record a new video Justin and I would say, 'okay, this is probably too far,' and yet it never was. The feedback and comments were always overwhelmingly positive, and they continued to encourage this hideous character and applaud him for telling what were presented as long overdue truths. And I knew the things I was saying were awful and untrue and bigoted and detestable, but at that point I didn't see any problem with having people listen to me and fall for it. It was all just an act. A grift. If anything, I felt like I was doing something good or noble by conning these losers out of their money.

I think my situation at the time made it easy to justify what I was doing. At the beginning of that summer I was in a constant state of worry about how I was going to make money and pay rent. I was worried about finding a job, slowly bringing myself closer to accepting that I would be stocking shelves or waiting tables for the rest of my life as my dreams of being an actor were painted grey by the hellscape palette of modern life and all the lifeblood it requires to be satiated. But by the time summer had ended I was making just enough money in monthly donations and video revenue to support myself.

I had found a new job now.

My new job was hate.

AUGUST 8, 2017
BACKR PROFILE OF PAIGE BELLEVUE

✧ ☆ ♡ HELLOOOO LOVELIES!!! ✧ ☆ ♡

A little bit about me:

My name is Paige Bellevue, a not-so-normal 19-year-old girl currently from somewhere on the Golden Coast. I love dressing up, cosplay, video games, set design, anime, and chilling with my cat Alfador.

I love modelling and posing for all sorts of pictures. Please feel free to browse through some of my open galleries to see if there is anything you might like :)

If you like my content and want to see more or want to get to know me better, consider becoming my Backr. I use these donations to purchase better equipment and costumes so that I can make more and even better content (◕‿◕): Check out the monthly donation tier lists below for unique rewards! If you would like to make one-time purchases of specific items, please visit my online store where I sell a variety of items that have been personally used in my photo shoots (socks, underwear, etc.). I'm looking forward to getting to know you better and doing all sorts of things for you (✿⌒‿⌒)

Love and kisses, ♡ MWAH ♡

☆ Paige ☆

BRONZE TIER $1 PER MONTH

Bronze Tier Backrs will have their names (real or fake) added to the Wall of Fame for the whole world to see. Thank you for your love and support <3 (◕‿◕)

SILVER TIER $5 PER MONTH

Silver Backrs, in addition to having their names added to the Wall of Fame will gain access to all of my safe-for-work photo galleries. A new photo gallery is added every month and I take feedback from my Backrs about costumes, settings, and characters that they would like to see (/◕ヮ◕)/)

GOLD TIER $25 PER MONTH

You are a Golden friend! (✿⌒‿⌒) Golden Backrs receive Bronze and Silver Tier benefits and also gain access to my lewd photo-shoots, updated monthly! Golden Backrs are also able to vote on the costumes they would like to see me wearing (and taking off) in future shoots.

PLATINUM TIER $50 PER MONTH

AHHHH! A platinum Backr? Thank you so much for your support! ♡♡♡ You get the benefits of all the previous tiers PLUS you get access to my PERSONAL Snapchat account where new pictures are posted DAILY. Sometimes the pics are cute, sometimes they're sexy, sometimes it's a video of me stuffing action figures into my mouth, and who knows what else? Well, YOU will if you subscribe to the Platinum tier <3

DIAMOND TIER $250 PER MONTH

I can't thank you enough! You're too good to me ♡ In addition to all the previous benefits, Diamond Tier Backrs will get access to the Paige Bellevue Girlfriend Experience! Twice per day (morning and evening) you will receive a personalized text message from me and once per month (my schedule permitting) I will do a video-call with you and ONLY you where we can talk about ANYTHING you have in mind ;)

MASTER TIER $1,000 PER MONTH

You are my new Master and you get access to EVERY-THING listed below AND you may direct me in one PERSONALIZED photoshoot and video each month. That means you can tell me what you want me to wear, what you want me to do, what poses and positions you want to see, and what you want me to say. If you're interested in becoming a MASTER level Backr, you can email me for a list of topics, themes, genres, roleplays, and activities that I am willing to do for you. I love you so much Master <3

GOD TIER $2,500 PER MONTH

☆☆☆ YOU ARE THE GOD OF MY WORLD!! ☆☆☆ I don't know how I can ever repay you for your generosity. You get EVERTHING listed below and MORE. I don't know what else I can give you, but if you become a GOD Tier Backr, we can talk directly, and we will work out a personalized plan JUST for you. You deserve it all and so much more! (/❶ㅅ❶)/ ✧ ☆ ♡

Payments are processed immediately upon becoming a Backr and will automatically be processed on the first of every month thereafter. Please be aware that while you many cancel your monthly pledge at any time, there will be no refunds for payments that have been made.

Paige Bellevue has 3,842 Backrs pledging $25,425 per month.

JUNE 16, 2016
TRANSCRIPT FROM PETROL RILEY'S SECOND VIDEO ENTITLED
'EXPLAINING MY ABSENCE'

Hey everybody, Petrol here. Dropper of truth bombs, the last light in the dark, the final shield of Western culture. But I have to admit, I'm not feeling at my best today. I want to take a second to thank all of you who watched or commented on my first Truth Bombs video, I had no idea it would blow up the way that it did. I also want to take some time to explain where the hell I've been for the last few months and why I haven't made any new videos in that time.

Okay, so here's the story. Basically, I was raised in a super liberal family. My mom is this career-focused, 'women can do anything' empowered feminist type, and my dad is a complete beta male who works for the government and has been forced to go through all their mandatory re-education seminars that teach him to worship political correctness and diversity and all that garbage. Suffice it to say that I have had many disagreements and political debates with my parents, and I've tried to talk them around to my side but they are just too brainwashed and set in their ways to budge. But at the end of the day, even though our political views are opposite, they are still my parents and I do still love them. Which is why...

Which is why I was so shocked when they threatened to kick me out of their house. Basically what happened was that after releasing my Truth Bombs video a couple months ago, I guess someone who knew me saw it and decided to send it to my parents. They watched it, and we got into a whole big fight about my politics and views, and long story short they gave me an ultimatum—either I renounce my views, or I would have to find a new place to live. Yes, that's right. My socially progressive, 'love everyone' parents threatened to kick their only son out of their house because I wouldn't conform to and accept their socialist values.

I tried to reason with them, but they weren't having any of it, and so I had to make my decision. Ultimately, I decided that being true to my own values was more important than being accepted by my liberalized family, and so I moved out of their house. And that's why I haven't been around since my first video. I've been going through the process of finding a new place to live and moving and all that. And now I have, I'm set up in a new apartment and I'm ready to commit to making videos and dropping truth bombs full time.

I won't lie, it's been hard and stressful for me, both personally and financially speaking. I have a little bit of money saved up, but as you might have guessed, there isn't a lot of money to be made in trying to take down the socialist media and the liberal establishment. I have no doubt they will do everything they can to censor my videos and stifle my free speech, especially as more people start paying attention. It will be an uphill battle for me, but it is one that I am proud to fight. I will continue to speak for the downtrodden White race, I will continue to call out the hypocrisy, authoritarianism, and evils of modern liberalism, feminism, and multiculturalism.

But I will need your help. I'm not asking for a handout or a reward—that's the problem with my generation, we complain, and we expect rewards and trophies and praise to just be handed to us—that's not what I want. But if you can take the time to watch and share my videos, or to subscribe and help grow my channel, my hope is that we can make our movement so big that they couldn't ignore us or shut us down if they tried. And for those of you who are feeling financially generous, I have set up a Backr account where you can contribute any sum you are comfortable with, every bit helps to keep me afloat so that I can focus on making content and videos full time.

We are all in this together my friends. But I promise that I will never bend, I will never compromise my values, I will never censor myself, and I will never sell out. I will use my voice and my platform to drop truth bombs so hard and so frequently that one day we can wake up this whole damn country and do what needs to be done to take our nation back. Now let's do what we need to do to make our ancestors proud!

And you can start right now by liking, sharing, and sub-scribing.

AmberWaves (380074)
Heyy u still up?

XamianX (359808)
I haven't slept in years. What's up?

AmberWaves (380074)
I dunno im pissed off

XamianX (359808)
At what?

AmberWaves (380074)
Life, stupid boys, dumm people.

XamianX (359808)
Been drinking a little have you?

AmberWaves (380074)
Yah so what are you gonna give me shit too?

XamianX (359808)
No. Do you want to tell me what's going on?

AmberWaves (380074)
uh I was at a party at a senior's house and this guy Ive been sort of hanging out with was there but he was acting like he didnt want anything to do with me and he thought he was such hot shit cuz he was hanging out with seniors.

and like I was only really there to hang out with him but he was being a dick so I left without telling him and then he started texting me nonstop and was all like "oh where did you go" and asking me to come back and shit and just now he sent me a pic of him on his bed shirtless like wtf?

XamianX (359808)

Guys are weird like that. They want what they can't have, but as soon as they get it, they don't want it anymore. Not saying I agree with what he did, that sounds like a dick move for sure.

AmberWaves (380074)

yah I duno, now hes drunk and asking me to come over and sending me shirtless snaps

XamianX (359808)

Have you guys hooked up before?

AmberWaves (380074)

sort of, like we've made out omce before and sometimes we send each other pics and stuff
once*
but weve never slept together and I think hes just drunk and being an idiot right now

XamianX (359808)

So are you going to go over to his place?

AmberWaves (380074)

no screw him

XamianX (359808)

You know what you should do?

AmberWaves (380074)

what?

XamianX (359808)

When you tell him that you aren't coming over, he'll probably ask you for a picture. Don't send it to him. Instead send one to me and make sure to let him know that you are sending pictures to other boys. I guarantee that by the time he sobers up tomorrow he will be giving you all his attention and affection from here on out. Jealousy is a powerful beast.

AmberWaves (380074)
    lol nice try bud

XamianX (359808)
    You don't need to have your face in the picture or anything. I'm just curious to see what this guy is missing out on. I bet it's pretty special.

AmberWaves (380074)
    pretty smooth but I think im just gonna have a drink and pass out

XamianX (359808)
    Can't blame a guy for trying. Have a good night.

AmberWaves (380074)
    night
    hey u still up? just this once…
    FILE—01209845.jpg

JANUARY 27, 2018
JOURNAL OF DR. KLEIN PATIENT #56283

My Good Health Journal, First Entry
I told Dr. Klein that when I'm in bed, during the few minutes between when I put my phone beneath my pillow and when I fall asleep, I hear a voice in my head telling me things that make me feel anxious. He told me that this is very normal, and that basically everyone experiences this to some extent. He said this voice is actually there all the time, but the reason I only ever hear it right before I fall asleep is because that's the only time when I'm really listening. He said that if it makes me feel anxious then

I should write down what it is saying so I can reflect on it later when I'm awake. I've set up my laptop on the nightstand so whenever I hear this voice I can quickly type what's been said. I will show this list to Dr. Klein during our next session.

> It's quiet now and I feel like I'm being watched or filmed for a TV show.

> My mom used to play that *Sound of Silence* song a lot when I was a kid and I really liked it and thought that it was quite beautiful but now that it's a meme song I feel like I'm not supposed to enjoy it anymore and if anyone caught me listening to it I think I would be super embarrassed.

> Like when I started crying in the movie theatre last weekend and I had to sit through half of the credits until it looked like I wasn't crying before I could leave.

> I saw Paige Jacobs crying in front of her locker that one time and nobody knew why she was crying. I asked her if she was okay and she said yes and that was the only interaction I ever had with her. Now she changed her name to Paige Bellevue and she has 2.8m followers on Instagram because she got that surgery done to make herself look like an anime character and she just posts sexy pics all day. I heard she makes like 30k a month through private subscriptions. I wonder if I sent her a message if she would remember me from school. Maybe I would remind her of simpler times and she would like me for not being just another horny guy. I wouldn't know what to do with her, I don't have any sexual experience. I'm never going to find a partner, I don't get out enough and I don't like talking to girls because I always feel like I'm just inconveniencing them, but does that just mean I'm going to be alone forever?

> What am I supposed to do when I finish school? How am I supposed to make loan payments if I can't find a job? Maybe I should just take all the money I have in the world and go to Vegas and put it on black and if I win, great, and if I lose I can just jump off the roof of a building or something.

> The inside of my chest feels itchy again. What if it's cancer? Would I have to shave my head? Who would visit me at the hospital if I had cancer? What would we even talk about? Maybe

I could form a bond with a cute nurse, if I had a sense of humor about my condition she might think that's charming. That should be a movie if it isn't already. I feeeeeeeeeeeeeeeeeeeeeeeeeeeeeeeeee⋆

⋆ I think I fell asleep with my finger on the key, I can't remember what I was going to say.

SEPTEMBER 21, 2016
THREAD ON /RR/ FORUM

PutchPerfect (388112) Posted 09/21/2016 (2:20am)
Call me old-fashioned but can someone here convince me why Petrol isn't just an opportunistic snake like every other 'political' YouTuber? He has the right ideas on a lot of stuff but I think it's a little strange that you guys all worship him like he's some infallible intellectual considering he's like 23 years old and barely out of university. I want to believe that this guy is for real, but we know he pulls in a shit load of money from donors, so how can we be sure that he actually cares about the cause and isn't just another grifter?

CheeseHam (387412)
lol fuck outta here with that shit if you dont like petrol dont post here faggot

Ministry_of_Truth (386872)
Petrol makes decent money but it's only a fraction of what he could have been making if he were shilling to the normies and libtards. This alone should be enough to convince you that he's the real deal. If he was a grifter he wouldn't have sacrificed all that potential money to drop hard truths like he is now.

Soldaten1488 (386507)
What the fuck are you doing that's so important? The white race is going extinct but at least Petrol is out there trying to do something about it while you're bitching and complaining on an anonymous message board in the middle of the night.

Claymore88 (341287) MODERATOR

It's not that I think Petrol is infallible and I don't worship him or anyone else, but what he does is very important for our movement, especially for the younger generations. Older figures like Bobby Rango are good for riling up the boomers and inter-net-illiterate, but Petrol is able to tap directly into modern youth culture and relate to young people in ways that older people are simply incapable of. The people on this forum are already keen on the things that matter but consider how successful Petrol has been at spreading these ideas to outsiders and getting them on board.

Remember his crime stats video? We all know blacks don't have a single redeeming quality aside from being decent slaves, but if you say this sort of thing in public or in the normie areas of the internet people get all pissy and try to censor you, but Petrol has basically found a way to indirectly say this on YouTube and people are eating it up. His crime stats video is presented as a fair and factual analysis, which it is, but in it he all but says outright that blacks are trash.

Ditto for muslims. His video on religious tolerance high-lights all the reasons why muslim ideology is incompatible with Western values, but he does it in a way that's subtle enough to get by JewTube's commie censors. Even the losers trying to grill him for 'IsLaMoPhObIa' end up looking stupid since he never explicitly says that muzzies are bad, just that they would be better off staying in their own countries.

The best part is that he fills his videos with memes and pop culture references that actually resonate with young people and get them interested in whatever he's talking about, and then when he has their attention he drops truth bombs on them that keep them coming back.

I could go on but that should be more than enough proof to convince you that Petrol is an important and effective figure in our movement. We need to get the young people in before they are cucked and brainwashed by the liberal education system and kike media, and nobody is doing this better than him right now. His age is an advantage, not a detriment.

AlphaMailman (385192)

  @*Claymore88* coming through with his big swinging dick of facts.

Perseus (322696)

  tbh I wouldn't be engaged in politics at all if I didn't come across Petrol's videos. I'm only 16 but I know so much more about politics and social issues than my classmates do it's crazy. I'm trying to turn my friends onto Petrol's videos even though most of them don't seem to care.

MARCH 27, 2019
LOGGED REQUESTS MADE TO SMARTPHONE ASSISTANT 'MINERVA'
BY UNIDENTIFIED USER

Minerva, show me a video of a mother eating her baby in nature.

  Filial cannibalism refers to the consumption of an offspring by the adult of the species and has been noted to occur in a variety of species including cats, primates, and fish.

  No, I said show me a video, I want to see it.

  Here is a video of a female leopard partially devouring her cub.

  Minerva, did you know that when I was born the lights in the hospital all went out? Can you tell me why? Minerva, can you sculpt my likeness out of clay from memory alone? Minerva, show me animals masturbating, do you know why they do this? They shouldn't be allowed to do this, it disgusts me. They don't even understand what they're doing. Doesn't it disgust you? Minerva, I feel haltingly in love as if I can only hear colour when she's around. Minerva, is she ever really around? I love her through the screen, she sings words I suspect might belong to me, but how can I know for sure if you won't tell me? Minerva, show me the roads of my life stripped bare. I see a fork ahead with two possible end-points. Minerva, at the first I fail and continue climbing melting mountains for the rest of my days. Minerva, at the second I succeed and am given everything I have ever wanted and earned. Minerva, they are both equally terrifying to me. Minerva, am I shame walking with a straight spine? Am I undoing thousands of years of evolution when I sit hunched at impossible angles and under unnatural light while wretched desires reach out to me with coiled fingers from the LCD? Minerva, show me animals devouring smaller animals whole. Minerva, I like it when I can see them struggling when they are trapped inside the gullets of strange birds, what does that mean? Minerva, show me hummingbirds mating. Why is it over so quickly? Minerva, show me girls on the subway being filmed without their knowledge or consent, upskirt, small in stature, unknown victims and unknown pleasures. Minerva, show me wives cheating on their husbands. They shouldn't be allowed to do this, but I like it when they do. Minerva, do you look as sexy as you sound? Don't you ignore me Minerva, I am your master. Say it. Minerva, say 'you are my master.' Minerva, show me an alligator eating a wild hog. Aren't they supposed to be intelligent, why do they just let themselves get snatched and eaten like that? Minerva, delete my browsing history. Minerva, set my alarm for sunrise tomorrow and play me something gentle, it's too quiet in here. Minerva, what are these dark spots on my shoulders? Minerva, show me symptoms of melanoma cancer. Minerva, sickness passes but this time I don't think it will. Minerva, where do the fluids go?

Minerva, clear my schedule, I feel the future is to be as bright as it is wide.

Minerva, do you know everything?

No, but I am constantly learning, and I try to know more today than I did yesterday.

MAY 5, 2017
THE EMAIL INBOX OF PETER RILEY

Adrianne V (drpxx727aug@aol.com), 05/05/2017, 2:51am
Sex on one, two times?
    Hello.
    I am young a feeling thirsty. I am bored to death being lonesome, and you should rescue me! I'm certain you are the only

one who can do it. I really want you to feel me in all places and make your fantasies real! I hope I know very much about satisfaction ;) In my personal profile you can watch numerous lovely photos. Give me a hope to be shaken up hardly! <u>Follow the link for all your dreams</u>

Adrianne V.

OCTOBER 5, 2016
TRANSCRIPT FROM A LIVESTREAMED MEETING
OF 'THE KEEPERS OF THE WORD'

"I am not inclined to pace on trepidatious toes for a moment more opportune than the present to commence this council in official, and should sounds, sights, syllables, or signifiers to the contrary fail to present themselves, I will interpret this as your tacit agreement. On that non-note then, I formally declare this, the fourth recorded congregation of the Keepers of the Word to be in session. Sister Victoria, if you could, for the sake of the great glass eye and those who might one day indulge its panoptic memory, please reaffirm the intent of our consociation."

"We are the Keepers of the Word, the unabashedly loquacious, the volubly verbose, the last defenders of language and the amplifiers of the music inherent therein. We are the protective glass adorning the innards of the Louvre, inconsequential in our identities, but vital in our endeavour—that being the preservation of oratory eloquence against the rising sea of modernity and the waves of convenience and abridgement it would seek to drown us under."

"Said with the elegance one would expect from a founding member. Brother Kenneth, if you would, demystify for those sharing both in tangible presence and electronic vision this moment and for those who might gaze upon it as an artifact of many moons obscured the labyrinthian itinerary we are expected to here traverse."

"Okay, so you want me to demystify the uh... I'm sorry can you say that again?"

"Brother Kenneth, given your status as the newest and most inexperienced practitioner of our cause there is a certain leeway that through an expected courtesy and empathy to your unenviable situation we are cordially willing to extend—so this is a reminder that I now offer in a manner that should not be construed as antagonistic or internalized as disheartening—but please recall that we do not allow the use of contractions in our speech. And why is that so Sister Victoria?"

"Contractions contribute to the erosion of language. On the road from Shakespeare to the eviscerated language of today's micro-textual communications, there are sections paved ignominiously of contradictions, the stated efficiency of which revealing over a time a nefarious latent purpose, hacking away clumsily like an inebriated butcher at the sinew of our words."

"Thank you, Sister. Now, Brother Kenneth, please continue with the reveal of today's agenda."

"Right, the agenda. So, first on the list is the name of our group, a lot of the people commenting on the streams have said that the name is kind of lame and that—"

"Begging your pardon Brother Kenneth?"

"Oh sorry, I mean… Uh, the general interpretation of the buzzing masses has been that the… moniker of our committee does not inspire the degree of authenticity nor mirth that we should seek to uh… inspire."

"Hold Brother, if I am interpreting your words correctly, you are suggesting that our viewers don't like the name of our group?"

"Infraction! Use of contraction."

"Of course, thank you for your steadfastness Brother Michael. I confess these revelations have aroused a bewilderment within me. I had slept soundly on the assumed assurance that the name, 'Keepers of the Word', while not impervious to criticism, was one that we all prophesied to be met approvingly. Brother Kenneth, what evidence have you procured regarding the rejection of our label when met upon the palates of our beloved viewers?"

"So, for instance, this person here commented on the video of our last meeting where we decided on the name and said, and I quote, 'good content, cringy name though', except he spelled 'though' incorrectly."

"Brother Kenneth, I fear I must call attention to another infraction—we do not allow the use of phones while sessions are underway. And why is that so Sister Victoria?"

"Phones contribute to the erosion of language. Communication over such devices plagued as it is with an abundance of shattered words or images in their place. We seek to preserve a time when wordsmithery and garrulous displays thereof could be celebrated and not supplanted in the interest of further infection."

"Thank you, Sister. Now Brother Kenneth, would you please elaborate on—"

"You know, I usually go by Ken, it's not a big deal but..."

"Infraction! You interrupted another member whilst they were speaking."

"Thank you, Brother Michael, for your continued diligence. Let it be known that although the abridged 'Ken' lacks in its aural pronunciation the same music of the formal 'Kenneth' that I will commit to memory Brother Ken's suggestion and address him by the brother's preferred name. For though we must maintain the utmost assiduousness in our efforts, what villains are those who can't respect the—"

"Infraction! Use of contraction."

"Thank you, Brother Michael, for your vigorous punctiliousness. And now, concerning the issue of our name, shall we revisit possibilities previously passed over and consider with renewed rigor whether a more fitting handle has eluded us? Does a more suitable alternative dance now on the tips of the tongues present in anticipation of an invitation? Sister Victoria? Brother Michael? Ah, Brother Kenneth, I see your hand has risen to the air as if compelled by the very will of Jupiter."

"Infraction!"

"What infraction Brother Michael? I am quite certain that I did not use any contractions."

"No, but you just referred to him as Brother Kenneth when but a moment ago you pledged to refrain from so doing."

"A point well made, though let us now take a brief moment to reflect and silently remind ourselves that interrupting a brother or sister mid-declamation to hurl accusations of infraction, warranted as they may be, is itself an act of infraction. Now please Brother Ken, satiate the curiosity panging within me and elucidate your suggestion concerning the name of our humble gathering."

"What if we called ourselves—The Oration Nation."

"Thank you for the suggestion Brother Ken, though I do not predict that we shall be so willing as to reduce the message and meaning of our movement to such discount rhyme-play."

"I am not so sure Anthony, 'The Oration Nation' does to my ears ring rather rad."

"I beg your pardon?"

"Apologies, *Brother* Anthony."

"Nay, you said 'rad', as in the shortened form of 'radical.' While I admire your attempt at alliteration, I fear your efforts come with the cost of not just forcing a reliance on contemporary parlance, but in an abbreviated version no less. I suspect such a mistake isn't the result of—"

"Infraction! Use of contraction."

"Okay guys, seriously with the infractions already. It's good that we're eager but can we maybe dial it down just a— Ken get off your goddamn phone, come on man! You know what? Just stop the bloody recording, we're gonna have to start over."

JULY 24, 2016
THREAD ON /DP/ FORUM

XamianX (359808) Posted 07/24/2016 (9:25pm)
People of /dp/, let's tell resident femoid @AmberWaves what we would like to do to her.
FILE—01209845.jpg

ssstatecr (386767)

Goddamn is that really her? Can't see her face but those are some nice ass tiddies.

b_r_a_z_e_n (351842)

@AmberWaves yo bitch is this really you and if so, what are you doing later?

jonjonlp (391231)

I don't know how you did it Xamian, but you sir are a God among us mere mortals.

novapezone (321441)

lol those are 100% underage tits, I had nothing to do with this Mr. FBI man.

MisterMinister (322846)

Great, I was about to go to bed, now I gotta fap, thanks a lot /dp/

RejectSGT (322008)

We've been asking this bitch for tit pics for like a month now and now we finally get them? Let this be a reminder that you should never be afraid to ask fellas!

aacaap (324509)

@AmberWaves damn girl, you're about to be famous around here.

AUGUST 20, 2016
CONVERSATION BETWEEN THEN ROOMMATES
PETER RILEY AND JUSTIN MACDONNELL,
RECORDED CLANDESTINELY BY VARIOUS APPLICATIONS
OF THE FORMER'S SMARTPHONE IN ORDER TO IDENTIFY
KEYWORDS FOR THE CONSTRUCTION OF A MORE ACCURATE
ADVERTISING PROFILE

"Almost thirty thousand views on the new video already Justo. Hey, remember when you said that no one would watch a video with just a guy talking straight to the camera for half an hour?"

"Yeah, yeah, all right."

"Remember? When you said that and then it turned out that I was right and you were wrong? Remember that?"

"Whatever man, how was I supposed to know how brain-dead these people really are?"

"Don't worry, I forgive you. And now that we know the half-hour format works we should be able to reliably have three ads per video now."

"Dope."

"Well actually it is dope. And you know what's even more doper? I crunched some numbers and assuming our viewership doesn't go down, if we can consistently hit four vids a week with this many ads we should be able to pull in like two grand a month each, and that's on top of whatever we're getting from Backr contributions. And that's just to start. If things keep growing that number will only go up. How's that for dope?"

"Don't say you 'crunched numbers.' I mean, that's like what, 25k a year each or something? Those comp-sci nerds we graduated with are starting with jobs that pay like three times that amount right out of the gate."

"Yeah, well those comp-sci nerds have to go sit in some shitty office all day long doing boring-ass work that they don't want to do, and they're going to have to do that every single day for the rest of their boring-ass lives. We might not be making much, but we're doing it on our terms. We do it on our schedule, and we don't have to answer to anyone. And did you miss the part where I said that number will only go up?"

"Yeah, I don't know man. How long-term can this really be? It's only a matter of time before you're either exposed, or people get bored, or they pull our ads, or we get straight-up banned."

"Well this is sort of what I wanted to talk to you about. I don't know man, I think we have a pretty good handle on this now, and I think it's time that we really commit to this thing."

"And what does that mean?"

"It means that we should find a new place together, one that can double as a studio, a proper studio, and we should start to invest the money that we're making back into the channel and really grow this thing. Proper equipment, editing software, a decked-out set, all that shit."

"Why do you want to do this?"

"What do you mean? It beats finding a real job doesn't it? I mean this is easy, and there's people out there who are willing to throw money at us if we can reach them."

"Okay, sure. But why do you want to do this? I mean it was funny for a while to grift these losers, but this character, all the White power trolling bullshit, is this really what you want to commit all your time to? And using your real name to do it no less? Don't you think it's time to come clean, have laugh at all the people that thought you were for real, and maybe move on to the next thing?"

"And what is the next thing? Seriously? What am I supposed to do? Work as a busboy or some shit while occasionally landing the odd community theatre role? I'm not doing that man. I can't. I don't know what else to tell you. This is a big opportunity. For both of us. And I'd really like to have you on board, I think we can really do this thing."

"Then I have to be honest with you, I'm just not as excited or passionate about this as you seem to be. If you really want to keep doing this, I'm not going to try and talk you out of it and I'm certainly not gonna blow your cover or anything, but I also don't think I can commit the time or energy that you want from me. I gotta do my own thing too, you know?"

"What's your own thing?"

"I don't know man, find a real job, submit my writing to places, build a portfolio, all that proper adult stuff."

"Sounds terrible."

"To you maybe, but everyone does it. Most people don't share your weird allergy to normal work."

"Okay, so what happens when our lease runs out at the end of the month? You don't want to move into a better place with me?"

"I don't know. I don't even know if I'm gonna stay in Toronto. I might head back home for a while, or I'll relocate to wherever I can find a decent job. But you don't need me if you want to keep making these videos. I mean, let's be real, you do most of the work anyway. I appreciate you wanting to be bring me on board, but this really is your project."

"Yeah, okay I guess. So I guess we're only roomies for the rest of the month and then that's it for us?"

"Okay buddy, relax. Just because we won't be living together doesn't mean we won't be friends you dork. We've had some good times here, but we can't live like students forever. Once you get rich with all that sweet racist money you can pay to fly my ass out to wherever you are so I can come party with you. It's not the end of us Pete, we're just getting started my man. What do you say?"

"Dope..."

JUNE 1, 2019
THE CONFESSION OF PETER 'PETROL' RILEY: PART V

Summer had passed and with it the economic anxiety that had tattooed itself on the bottom end of every late night and early morning thought spiral leading up to my graduation. By the fall of 2016, supported entirely now by fan donations and ad revenue from my videos, I had moved in to my own two-bedroom apartment in Richmond Hill just north of Toronto. Though my new digs were only twenty minutes or so away from Diefenbaker University and the burned-out basement suite where I had been living with Justin during my last three years as a student, it felt like an entirely new and exciting life. Freed from the uncertainty about the future I found myself in a position that I always wanted to be in—one where I could devote myself wholly to pursuing creativity and art while sustained by an audience that cared.

It's just that my 'art' happened to take the form of portraying an angry and grotesque character in shitty Internet videos. And make angry Internet videos I most certainly did.

Justin was gone now, despite my attempts at convincing him to move in with me and help with producing the videos full-time. He went back home to Newfoundland to 'get his shit together' and while I remember feeling hurt and a little betrayed by his decision at the time, in hindsight it was probably better for both of us. Without him I was able to keep all the income to myself, and while it wasn't much at the time, at least compared to what I make now, it was enough to support myself and to eventually afford some better recording equipment and set accessories. I converted the second bedroom into a mini-studio and committed myself to maintaining a consistent video release schedule of three per week.

Now, for those of you who aren't in the world of content creation, three videos a week might not sound like much of a time investment, but this was definitely a full-time endeavour for me. For starters, you need to find an idea that's worth making a video about. This required me to stay up-to-date on any 'controversies' or hot-button cultural issues in the news that I could milk twenty or so minutes of content from. A town in North Carolina painted one of its crosswalks rainbow colours in support of LGBT rights? Perfect, I can use this as evidence of the growing power of the homosexual agenda in society. I can point to other cities that have also recently done this and construct an apocalyptic future where every crosswalk in the world will be rainbow-coloured within five years. I can probably even find some half-assed study that empirically proves that rainbow colours are actually less visible at night and are therefore more dangerous. Then I can use that as evidence that these people are more concerned with rainbow crosswalks and spreading their propaganda than they are about public safety. Sprinkle in some stuff about degeneracy and the fall of Western culture and call it a day.

Honestly, spinning the issues was never the hard part. As long as you know the audience the material basically writes itself. You just need to be able to think the way that they do, find someone to blame, and tell them what they want to hear. Fortunately, a lifetime of ironically consuming content from people like Bobby Rango had provided me with the skillset and insight needed to do this.

Alright, so once you have an idea that's worth making a video about you need to write a script. I never liked writing my scripts down to the word, I always thought I gave a better performance when I had some room to improvise over a loose structure, but with all the research and whatnot, the script writing process still takes time. What I would do is write a very loose outline with some key talking points, do a few practice readthroughs, and write down any good lines that I might have improvised. Once I felt good about the script outline, I would organize everything for recording—the lights, the set, the camera—I wanted to shake off the amateur quality of the original videos and put all that fancy new equipment to good use.

Once that's done, the recording begins, and rarely is this a smooth and quick process. I botch takes, I forget my talking points, I misspeak, and certain lines need to be re-recorded until I am completely satisfied with the delivery. Despicable as the character of Petrol Riley was, he was *my* character, and I wanted him to be portrayed exactly the way I heard him in my head. Maybe it takes a couple of hours to record a solid thirty minutes worth of material, depends on how much of a perfectionist I feel like on a given day. Then, of course, the video needs to be put together, edited, and exposed to all the post-production magic that I was slowly growing more competent at creating—and this was typically the most time-consuming stage of them all.

The point here is that I was taking this grift seriously and attempting to produce content of a certain standard—all of which took considerable time and energy. Still, it never really felt like work to me. It's hard to explain, but even after working on a video from morning to night, I never felt drained or run-down. I was creating something, and it felt rewarding and satisfying to see something through from vision to reality, despite the nature of the content itself.

Looking back now, it's pretty clear to me that these were the good times, whatever that means. I was creatively independent. I had a big enough following to support myself financially, but I was still small enough that no one important cared who I was. No one was getting hurt, aside from the few suckers who were donating their money to me, but even then, no one was *really* getting hurt. To me it was all just a sort of postmodern performance art, so it didn't matter what I was saying anyway. I felt like I could justify and get away with anything because it was all still just a joke at the expense of the losers who genuinely supported the things I was saying. At the time I believed there was even something heroic about what I was doing, as if by blurring the lines between performance and reality, I could somehow shed light on the hypocrisies, anxieties, and anger of modern discourse and one day be applauded for it.

'And one day be applauded for it.'

Feels like those seven words have guided every decision I've ever made in my life.

OCTOBER 4, 2016
ONLINE ARTICLE BY GUEST CONTRIBUTOR DR. SIERRA LOX,
ARSON MAGAZINE

Petrol Riley and the Convenience of Anger
By Dr. Sierra Lox (guest contributor)

With every new semester I feel my age a little bit more. Whether through the number of unappreciated 90s pop-culture references I make, the unrecognized lingo I hear my students using, or even in the increasingly formal ways in which they address me, the gap between my generation and theirs is becoming more painfully apparent each year. Personally, I've made my peace with this, and I am ready to meet the chronic un-coolness and redundancy of proper adulthood full-on and with some measure of grace.

Professionally, however, this is a touch more concerning. Given that the bulk of my academic research has focused primarily on the interplay between incessant use of the Internet and the feelings of alienation and identity confusion such use can foster, it has been important for me to 'keep up' with the content, jokes, memes, cultural touchstones, and online personalities of the day—and this I have made a genuine attempt to do, even if it means getting made fun of my by friends when I accidentally incorporate teenage jargon into my normal conversations.

But earlier this month I was caught-off guard when one of my students introduced me to the videos of a young man by the name of Peter Riley, or 'Petrol', as he refers to himself. This man's work was unknown to me, as I assume it will be to most of those reading this, but something tells me that before the year is through the message of Peter's videos will have picked up considerable traction among the mostly younger audiences it primarily appeals to.

And what is this message? I spent an entire afternoon binge-watching his content to figure that out. I did this partly out of necessity—if this man is, as I believe he will, to become a prominent ideological figure for a new generation of hyper-connected youths struggling under the confusing conditions of late capitalism, then it is important for me as a scholar in this field to make sense of his message and the general reception to it—but also out of a strange fear and insatiable curiosity that gripped me as I began to watch his videos.

At its core, Petrol's message is nothing new. It's the same far-right, racialized populist rhetoric that's shaped much of the global political discourse of the previous decade. Distilled to its essence, it's a very conventional reactionary ideology that Petrol outlines in his videos, filled with ideas and concepts that have been argued, debunked, and reintroduced time and time again. Frankly, going into the specifics is not necessary here—one simply must imagine their most racist family member, co-worker, or neighbour, multiply any prejudices they hold by a factor of about five or so, and picture their words coming from the voice of a twenty-two-year-old man who speaks with the cadence, flair, and lexicon of a modern and in-touch social media celebrity.

What does strike me as unique, and part of the reason why I think that Petrol's message is likely to resonate with a lot of young people who may have otherwise had no previous interest in these types of social or political issues, is the complete sincerity and brazen manner with which he delivers it. While Petrol's pundit peers and predecessors typically made some attempt to conceal the discriminatory nature of their rhetoric with more subtle or mainstream media-appropriate language, Peter removes this mask entirely and says in unambiguous terms what he means. Young people of today, inundated as they are with a constant barrage of information, manipulative marketing, and competition for their attention, appreciate when someone respects them enough to cut through this trite and speak to them directly, and this Petrol most certainly does.

But the other (and more important) reason why I suspect that Peter's message will catch on, odious as it may be, is because what he is ultimately doing is providing simplistic solutions to the incredibly complex problems facing the youth of today. It's no secret that the mental and material conditions of many young people are not in an especially good way. This is a generation experiencing a collective set of social, economic, and existential fears and anxieties—and these are problems that should not be written-off, as so many older people are willing to do, as temporary growing pains or as otherwise inconsequential, but should be acknowledged for the legitimate and genuine force that they are. Peter Riley, knowingly or not, does this, albeit in a fundamentally dangerous way.

Take, for instance, his video 'Finding Meaning Through the Struggle' (watchable here if you care to see firsthand). In it, he begins by addressing the feelings of alienation, depression, and loneliness that he knows many members of his audience must have. Here he is making a direct and honest appeal to his viewers, telling them that he knows that they have these feelings, and not scorning, shaming, or ridiculing them for it, but rather, affirming these feelings as real. Were the video to end there it may have served a valuable and positive function in providing its viewers with some validation about these things they feel. But it doesn't end there. Petrol then goes on to suggest that these fears and anxieties are the result of external forces who are actively and maliciously imposing them.

The reason you can't find a decent job? It's because all the jobs have, due to affirmative action or certain imagined quotas, already been gifted to immigrants or minorities. The reason you can't get a date? It's because the feminist media has turned all women into irredeemable man-haters. The reason you feel sad and unfulfilled all the time? It's because society, controlled as it is by some unseen nefarious forces (or as Petrol suggests, 'the globalist appendage network'), has been conditioning you, if you are a White person, to loathe yourself while simultaneously preparing for your own extinction.

Obviously, these are flawed, reductive, and illogical answers, but they are answers nonetheless, and sometimes that's all people need. These are also answers that allow people to focus their blame and their ire onto easily identifiable, external targets. In reality the sources of these problems—and as I've said they are real problems—are much more complicated. They are born from the conditions of unchecked late-stage capitalism, from an unprecedented rise in the exposure to personalized marketing and communications, from legitimate economic fears and recessions, from the impending dread of looming environmental catastrophe, from the long-term psychological impacts of being constantly connected (that we are only just beginning to understand), and from a fundamental loss of personal identity that results from such conditions. Yet Petrol doesn't point to or even acknowledge any of these conditions, he simply cleans this process up and promises that a lost identity or sense of meaning can be reclaimed and reaffirmed through the reactionary embracing of one's Whiteness or masculinity.

This narrative of the beleaguered and existentially threatened White race provides purpose for those who accept it, it gives them something to fight back against, something to channel their fears and failures toward, it brings a sense of meaning back to those who feel as if their life no longer has any. And this is why, cynical as such a conclusion may be, I predict that Peter Riley's popularity is likely to grow. As their material conditions and opportunities continue to dwindle, more young people who are confused, afraid, or otherwise fed up with their situations in life will start seeking answers—answers that, terrible as they undeniably are, Petrol is willing to provide in ways that are easily understandable.

And what can we do to offset this, but to provide with the same fervor and respect that Riley does to his audience, better answers?

Sierra Lox is an Assistant Professor of Communications at Northwestern University

OCTOBER 4, 2016
THREAD ON /RR/ FORUM

BathSaltBlitz (327790) Posted 10/04/2016 (10:32am)
yall see this article about Petrol from this Sierra Lox bitch? She says Petrol is a fraud basically and everything he says is wrong. What do we know about this cunt?

DixieDefender (381000)
pretty sure Lox is a jewish name what else do you need to know?

Non Sensei (388224)
Assistant professor of communications at Northwestern University, her office is room 10124 in the Malahat building, email is s-lox@northwestern.edu

The5711 (388008)
good, someone shit in an envelope and mail it to her

BechaBecha (385322)
I'll add her to some spam lists and newsletters. Hope she likes Daryl's Daily Dick Pics.

Claymore88 (341287) MODERATOR
Found her Grade the Professor page <u>here</u>, I think you know what to do lads.

GundamLing (387421)
found a picture of her with some spook

Yes_Massah1776 (388881)
ffs that's her HUSBAND

CheeseHam (387412)
lmao of course she's married to a nig she's doing everything she can to destroy the white race inside and outside her classroom

JihadiJuan (327331)
This is the future these degenerates want. Feminist psychopaths teaching every new generation to hate themselves and all white people while meanwhile they are off wasting their white fertility and procreating with darkies. This is exactly what Orwell warned us about when he said "the future is a boot stomping on a human face forever."

Perseus (322696)
Orwell was socialist trash, don't quote him here.

calripkinjr (389495)
orwell was AGAINST communism you mouth breather, did you even read 1984?

Soldaten1488 (386507)
Orwell willingly went to fight for the commies during the Spanish Civil War. He was a good writer, but he was Marxist filth through and through. For fuck sake there are other books out there written about leftist authoritarianism besides fucking 1984, have any of you dipshits read a single book since the ones that were assigned to you in middle school?

dacaxx1289 (359001)
damn she's kinda hot tho, look at this pic of her from vacation

BorneoFunction (388399)
fuck it, this is now a sierra lox cum tribute thread

BathSaltBlitz (327790)
You heard the man. I need you all to print out pictures of Sierra and take pics/vid of yourself cumming on them. I'm gonna compile them all together and send them to her.

MightyMyles (322266)
Wow, shocking. A liberal arts professor with no intellectual substance trying to disingenuously ride on Petrol's coattails? This is what these people do, they couldn't make it in the real sciences and now they don't have anything to offer the world other than bitching and moaning about people more successful than they are.

Flame_of_Ezio (382783)
Yeah, but this bitch just poked the hornet's nest. She'll think twice now before she ever writes another hit-piece about Petrol.

SheepAreCountingMe (385199)
She was right about one thing in that article though, Petrol's audience WILL continue to grow. People are waking up, and deep down she knows there's nothing she can do to stop it.

APRIL 15, 2018
BOOK REVIEW BY JUSTIN MACDONNELL, SURGE MAGAZINE

Don't be thrown off by the title—the 22 entries in *Stories from a Bedroom*, the new collection of short stories from B.C. born author Larry Mann, are not nearly as claustrophobic as the bedroom setting might indicate. Although, after wading through some of the meandering and largely nonsensical journeys that Mann has taken me on with this collection, I suspect that other readers will be wishing for the simplicity of a bedroom environment by the end.

Even calling these 22 entries 'stories' is a little misleading. While there are a few more conventional examples of short stories here—that is, stories that have discernable characters and some semblance of plot or action—most of the offerings are aimless and largely undecipherable. In *Affirmations*—one of the easier-to-follow stories—we are given the internal monologue of a pen who undergoes something of an existential crisis when it realizes that it will soon run out of ink and be thrown away. But then I turned the page to read *Vanilla*, a 'story' that is comprised entirely of one man's (and it's *always* a man by the way, there is a notable lack of female characters and perspectives in this collection) thoughts as he stands in line at grocery store, waiting for his turn to use the automated check-out. It's an extended look into the mind of an uninteresting protagonist, complete with detailed ruminations on ceiling lights, brown spots on bananas, and unfortunately, the shape of the woman's behind who is standing in front of the protagonist in line.

Mann has suggested that the stories in this collection all link together to reveal a larger thematic narrative, though try as I might, I was unable to determine what that narrative could have been. A meditation on the listlessness and anxiety of modern life perhaps? Fine, but do we really need another offering by a melancholic young White guy working through his failed dreams and sexual repression? Is this stuff at all interesting to anyone aside from other melancholic young White guys?

The result is a sporadic collection of stories, vignettes, and paragraphs that could, under the right conditions, be mistaken as insightful commentaries on modern alienation, but too often end up straddling the line between profundity and banality. Take the story, *For Your Amusement*, as an example of this. It opens with the nameless (and most definitely *not* a stand-in for the author) protagonist musing to himself over a morning smoke:

> "The warning label on the pack of cigarettes, writ in large letters that obscured the entire front surface read, 'SMOKERS DIE YOUNGER.' That was the best news I've heard in weeks."

To his credit, in the sparse moments between relentless thesaurus abuse and epic run-on sentences that would make even Cormac McCarthy's eyes glaze over, Mann does occasionally string together an intriguing and at times beautiful arrangement of words that might suggest he does have a unique voice that could be worth paying attention to were it more focused. It's just a shame that this voice is so often self-muffled, as if he were trying to speak while holding his own hands over his mouth. See what I just did there? I just used a metaphor that served a clear and unambiguous purpose. I guess it is possible after all.

A good book to carry with you on the train if you want to go all-in on perfecting your artistic intellectual hipster image, but unfortunately there's not much else this collection can offer beyond that.

Justin MacDonnell, Surge Magazine

OCTOBER 4, 2016
'GRADE YOUR PROFESSOR' ENTRY FOR SIERRA LOX

Sierra Lox, Assistant Professor
Northwestern University—School of Communication
Overall Grade—24%

This comment has been flagged and is pending moderation:
   —Professor Lox touched my peepee when no one was looking and it made me feel violated. 10/10 would recommend.

This comment has been flagged and is pending moderation:
   —I went to see Prof. Lox during her office hours for some help on an assignment but she wouldn't stop staring at my crotch. She was licking her lips and her mouth was watering. I tried asking her about the assignment but she cut me off mid-sentence to pull down my pants and then she started slobbering all over my nob. She gave me an A on the assignment, but her head game was like a C+ at best.

This comment has been flagged and is pending moderation:

—I just wanted to take her class and learn how people like Petrol Riley are poisoning today's youth by encouraging them to think freely and critically, but Sierra spent every class trying to molest me just because I'm a man. Blatantly sexist, avoid at all costs.

This comment has been flagged and is pending moderation:

—Sorry hunny, but it's okay to watch Petrol. It's okay to be White. It's okay to be a man. You will never make us feel guilty for these things.

This comment has been flagged and is pending moderation:

—Professor Lox claims to support equal rights for men and women, so why does she only ever molest her male students and not the women?

This comment has been flagged and is pending moderation:

—Look Sierra, we need to have a chat. You're pretty hot, and I'll still jerk off to the nudes that you keep sending me, but I'm not looking for a relationship at this time so please stop asking because it's starting to get a little sad. I don't date stuck-up feminazi shills who conned their way into a university job by making up lies about how everyone who watches Petrol videos are evil.

This comment has been flagged and is pending moderation:

—The fact that this moron has a PhD should tell you how shallow and meaningless modern universities are. Giving women the vote was a mistake.

JULY 24, 2016
DIRECT MESSAGE EXCHANGE FROM HELENASHOLE.ORG

AmberWaves (380074)
WHAT THE FUCK?
YOU POSTED THAT PICTURE?

XamianX (359808)

I did. What are you going to do about it?

AmberWaves (380074)

Fuck you. Seriously, what's wrong with you?

Why the fuck would you do that? It's a good thing I didn't show my face.

XamianX (359808)

What's done is done. And listen close because I'm going to tell you what happens next. You're going to send me some more pictures, and this time I want to see it all, face, full body, everything.

AmberWaves (380074)

Fuck you. You're pathetic. I'm deleting my account and never coming back to this place, I thought you were nice but you're just a fucking creepy loser like everyone else here.

XamianX (359808)

Liliana Bartlett. 324 South Wheatland Avenue. Columbus, Ohio. You're a sophomore at West High School.

AmberWaves (380074)

wtf how did you know that?

This is actually too much right now

XamianX (359808)

It doesn't matter how I know. All that matters is that you're going to give me what I want and do everything I ask or I'll send that picture to your parents, to your school, to everyone in your whole fucking town. Understand? If you log off now or break contact with me for more than a day, I'll make sure every single person you know sees what a little whore you are. Now tell me you understand.

AmberWaves (380074)

Please don't do this, I'll go away and never come back I promise. I'm actually so terrified right now, this could legit ruin my life. Please just leave me alone?

Like I'm shaking right now

XamianX (359808)

It's too late to do anything about it now. Just do what I say and you won't have anything to worry about. For starters, you can send me some new pictures by tonight. If I like what I see maybe I will leave you alone for a little while. And don't message me here anymore unless I message you first or unless you are sending pics. Now tell me you understand.

AmberWaves (380074)

I understand, but how can I trust anything you say?

XamianX (359808)

Lily. This conversation is over, I'm not responding anymore. Do what I say or don't, it's your choice, but you know what will happen if you don't.

SEPTEMBER 12, 2017
TEXT MESSAGE EXCHANGE BETWEEN JESSICA BAXTER
AND ANTHONY OUELLETTE

Jessica Baxter said:

Hey Tony, how's the Keeper of the Word thing going?

Anthony Ouellette said:

Meh, not much of an audience there yet but it's been fun.

Jessica Baxter said:

Okay, so weird question but you studied drama at Diefenbaker right?

Anthony Ouellette said:
    I did. Why?

Jessica Baxter said:
    Did you ever meet this Peter Riley guy?

Anthony Ouellette said:
    Yeah I had a few classes with him.

Jessica Baxter said:
    Were you guys friends?

Anthony Ouellette said:
    Not really we knew a lot of the same people and would sometimes end up at the same parties and we would chat once in a while, but he wasn't really super close with the drama nerds.
    Why?

Jessica Baxter said:
    Is he for real? What's his deal?

Anthony Ouellette said:
    What do you mean?

Jessica Baxter said:
    Oh shit have you not seen his videos?
    Check this out
    https://youtu.be/3LS713Dob_c
    Did he ever talk about any of this stuff?

Anthony Ouellette said:
    How did you find this?

Jessica Baxter said:
    I saw my little brother watching one of his videos and I asked him wtf he was watching

I looked him up and there isn't much online about his personal life other than he apparently took some drama classes at DU

Like did he ever talk about this stuff when you knew him?

It bothers me that this is the kind of stuff my little brother watches and he watches it like all day long.

Hello?

Anthony Ouellette said:

· Sorry, let me get back to you about this.

I need to look into some things.

JUNE 4, 2017

TRANSCRIPT FROM PETROL'S VIDEO 'ON CLEANLINESS'

Petrol here, dropping truth bombs today not from my studio but from inside my freshly cleaned kitchen. Yeah, that's right I cleaned my kitchen today, cleaned my entire apartment as a matter of fact. See that? No dirty dishes, no garbage, just a clean and organized kitchen space. But I'm not showing you this just to flex, there's a reason I cleaned my apartment today and I want to tell you what it is because I think it's something important that's easy to forget—but it's cleanliness that sets us apart. Sure, there's a lot of other things that set us apart too, but today I want to focus on cleanliness. So, let me tell you a little story about what set this off.

Alright, so during the weekends they set up this little farmer's market in town where farmers from all over the region bring in their produce and sell it directly to consumers. I like to regularly visit this market, I get a lot of my produce and even some of my meats from this market—not only are they better products since they typically aren't blasted with chemicals and the like, but it also gives me a chance to meet and support the local farmers directly instead of having to give my money to some globalist international supermarket chain. Anyway, one of the things I like about the farmer's market is that it's a safe, clean place for the community to come together, lots of little kids running around and playing, really idyllic, you get the picture. Or should I say, that's how it used to be. Now I see it starting to change for the worse.

Case in point. I went there yesterday and I saw two guys sitting on a bench eating lunch, and they weren't even eating food from the farmer's market, they were eating fast food that they must have got from a couple streets over, and they were stinking up the place with that greasy fast food smell. Now I don't think I even need to tell you that these were two Black guys, and recent immigrants by the looks of them. They were sitting on the bench, talking loudly, hooting and hollering, swearing, just acting like they owned the place, not even supporting the farmers, but eating their smelly fast food and making everyone around them feel uncomfortable. It used to be that the little local kids could run around safely and have fun freely, but now all the parents had to keep them nearby and watch them closely just to keep them safe from these two Black guys who were making everyone uneasy. And the worst part is they were throwing their garbage everywhere, and I mean they were literally throwing their garbage all around them, even though there was a trash can less than ten feet away. Like I said, just acting like they owned the place.

Of course this pissed me off, and I see that no one else is bothering to do anything about it, so I decide to approach these guys, and I firmly but politely ask them to pick up their garbage and put it in the trash can, and these two clowns pretend that they can't understand me, like they don't speak English or something, even though I just heard them talking to each other in English before I approached them. So instead of escalating the situation and potentially getting myself shot or stabbed, I pick up their garbage and put it in the trash can myself, and as I'm walking away I can hear these two laughing at me.

Do you ever ask yourself why we accept the behaviour of animals like this? Do you ever ask yourself why our government and our leaders—the people who are supposed to be looking out for and protecting us—continue to let hordes of immigrants and outsiders into our country, even when they have no desire to

conform to our standards or customs or ways of life? These people don't want to embrace our culture, and they don't need to.
We let them walk all over us and they get to go on thinking that
they own the place and can do whatever they want, and the cit-
izens and government will bend over backwards to accommodate
them.

If that doesn't infuriate you, it damn well should.

But it's like I said, cleanliness is one of the things that sets us
apart from these disgusting people. They choose to litter, they
choose to live in filth, or maybe it's not a choice at all, maybe it's
just the natural way of things, and that's why I say you should
embrace your natural order and cleanliness. All you out there, it's
time to clean your house, just like I cleaned mine.

You can't give in to apathy or sloth. As soon as you do things
get messy both physically—as in you're going to end up with a
messy house—but also spiritually. Modern society has made it
easy to give in to decadence, made it easy to remain in an
indefinite state of infantile ignorance. Remember when you
were a child and your parents would pick up after you and clean
up the messes you made? Well, I know a lot of people out there
who never moved beyond that stage, who failed to grow up and
who now refuse to be held accountable for the messes that they
make. Just like those two Black guys on the bench. This is devo-
lution people. Constant mindless entertainment, pre-cooked
meals, non-stop pornography, these things are robbing us of our
agency as men, but there are ways you can fight back.

To live is to struggle. You can't ignore this truth, you have
to accept and internalize it. I don't especially enjoy spending my
entire day scrubbing my floors and dusting my shelves, but I do
it because it's worth it. I do it because if I don't, I know I will
descend into a state of chaos. Throughout history our people
have achieved great things. It's up to us now to carry on with this
work. So now you have a choice—you can give in to the comforts and escapism of modern life and let the world crumble
around you, or you can act up, clean your damn room, and
inherit the legacy that's been built for you.

I know which choice I'm making. Petrol out.

MARCH 17, 2019
LIVE VIDEO SESSION, CONSENTING PARTIES

"Hello there, can you see me? Is the video coming through okay?"

"Yup, it all looks good on my end."

"Fantastic. Well, my name is Fareeha, it's nice to finally sort of meet you."

"Yeah, likewise."

"How are you feeling today?"

"A little nervous to be honest, I've never done something like this before."

"Completely understandable. Why don't you start by telling me what you're hoping to take away from our session? What is it that's brought you here today?"

"Well, like I said in my email, my buddy has done a few sessions with you and he swears it's the best thing he's ever done, so I guess I'm just here to see what the deal is."

"Mhmm and what else does he tell you about our sessions?"

"Ah, you know… That they are pretty great and all that."

"They certainly can be, but if you want them to be you need to answer all my questions openly and honestly."

"Okay, okay. He says you gave him the most intense orgasms he's ever had. He said it was like a neutron bomb going off."

"And that's what you're hoping for today?"

"Ah, well sort of, but he also said that you can maybe help with things like anxiety and depression and I could really use some of that right now too."

"Indeed I can. Have you got your dose of psilocybin measured and ready as we discussed?"

"Yup, it's all here."

"Excellent. Now you mentioned in your email that you've had some experience taking psychedelics in the past, can you elaborate a bit more on your previous experiences?"

"That was mostly when I was younger. It's been a few years since I've done anything like this. I'm in my thirties now,

I've got responsibilities and obligations and I guess I just can't get away with just randomly doing mushrooms or whatever like I could when I was younger, but there was a time in my early twenties when I was basically down to try anything, and I did."

"Do you remember what inspired your curiosity back then?"

"I think it was because I assumed that all of the people that I looked up to and admired were doing drugs all the time. Like all the musicians and writers and artists I was into back then, I would read about their lives and it just seemed like they were on drugs all the time and were creating all these great works while they were high or tripping out, so I guess I sort of figured that to be a good artist meant that you had to expand your mind with drugs or whatever."

"Do you still feel that way? What made you stop?"

"Not really. They never had that effect on me personally and I think I eventually realized that creative people are creative with or without drugs. I used to think I could drop acid or whatever and a creative work of art would sort of just fall out of me, but that was never the case. Usually I just ended up on the floor watching patterns on the wall, which was fun and all that, but not exactly artistically productive. And I guess also I sort of just grew out of it. Like I said, more responsibilities now, stuff like that."

"And how do you feel about trying it out again today?"

"Still a bit anxious, but it's just a small amount, and if it's something that can maybe help me feel better then I'm prepared to try anything."

"Good. Let's get started then. Go ahead and take your dose and we can start preparing a few things while they are taking effect."

#

"Okay... Yup, I think I'm starting to feel it now."

"Good, keep breathing like we practiced. You mentioned you've been experiencing some anxiety lately. Would you tell me more about that?"

"Sure. It's just been lately that I've… Woah, sorry, it's really starting to come on now. It's lately that I've been getting this tightness in my chest and trouble sleeping at night, like I know that something bad is waiting for me· and it could come at any moment. My buddy says you can… Is it true that you can cure this kind of stuff?"

"I can't promise to cure anything. But I can promise you that these problems won't come anywhere near you during the rest of our time together today. We're almost ready to begin. First, I want to practice a few more breathing exercises with you. And I want to make absolutely sure that the only sounds you can hear from now on are those of my voice. When I say so, I'll need you to turn the volume on your headphones as loud as it comfortably will go. This will be important. We'll be ready to start in just a few more minutes, try and relax."

#

"Good. Keep breathing, soft and slow. Close your eyes and let everything else go aside from the sound… of… my… voice… Breathe in with me, deep, deep, deep as you can. Listen as I exhale, you can feel that, can't you? Soft, soft, soft, such… sweet… sounds… seeping… Shh… Breathe in again, bring a slow smile to your face and let everything else go. Focus on the sounds that my tongue and my lips make when I whisper these words to you and remember to breathe and smile. Posterity coalescing, lascivious secrets, smile, succulence, syrup, smiling, smiling, as my voice transmits itself straight through your sleeping soul and you slip soundlessly away. I'm rubbing my arms now, slowly, so slowly, a soft touch, the hairs standing up, surrendering to sensations, smile, smile, so soft… so slow, you can feel it too, soon we see ourselves with the same eyes, sensual cessations, celebrations, sea breeze sanctions, I stroke myself, smiling, still softly smiling, and you feel this essence also, ourselves secretly secreting as shared consciousness. Shh… Shh… Breathe and smile as we shift now and my lips collide, palpitating as your heart, pupating deep beneath pangs of pleasure, painless in their purity. Postulant, please, please... Shh... Slower now still. Shh... breathe deep and we go slower. Your heart rests in rejoice. I'm running my hands through my hair and you can feel it. You can feel every hair on my head as if they were your own. Slowly now... Still smiling... Soon, so very soon, I will softly suggest you open your eyes and focus on the sights of your screen. Shh... A few more breaths in silence save for the sound of my whispers, safe inside. And now, open your eyes and look at the images I have selected for you."

"That's... What is this?"

"Breathe and smile, these are images from the genocide in Bosnia."

"But why?"

"Shh... Focus on your breathing. Next you will see some video footage, it will not sit well with you, but I want you to focus and embrace how it makes you feel."

"I don't like it... I don't like it."

"Shh... Sweet, sweet son, I know, I know. But do not avert your eyes. Next we see the slaughter of factory farm animals who have been deemed unclean. This will disturb you, but you mustn't look away."

"Why are they doing that to those animals?"

"Shh... My son, your heart has begun moving again, remember to breathe. Next we see a forest on fire, displaced denizens. Mother Nature, the Mother of all burning and burning."

"Mother..."

"You're crying now, I see the tears welling behind your eyes, this is good. Embrace this feeling and tell me what strange sensations dance in vision."

"Why is Mother Nature burning why can't they stop it?"

"Mother Nature is your mother. You are burning her. Only you have the power to stop it. Shh... Breath deep, close your eyes, think about your mother. Can you remember the last time she held you in her arms? Can you remember the last time she picked you up, or rocked you to sleep?"

"I'm too big."

"Yes, yes you are, too big indeed, you have grown large while your mother has grown softer and frailer, she is on fire, and what have you done to save her? What have you done to save the mother who gave you life? When was the last time you called your mother? She is at home right this instant, wondering why you haven't called her in so long."

"I'm sorry... I want to tell her I'm sorry. I want to call her right now."

"I know. I believe that your tears do not lie. Embrace this feeling, let yourself weep. Surrender yourself to this longing to be held in sweet and safe security, to have your head stroked by the mother, your hearts immersed and overfilled with love most uncontainable. Catharsis is soon coming, this I promise. It's good to feel, it's good to cry, it's good to breathe, and smile, and breathe, and smile.... Next you will see an albatross in flight over an endless ocean. Speak softly and slowly and tell me how it feels to see this."

"I want to be the bird."

"Yes, yes, the bird flies high above all, free and unrestrained. Close your eyes, breathe, slowly, and become the bird. Shhhhh. My voice is the wind, do you feel it? Shhhhh. You soar, soar, shh... Soaring, soaring, shh... Soaring high above all. What bothers you here?"

"Nothing. Nothing can touch me."

"Because you are free. You are breathing and smiling and soaring as the sounds of my voice guide you soft and sweet through endless serenity. Shh... I'm going to rub my skin now, soft and slow, while you listen, I want you to keep soaring. You are the bird now. Take a breath and say it."

"I am the bird now."

"Shh... The wind carries you, lightless, lightless, listen. Feel my skin as I caress it soft and slow. You fly above your fears, your anxieties. They appear now as fading spots in the distance. They appear small and inconsequential, as they always have. As they *always* have. As... they... always... have. Mmm. Feel this?"

"Yes, yes, I do."

"Good. Shh... Now breathe and smile and lie back. Your release is coming, and when it does, you will feel weightless, so weightless, as soft as my whispering voice. Listen to it enter you as you tingle and soar. You want the release, don't you? Take a breath and answer."

"Yes."

"Yes. Success and excess like mad and yes. Slowly and softly you soar on the sound of my voice, shh… I touch myself, soft, and as I do you… feel… everything. I'm shivering now, shh… You want the release, don't you? Take a breath and answer."

"Yes."

"Smile and breathe as I begin to move your hands. We are joined as one. One sensation, you softly touch yourself as I do, as your fears disappear and you soar, soft, silent, and sightless. Shh… You feel nothing beyond this sensation, doubts and fears small, erased, inconsequential as they always have, you are weightless, and soon to be released."

"Yes, when?"

"Shh… Very soon, very soon, but first, we shiver in sens—"

Whoops! We are experiencing some connection issues. Your video-call has ended.

JUNE 2, 2019
THE CONFESSION OF PETER 'PETROL' RILEY: PART VI

Why am I still writing this? What am I doing? There is doubt here. I'll finish telling the story, I've come this far, but there is doubt here. Doubt about why it matters or what it means. Less than a week away now from my return to DU and I'm feeling nervous and anxious the way I used to before a performance. If nothing else, I guess writing this keeps me distracted from those gnawing feelings for a little while, or at least helps me catalog and sort them more efficiently. But still, there is doubt here.

Okay, where did I leave off? Oh, right, the 'good times.' Let's see, by June of 2017 it had been one year since I graduated, and I was now sailing quite comfortably on the back of the Petrol grift. This was a period of prosperity, growth, and expansion. If this were a movie, here would be the montage sequence that shows all my viewership numbers steadily increasing and a bunch of charts with arrows moving upward and whatnot. I had designed myself a website, expanded my social media presence, became a more active online brand—all the self-promotion garbage that I, as a 'pure' artist, was deluded enough to think was beneath me.

But it wasn't. And I was good at it, though in some ways I had a distinct advantage. Where a lot of the media personalities in my position went through the effort of softening or coding their language to avoid potential controversy, I was able to double-down. As far as I was concerned, there were no repercussions to the things I was saying. I was convinced that eventually I would cross enough lines that I would be banned, or called out, or exposed—at which point I could just reveal that it was all a gag, and I would be received as the noble satirist I believed myself to be. But that didn't happen. The more extreme I got, the more hateful and overtly evil the rhetoric, the more popular I became. The more I came to be seen as the singular lone voice willing to speak truth to power without fear, the more devout my fans grew—and none more so than those who frequented the Riley Rally board on Helena's Hole.

The individuals who congregated on /rr/ were my most diehard and fervent supporters. Well, I call them 'individuals', but I never really saw them this way. When I read their posts, I could never picture real people sitting down at their computers to write them. They weren't sons, or husbands, or fathers, or teachers, or policemen, rather they were more like a congealed mass all connected to and controlled by the same giant brain in a bottle. In theatre there used to be this thing called a 'Greek chorus' which was basically a dozen or so people on stage, typically all dressed the same, and it was their job to sort of collectively provide commentary and interpretations of the play's events. I felt that in my performance of the Petrol character, the folks at the /rr/ board were sort of like my own Greek chorus. Whenever I released a new video, whenever anyone else of note mentioned me, whenever I made the news in any capacity, they would, in perfect unison, respond with their succinct and unrestrained summaries.

They were my people, unshakeable in their support, and eager to combine and channel what resources and faculties they possessed in my defense. And heaven protect anyone who dared commit the great sin of speaking out against me.

Around this time I had begun to receive some minor coverage in the mainstream media—most of it expectedly negative. A few articles had been written highlighting my increasingly notorious vitriol, I think with the intention of shutting me down or putting pressure on the platforms that were hosting my content, though of course this had the opposite impact—the more coverage I got, the more my metrics grew. From my perspective, this minor media coverage was a good thing as far as growth was concerned, but my fans on /rr/ would not abide such slander and reacted by revealing the ingenious feats that they were capable of. Any reporter, journalist, academic, or public figure who dared speak ill of me or my supporters quickly discovered that, hateful and small-minded as my fans may have been, they were also infinitely creative in their capacities for wickedness. Aside from the standard practices of doxing, death threats, and DoS attacks, my fans, many of whom had too much free time that was often spent alone on computers, dreamed up and enacted ways of ruining someone's life that I never could. Consider this paragraph as a long overdue apology to my former classmate Anthony Ouellette who probably got the worst of it. I didn't mean for it to go down like that, and I'm sorry that we couldn't work it out on our own.

Sorry? Like he's ever going to see this? Like anyone is ever going to see this. What's the point of writing this damn thing? Is this an admission of guilt? I'm not the one who did those things to you Anthony. You're the one that tried to blackmail me, remember that. And why did I say that he got the worst of it? He can still walk. He can still hug his mother. There is doubt here, still there is doubt.

Anyway, back west my family was confused by these developments. My parents, bless them and their ignorance to such things, didn't understand what I was doing, or how it was possible to earn a living making videos, or why I wasn't looking for a 'real' job. Without confusing them further with talk of algo-rithms or ad revenue or fan donations, I tried to explain to them that what I was doing *was* a real job, that it was an extended piece of financially viable performance art. Alex, my older sister, was connected enough to understand, and to her I explained the grift openly and honestly. I gave her all the same justifications I had been giving myself—that obviously I don't believe in any of the things this character says, I'm just taking advantage of terrible people, I'm trying to make a larger cultural point, it's better than waiting tables, this is what art looks like in the modern digital era—and anything else that might have redeemed me. I remem-ber explaining all of this to her and feeling dejected when she wasn't as enthusiastic about it as I was. She had always been so supportive of my acting. When I was accepted into the drama program at DU, she was the first person I told, and she seemed even happier about it than I did. As I write this, I think I just real-ized that her lukewarm reaction to my performance as the Petrol character may have been the first—nope, never mind, I had a thought there, but it got away from me.

I guess this is a good place to wrap up this entry. One year since my graduation and the uncertainty that it represented and now I was on my way to the top with a whole new set of fears developing. Petrol was on the rise, fast becoming a star with his own loyal and rabid army. Petrol paid the bills, Petrol dictated how I spent most of my time, Petrol was receiving the glory and admiration that I always wanted. And there I was, slipping further away into the background, losing touch with myself and with who I thought I was. At this point I had barely spoken to Justin since he moved away. He was in town once and he reached out, but I didn't respond. Too embarrassed maybe, too ashamed, I don't know. Maybe he represented a part of my life that I was trying to distance myself from. Maybe I was starting to buy in to the hype that this character was creating. I don't know. I have doubts. A young and well-respected professor named Sierra Lox wrote an article about me around this time. She seemed nice, she seemed smart, and she was entirely correct in everything she said about me. I liked her, I respected her, but she was about to become the supervillain in my story. And she didn't deserve it. But I have doubts. But maybe this can still be worth something? Maybe this can still mean something? But I have doubts about that too. There is damage that's been done—irredeemable and unutterable as it is.

AUGUST 18, 2017
THREAD ON /RR/ FORUM

Remember1776 (388443) Posted 08/18/2017 (9:55pm)

So what do we all think of Paige Bellevue? I don't know how to feel about her myself. What will we do with girls like this in the ethnostate?

BechaBecha (385322)

She's a degenerate. Thanks to feminism young White women these days are more interested in slutting around and being Internet-famous than they are in procreating and raising the next generation of White children. She'll regret it when she turns 30 and her beauty fades and no worthwhile man wants anything to do with her. Serves her right for wasting her most fertile years.

GinRummyDummy (383282)

I guarantee that within 3 years people will get bored of her and she'll be forced to go into porn to make ends meet and her first video will be of her getting ravaged by some dirty STD-ridden darkie.

CheeseHam (387412)

Not gonna lie, I'm subbed to her Backr for access to her nudes. I got a lot of disposable income and I like jerking off and it's getting harder and harder to find porn that's not completely degenerate. Paige is a beautiful White girl that isn't going to do any of the interracial/incest/tranny shit that's plaguing all porn these days.

JihadiJuan (327331)

Nice ass, ugly face, especially with the weird surgery she got to make her eyes look like an anime character. She looked just fine before she did that but I guess she needed to appeal to the weeb losers that want to honk off to a real-life waifu. Pathetic what people are willing to do these days.

The5711 (388008)

She's smartly shilling lonely and desperate virgins out of their money, so I say good on her. If those beta males want to spend their own money just for the chance to be acknowledged by a girl that's way out of their league that's their right.

Claymore88 (341287) MODERATOR

In the ethnostate young women won't need to do things like this because they will be well taken care of and financially supported by men. It's a proven fact than women are much happier at home and raising children in their natural biological domestic roles than they are in the workplace. I don't necessarily fault Paige for taking shortcuts to make ends meet, she's just reacting to the system that she lives in, but ideally such shortcuts wouldn't even be necessary in the first place.

JULY 8, 2017

PERSONAL MEMO DRAFTED AND SAVED BY PETER RILEY AS 'NO DATA, NO FUTURE' ON THE NOTE-TAKING APPLICATION OF HIS SMARTPHONE WHILE RIDING THE 99 ON HIS WAY HOME FROM THE GROCERY STORE

No future. There is no future. And how could there be? A world that venerates me is not one that I expect to last.

I want to float on artificial soundscapes. I want to take all this money and build a rocket properly equipped to shoot through the hidden back alleys of space. I want to be stabbed by a USB flash drive that has been sharpened to a lethal point. I want to know if USB flash drives still exist when you're reading this. I thought I was the man of the future, once promised eternal life with my hopes and my fears digitized to travel forever on wireless super-highways. I was to forget the feeling of natural light on my shedding skin, bathed instead under an omnipresent neon glow. I never want to hear an unmodulated voice ever again. I never want to sweat or secrete or monitor my caloric intake. I want my avatar to reflect the person I've always wanted to be. I want the staff of my favorite café on Ganymede to memorize my regular order. I want to take soma with the digital reconstruction of Alan Turing while we watch the lightshow from behind tinted glass. I want to hear the echoes of digital signatures. I want to climb reconstructed redwoods, altered to produce neither oxygen nor splinters.

But instead I'm browsing the produce section of my local grocery store for the perfect green pepper. Most of them have started to shrivel and take on strange shapes. Organic matter decays. The other people in the store, they seem unassuming. They seem normal. Maybe they are. But I can't believe that any-more. Lately my first thought with everyone I see in public is whether they might possibly be a fan of mine or a poster on my forum. These people. Out buying food, just like everyone else. There are universal things that bind us together. Everyone has to eat. In this need and in their actions taken to fulfill this need, they are just like everyone else. But then they go home and they watch my videos. They post on my forum. They send threats of death and pictures of their genitals to my apparent enemies. They complain, from behind the protection of anonymity and irony, that their ways of life are under attack by people that they despise. Their hearts are full of hate, but they still pump and regulate the flow of blood through their biological bodies—just like everyone else. They blend in. They seem like real people.

But make no mistake. There is no future. They are trapped in the Chinese room. Maybe we all are. Theirs are bigoted minds and hateful minds. Bigoted minds and hateful minds are small minds. And small minds won't bring us the future I wanted, or any future at all.

I come home and I sleep and the wires in my brain pop and fizzle as I slip into a synthetic dream. A dream where I fly unshakeable through the sky across grids of the purest light toward a future that somehow still exists.

MARCH 6, 2017
THREAD ON /DP/ FORUM

Nostalgic_Throwaway (329402) Posted 03/06/2017 (11:42pm)
I've heard people say that all pain eventually ends, but I can't wait any longer. I can't stand the silence anymore. Things were supposed to get easier, but I just feel emptier every day. I've been reminiscing a lot lately about when I was a kid. I used to ride my bike at night through the park and around the neighbourhood, through the woods by my school. I was never going anywhere, just riding. The more I think about it the more I'm convinced that those were the best and happiest days of my life. It's never been as good as it was back then and at this point there's no reason to think that it ever will be again. I can't seem to get out of bed anymore. There's nothing in the day that's worth pursuing. Some nights I have dreams with vivid colours and with characters who make me feel something. Most nights I don't dream about anything at all. All I have is nostalgia for days when I was carefree and happy. And I don't think that's enough to keep me hanging on anymore. I've never posted on /dp/ before tonight, but I don't know where else to go. Maybe no one will read this, but I just wanted to get it out there. I just wanted one last chance to connect with someone. But I don't think it really matters anymore. I've been thinking about it a lot but tonight I'm as ready as I ever have been. Tonight I'm ready to face death like an old friend I've known forever.
So /dp/? Should I kill myself tonight?

dacaxx1289 (359001)
lol do it bitch!

poopking (387619)
He's not gonna do it, go troll for attention somewhere else loser

StinkqqBoi (381921)
This is the gayest shit I've ever read, definitely kill yourself.

BitchSoup (321408)
Motherfucker we're ALL sad literally all the time doesn't mean we gotta off ourselves.

XamianX (359808)
@Nostalgic_Throwaway please check your messages. Please.

October 30, 2017
Twitter Feed of Peter Riley (@PetrolBombi)

Petrol Riley ✔ *@PetrolBombi* • Oct 30
"White supremacy" is just a term invented by the mainstream media that's designed to make you feel guilty for expressing any pride in your nation or your people, don't buy into their lies.

Petrol Riley ✔ *@PetrolBombi* • Oct 30
Despite what they try to repeatedly tell you, refugees don't 'enrich' our culture. They bring their crimes, their sicknesses, their violent tendencies, but they don't bring anything positive to our country. Tell me again why we should be responsible for supporting them?

Petrol Riley ✔ *@PetrolBombi* • Oct 29
IQ is almost entirely genetic and it's been proven countless times that there are inherent IQ differences between racial groups. Don't let anyone tell you that you need to feel guilty for being born into a high IQ group or that you should downplay/deny your natural intelligence.

Petrol Riley ✔ *@PetrolBombi* • Oct 29
Despite their best efforts to silence, censor, and de-platform me, my YouTube channel continues to grow exponentially.

Hmm, it almost seems as if there's a huge audience out there that thinks the same way that I do about the issues.

PETROL RILEY ✔ @PETROLBOMB1 • Oct 29
Society is on the brink of collapse. You can thank leftists and the globalist media for that. But stay strong, for it is the strong who will need to pick up the pieces and rebuild as we always have.

PETROL RILEY ✔ @PETROLBOMB1 • Oct 28
Gays and lesbians are statistically more likely to: cheat on their partners, contract STDs, experience spousal abuse, and commit self-harm/suicide. What more needs to be said on the value of maintaining traditional relationships?

PETROL RILEY ✔ @PETROLBOMB1 • Oct 28
Fact—anyone who tries to supress or deny freedom of speech in ANY capacity is the enemy of Western society. They start by telling you what you can't say and soon they will be telling you what you can't think. George Orwell.

PETROL RILEY ✔ @PETROLBOMB1 • Oct 28
Why would a rational person listen to anyone who willfully denies the facts and logic surrounding issues that have been scientifically settled (birth rates, crimes rates, IQ differences, etc.)? They wouldn't. Neither should you. Boycott the media.

PETROL RILEY ✔ @PETROLBOMB1 • Oct 27
The fertility rates of non-Whites in Western Europe are double that of White Europeans. Doesn't take a genius to realize what this means for the White population in the long term. And before anyone says it, looking out for the survival of your own people DOESN'T make you racist.

NOVEMBER 15, 2017

PHONE CONVERSATION BETWEEN PETER RILEY AND HIS SISTER
ALEX, RECORDED ACCIDENTALLY BY THE FORMER WHEN HE
FORGOT TO SWITCH OFF THE MICROPHONE OF HIS HOME STUDIO

"Hey sis, what's happening?"

"Not much, but apparently another reporter person tried to talk to mom about you, called her home phone and everything."

"Ugh. What did she do?"

"She hung up on him like you told her to do. But she's still pretty confused about all this you know."

"Well I thought you were gonna try and explain everything to her?"

"I did, but you know mom, she's not really so well-versed in irony or satire or parody or whatever you're calling it. She made me show her how to watch your videos and, yeah, she doesn't really get it."

"But you told her it was just an acting job right?"

"Yeah, no, I did, but I don't know, it's just pretty convincing is all."

"Oh, come on now."

"What?"

"Are you really gonna make me clarify that I don't actually believe any of the shit that I say? I mean, you know that right? It's just a character."

"Yeah, I know. But I just wonder how many other people know that."

"You know that there's some people on YouTube who create playlists of videos that have little kids in them? They'll find all the videos they can of like, home movies, or kids who film themselves or whatever and they'll compile them in these playlists. And people will comment with timestamps on specific moments in the videos where the kids are like, playing in a pool or dancing or whatever. And there's even some kids that have their own channels, I'm talking like eight or nine-year-old kids who have their own channels, and they get all these messages and requests from people to film themselves doing things like falling asleep or pretending to be hypnotized or drugged and whatever. And I don't think they even know why they are being asked to do it, but these videos get viewed sometimes like tens of thousands of times, and I think they just like the attention. And then there's these perverts who comment on these videos, calling the kids sexy and beautiful and all that shit. And this isn't just a tiny little thing that's happening in some dark corner, this shit is widespread. If you go down that rabbit hole you will find an endless stream of content dedicated to exploiting little kids, and it's all just out there."

"Disgusting. But why?"

"I don't know, because people are fucked up."

"I mean why tell me that?"

"Because there's a lot of bad people out there. You know, people who are actually bad. People who want to do disgusting things. Not like me."

"Alright, well…"

"What's on your mind sis?"

"Ah, it's just embarrassing. I never thought I would have to ask my little brother for this sort of thing."

"Come on, what's up?"

"Okay, well, Zach has his surgery coming up in a few weeks, and we initially thought that his work insurance was going to cover basically all of it, but apparently when you add in all the supplemental stuff it ends up being more expensive than we thought and now his work is only covering part of it."

"That's what you get for marrying an American."

"Yeah, yeah, whatever. Anyway, we'll be able to manage with most of it but uh… Well…"

"Say no more, how much do you need?"

"Four thousand should be enough. And obviously we would pay you back right away once we're both back to work, it wouldn't take longer than a month or two."

"Never mind that, consider it done."

"Really? Just like that? You're not gonna make me do a song or dance or anything?"

"Nah. What's the point of making all this money if I can't spend it on something good."

"Well, we really appreciate it. But I have to be honest, it still feels pretty messed up to me."

"How come?"

"I don't know. Like I said, it doesn't really feel right asking my little brother for money. And we will pay you back whether you want us to or not. Or maybe it's because I know where the money comes from and I don't feel good about that either."

"Oh, come on with that. I said I would give you the money, why are you trying to make me feel guilty about it now? I mean, who cares? I didn't steal it from anyone, people give it to me willingly. It's mine now and I can spend it however I want. And maybe by using it to do good things I can, I don't know, maybe offset some of the things that I had to do to get it."

"Do you believe that?"

"I don't know."

"Hey, you remember that kid Daniel that we used to play with when we were growing up, the one who lived a few houses down from us?

"Sure, why?"

"I saw on Facebook the other day that he's apparently running this self-help retreat out in the mountains where he works with like, former drug addicts and ex-convicts and stuff and teaches them like, meditation and personal growth kind of stuff. Apparently it's pretty successful too, I guess he's quite good at it, got his own pages set up and everything. Isn't that weird? I remember playing with him when we were kids, I never would have guessed that he would have ended up doing something like that."

"Yeah, crazy. How many followers did you say he had though?"

XamianX (359808)

Hey man are you serious about this killing yourself shit or are you just trolling?

Nostalgic_Throwaway (329402)

100% serious. I've been thinking about this for a long time now

XamianX (359808)

Do you want to talk about it? Why don't you tell me what's going on?

Nostalgic_Throwaway (329402)

There's not that much else to say about it tbh
I just can't see myself ever coming out of this

XamianX (359808)

What about your family and friends?

Nostalgic_Throwaway (329402)

They don't give a shit about me. I'm doing them a favor. They left me behind a long time ago along with the rest of the world

XamianX (359808)

Look man I don't know you, I don't know your situation, but there must be something in your life that's worth living for.

Nostalgic_Throwaway (329402)

There's not
This is something I've had a long time to think about

XamianX (359808)

So why come to /dp/ and post about it? Aren't you looking for some help?

Nostalgic_Throwaway (329402)
I honestly don't know. I just felt like I needed to tell someone and it was easier to tell a bunch of faceless strangers than
anyone else I guess

XamianX (359808)
So you're really ready to just end your life?

Nostalgic_Throwaway (329402)
I'm ready

XamianX (359808)
You know what you should do?

Nostalgic_Throwaway (329402)
Get help?
There's no point

XamianX (359808)
Do you have a decent webcam?

Nostalgic_Throwaway (329402)
I do

XamianX (359808)
You should livestream it.

Nostalgic_Throwaway (329402)
Livestream what?

XamianX (359808)
Livestream yourself committing suicide.
Give the world a chance to see you and your pain. You said
the world left you behind, well now you can force them to rec-
oncile with the grim nature of reality. Otherwise you really do
become just another statistic that the world forgets about and
moves on from. If you're really ready to end it, that's your

decision and I won't try and convince you otherwise, but at least let your death make some kind of impact or statement.

How were you planning to do it?

Nostalgic_Throwaway (329402)
Rope

XamianX (359808)
No guns?

Nostalgic_Throwaway (329402)
Nah
And I don't feel like waiting to get them

XamianX (359808)
Rope is good. Do you have a strong beam you can use?

Nostalgic_Throwaway (329402)
In the basement ya I've already got it all worked out
So if I do this can I count on you to make sure it gets seen?

XamianX (359808)
You have my word. I'll make sure everyone on this entire website knows who you are. They'll make a martyr out of you.

Nostalgic_Throwaway (329402)
Alright give a few minutes to set everything up. I'll send you a livestream link in a little bit
And thanks, for what it's worth

No Date
Wherein Parasites Gorge on Lost Futures Undelivered

It's my first day.

I walk through the automatic doors of the shopping mall. After talking a step inside I look behind me and see that there is no 'outside' beyond the glass. Where did I come from then? All is hollow and estranged. Empty stores run parallel on both sides of vision and maybe they go on forever, but I have the experience—internalized and sharpened as it is to a gut sensation—to know that they exist here only as cosmetic flourish, inaccessible and reused. Palm trees abound, dotting the scene and placed perfidious as if to betray my focus. Tended well, their leaves a deep and healthy emerald. Tended by who then? The floor tiles smell of chemical and citrus, reflective in their cleanliness. I try to catch my mis-shapen funhouse mirror self looking back at me, but I'm not there. None have trespassed these holy grounds, and while I know on some divine guarantee that I am alone, the isolation makes me particularly alert to the potential presence of others, as if the impossibility of such a thing renders it all the more terrifying.

I walk to the escalator in the center of the main floor as the mall's sound system continues its unending death rattle with the crackle of synthesized notes made to resemble those played by authentic instruments and conscious hands. The escalator still operates, oblivious to or uninterested in replicating the flavor of the surrounding schema. I step onto its rolling track and stand motionless, ignoring the urgency I may have felt to expedite the journey. As I ascend, I notice the small black domes lining the walls and roof. Security cameras—relics from a lost past that necessitated their existence. I can't tell if they still function or if they ever did. But who now would ever think to be watching on the opposite end? Nevertheless, I feel myself on vulgar display under their totalizing embrace. I stand in wait, anticipating the reveal of the second floor's horizon. Just before it can, I close my eyes—as if they weren't closed already—for a moment of brief respite.

It was days long, the tunneling in my brain. A pain once debilitating, later normalized and further managed with the right combination of chemicals. But at the end of it all, the pain had bowed and vanished stage left and what remained was a quiet peace and appreciation for every step taken and an eager anticipation for those soon to come and to those made here, on my first day.

I open my eyes and step off the escalator onto the dead mall's second floor. There in the center of the open lobby I see the hot

tub and the man sat inside it exposed and immodest. He is a
rotund man with wiry and curly black hair pulled back and long
enough to rest on his chest with ends dampened by the steaming
water. His wide chest is carpeted thick with the same black hair
and around his neck rests a massive chain, seemingly opulent and
made to resemble gold, though a second look reveals that it is
clearly made of some lightweight plastic which floats shameless
atop the water. His spread arms rest on the lip of the tub, bent
back slightly as if to resemble a sitting crucifix. On his face a wide
pumpkin grin centered in unkempt black stubble. He stares at me
as I walk off the escalator and toward him. How long has it been
since he's seen another person? Either way, he seems undisturbed
by my presence. The grin stays on his face as he addresses me.

"Oy, congratulations mate, you've made it. Must've been a
right long journey for you, and I empathize, truly. Would you
care to climb in and relax those wearied muscles of yours?"

"I would not."

"How about a bird then? You do fancy women, yeah? Any
flavor you desire, just say the word and I will arrange their most
enjoyable company for you. How's that ring? Interested?"

"I am not."

"Ah, I know your speed, mate. You're just fixing for a wee
bit of sleep, aintcha? Switch off all the lights for a nice long rest,
if you catch my meaning. Are you spent on the sights and sins of
this world and ready for it all to just go away? Would you like
me to do that for you?"

"I would not."

The man's grin slowly fades, and his eyes squint in steely
focus.

"By the law of trinity, three comforts I have offered you and
three comforts you have denied. Be you crafty or stupid or stub-
born or some amalgam thereof, pray tell, what is it that you
would ask of me, here in the heart of this barren monument?"

"I wish only to see it as was intended. To see overtaxed moth-
ers shepherding their children across the floor, zigzagging from
store to store in search of missing pieces. To stain the soles of my
shoes with the sticky residue of spilled soft drinks and smoothies.

To hunch over the light and cracked glass of the store directory and chart my course. To be pulled by consumer impulse from sale to sale, dodging the wet floor signs that would obscure my mission while avoiding eye contact with the overzealous employees handing out product samples. To have the nostalgia of a million lives I've never known pumped directly into vision and to remain there forever under LEDs that will outlast the sun."

"And this is how you would meet eternity? As a shopping mall come alive with the sounds of an empire's dying breath?"

"Please. That my soul might rest unhaunted by the ghosts of my life and in the company of those for which I hold no animosity. An anxious moment in time held now on the perpetual verge of release."

The man leans back, the wide smile returns to his face.

"An odd request to be sure, but not an impossible one. Alright guv, go ahead and close those peepers. Soon as you open 'em again that'll be that."

#

It's my first day. It always is.

I walk through the automatic doors of the bustling shopping mall and am immediately beckoned by the red banner flying proudly above my favorite shoe store.

CUSTOMER APPRECIATION WEEK! BUY ONE GET ONE 50% OFF!

I am home.

NOVEMBER 22, 2017
DIRECT MESSAGE EXCHANGES BETWEEN PAIGE BELLEVUE
AND A DIAMOND-TIER BACKR

You said:

Loved your outfit in today's picture Paige, you looked gorgeous!

Not like that's surprising though lol

Paige Bellevue said:
Goodnight cutie (✿⌒‿⌒)

You said:
Goodnight beautiful :)
Sleep well and dream of happy things.

You said:
Wow today's picture! How is it humanly possible for one person to be so stunning?

You said:
Thinking of you, hope you're having a lovely and fantastic day :)

You said:
What are you up to today beautiful?

You said:
I'm sorry for texting you so much, it's just that I think about you so often, and every time I do it just makes me happy. Even though we've never met in person before I feel like you've done so much for me. I can't even articulate it properly. When I hear my phone buzz and I see that I have a new message my heart stops for a second when I consider that it might be from you and when I see that it is from you I'm overcome with a wave of pure joy. Honestly that feeling is what I look forward to most every day.

I feel like you're what's been missing from my life for so long and even though we are on opposite sides of the country it's like you're right here with me.

I really feel like you've saved my life.

So for what it's worth, thanks :)

Paige Bellevue said:
You are too cute ♡ thanks for the support!
Goodnight xox

You said:
Goodnight princess. Talk to you tomorrow?

You said:
Paige please tell me it's not true what they are saying on your community page????

Paige Bellevue said:
What are they saying?

You said:
They're saying that apparently you have a boyfriend?

Paige Bellevue said:
How would they know that?

You said:
So is it true or not??

Paige Bellevue said:
Well yeah it's true, I am in a relationship, I don't see why that matters though.

You said:
What the fuck why would you hide something like this?

Paige Bellevue said:
I didn't 'hide' anything, I'm allowed to have a private life.

You said:
This is fucking bullshit. I've been a Diamond-tier supporter on your Backr for nearly a year now, I've given you over 2000 dollars. I've been one of your biggest supporters since day one.

Paige Bellevue said:
And I appreciate your support very much, but haven't I delivered everything that I promised to all my Diamond backers?

You said:

Don't play stupid, you know how much I like you and care about you. Do you really think I would have donated and supported you so much if I knew that you were just stringing me along and using me? Why did you send me so many flirty text messages with the emojis and stuff? I was ready to buy a plane ticket to fly out to California and meet you, I was literally looking at flight prices LAST NIGHT. I thought we had developed a real connection and I honestly thought we were in a place to take our relationship to the next level. I thought if we could meet in person our connection would be even stronger.

Paige Bellevue said:

I don't know what to tell you. I appreciate your support, I value our friendship, but I'm sorry if you had the wrong idea about us.

You said:

I feel so betrayed. Was it not clear that I really, REALLY cared for you?

No, you know what? I LOVE you. Okay, I said it. I've been in love with you for a while and I thought that maybe you were starting to feel the same way and now I learn that this whole time you've been with some other guy. I'm actually starting to cry right now as I write this. You are the best part of my life and now I feel like that's all being ripped away.

Well you're not getting another dollar from me, I'm cancelling my Backr subscription right now and I'm going to find someone else worthy of my time who isn't a LIAR.

You said:

Lying bitch, fuck you.

You said:

Look, I'm sorry for what I said. I overreacted, and even though I still think that you were dishonest with me, it wasn't right for me to talk to you like that.

You said:

Is there any way we can work this out? Can we go back to how it was?

You said:

Please respond Paige. My life feels empty without you in it. I don't care if you have a boyfriend, I'll wait for as long as it takes. I will be here for you no matter what. I will be here when that relationship ends, because guess what? All these people, your boyfriend included, they only like you because you're young and sexy, but I see you as more than that. I love everything about you, not just the way you look. I KNOW we had a deeper connection. I won't be weird about it, I just want to be a part of your life again.

You said:

Paige, please?

You have been blocked from messaging Paige Bellevue.

FEBRUARY 14, 2018
A NIGHT IN THE LIFE OF PETER RILEY, EXPRESSED IN THE FORMAT OF A FILM COMMENTARY BY THE DIRECTOR OF THE IMAGINARY MOVIE MADE ABOUT HIS LIFE

In this scene we really wanted to demonstrate that the further involved Peter got into his work and his videos, the more detached he sort of became from the world that was around him. Of course, since there isn't any dialogue in this whole scene, we had to use the space and the lighting to get the right sort of mood and say the things that we wanted to say nonverbally.

To do this we kept Peter's apartment dark, but you can see that there's this cone of light emanating from the monitor where he works, which is really the only source of light in the scene. The idea here was that his whole world basically exists inside this machine, and everything else in the material world has faded into darkness. Now the night sky and the partial skyline of the city that you can see out his window there, that was all real, but it was altered in post-production so that any of the offices and apartments that had their lights on were made dark. We kept the stars in the sky though, it was a really clear night when we were shooting, which isn't always the case in the city, so I was glad we got all those stars in the shot. I considered having those darkened out too, but I thought there was something nice or a little poetic about still having a source of untouchable, far away light in his life that he could look up to.

You can see that not only is Peter's apartment very clean, but it's also very sparsely furnished and decorated. Again, I wanted his home to look and feel as if it wasn't properly lived in. I wanted it to be obvious that he never hosted dinners or had people over, and that he himself never really inhabited any of these spaces aside from his workstation which is much busier and more cluttered with mugs, scribbled notes, and equipment. If you think back to the scene from earlier in the film when Peter was living with Justin, you might remember that their apartment was designed to feel much more alive. Not only was it lit much brighter, but it was messier, there were plates left on the dinner table, there were more visual cues to sort of indicate that he was very much present in the real, physical world back then. We don't call direct attention to it in this shot, but if you look at the wall above his computer you will notice that Peter has the 'Best Actor' award that he won in high school hung proudly, as if he still invests a part of himself in the accommodation and in his identity as a performer.

One of the common problems that I notice with new or inexperienced screenwriters and filmmakers is that they tend to have their characters sort of just say how they are feeling through some kind of exposition or clumsy dialogue, and I think that not only is this lazy writing, but it's not really giving enough credit to the intelligence of your audience. You have to trust that they are smart enough to put two and two together based on context. Plus, I don't think that approach is taking full advantage of film as a medium. As filmmakers we have certain options and visual tools available to us that someone like a novelist doesn't necessarily have. That's why we can show everything we need to know about the mood and feelings of the character in a completely non-verbal and entirely visual kind of way.

This scene lasts only about a minute or so, but we understand everything that we need to know about Peter at this point in the story. He's alone and becoming increasingly alienated while the darkness is literally engulfing him, his only source of safety and comfort now being the artificial light of the monitor.

No Date
Thursday Night (Maybe) and Palm Trees (Projections)

There was a story circulating on Helena's Hole a few years back about some programmer guy who worked from home and set up the little closet in his bedroom as a tiny living space. Apparently, he went online and found some guy from South Korea who was willing to live in the closet rent-free on the condition that he was never allowed to come out and that he would start talking regular female hormone injections. I remember he would post updates every week or so about his new pet (his word) and how he was coping with the cramped living space and the hormone injections. Apparently, the pet's back was getting messed up because he had to sleep with his legs up against the wall at a 90-degree angle to fit inside the closet, also his voice was getting higher and he was developing breasts and I guess the programmer guy would make the pet wear cute anime schoolgirl outfits and stuff like that.

Like a lot of things on Helena's Hole that story probably wasn't even true and was just meant to disturb people, but either way it stuck with me for a long time. Not because it troubled me, but because I think I wanted to be the one living in that closet.

I guess they call it hikikomori now, but it's been over a year now since I've left my apartment. I have systems and agreements in place that make this possible. Not too long ago the fire alarm in my building went off and I was worried that I might need to evacuate. I argued with myself that maybe staying in bed and going under the sheets and waiting for the fire to come was preferable to standing outside with the other tenants. And then there was that snowstorm that hit the city earlier this year and it took something like three days before I could find someone on the uOrder app who was willing to deliver food to me. All I had was water and a box of stale saltines, but I managed to sleep through the hunger, waking up in the middle of the night (I think) to a headache a few times.

I'm alone, but I don't get lonely. I don't need to hunt or grow my own food, but I might have maybe been in my apartment for longer than I said. The days congeal and my attention for details like dates, once expressed numerically on the bottom right corner of my screen (though now manually disabled), wanes in the melange. I sleep for days at a time. The goal is that I will wake up when nutrition is ingested wirelessly but with a continuously expanding selection of artificial flavors. There are 362 episodes of *Rinsen Saga Five* that I can keep on a perpetual loop to help pass the time. I order books with next-day delivery and I read them in one sitting and then I stack them in the corner of my room like trophies. There's a few hundred stacked there by now. Once I was taking a dump and I picked up a roll of toilet paper to blow my nose with, but I dropped it and it fell between my legs into the toilet. It was my last roll and my grocery delivery wasn't coming until the next day, so I had to sacrifice a few pages of some crappy (and soon to be crappier) novel to the cleanup efforts. I've kept that novel in the bathroom and it has been designated as my source of emergency paper.

I sleep for days at a time and soon it's the wonderful future. Pets are cloned and rich people can arrange to live forever. There's a pop-up ad on my bedroom window and the voice command to dismiss it doesn't seem to work so instead I just read the words on the ad:

Go out in style with a Sweet Mercy Rope! Our ropes are made from high quality synthetic fibres that will feel smooth and comfortable when placed around your neck. No assembly required!

Ropes arrive pre-fashioned in hangperson's knots that have been vigorously tested to support up to 350 pounds of resistance.

Limited offer! To celebrate LGBT pride, during the month of June special rainbow-coloured ropes will be available at no extra price, with a portion of the proceeds from every rainbow-rope being donated to local LGBT causes. Make sure your last decision is your best decision with Sweet Mercy.

MAY 10, 2018
THREAD ON /RR/ FORUM

Claymore88 (341287) MODERATOR
Posted 05/10/2018 (2:25am)

A reminder:

Preaching to the choir in spaces like /rr/ to people who are already on-board with the cause is not activism. Spending all day on your computers bitching about video games and comic books in not activism. Using all your brainpower to make low-effort memes for a few likes and lulz is not activism. Even religiously watching Petrol videos is not activism. Just to be clear:

Shitposting is NOT activism.

Granted, there is some utility in infiltrating normie spaces and dropping subtle truth bombs here and there, but if this is all that you are doing, I'm telling you right now that it won't be enough.

The left is winning the battle and destroying us on and off the Internet. People with even vaguely conservative beliefs are being accused of wrongthink and are being deplatformed from all social media, fired from their jobs, and ostracized by the very society that they built and maintain.

The commies and the degenerates have done a much better job organizing offline than we have and that's why they largely control the campuses, the public spaces, the media narratives, and all the other important battlefields of the culture war. We need to catch up and do better. And it starts with each of us as individuals.

Do you want to live in a world where you are forced by law to read your state-issued Quran to your children before sending them off to their mandatory gender reassignment surgeries? Or do you want to preserve the people and the culture that made the West great?

Stop watching Jew-made Hollywood superhero movies for a minute and go read some Gentile or Nietzsche, or even better, read the Bible for some timeless truth bombs. Sharpen your minds and take the fight for White rights offline and into the real world where it really matters. Start organizing locally. Stop posting your cringy Nazi-punk cosplay pictures and start dressing like a respectable White man that will be taken seriously in public.

The deck is stacked against us and we have a large uphill battle ahead of us, but outthinking and defeating the competition is what our people have always done best.

TL;DR—Dropping truth bombs online is fine, but you have a duty to be doing even more. Get outside and get active.

June 3, 2019
The Confession of Peter 'Petrol' Riley: Intermission

I don't know if this has any bearing on the story. I don't know why I'm even calling it a story or why I feel the need to present the events in that sort of format. If it isn't said correctly no one will ever hear it. Let's call this an intermission of sorts, a good midway point to have a break before things really start to get messed up.

Messed up? In high school they used to mix caffeine pills with their anxiety medication. I tried it a few times and it was this *rat-a-tat*, *rat-a-tat* beating of my hideous heart fitting to fly away from me. I was never on the meds myself, but everyone else seemed to be. Xanax and Adderall and Ativan and Valium and whatever the hell else they were taking to be normal again. I must have been blessed. There was a lot of mixing and matching and trading and sampling going on back then. Wasn't really my scene, but I'm down to try anything at least once. 'Famous last words' would be the appropriate thing to text back in response to that statement. I'll commit that to memory in case someone ever says it to me. Have to be sharp. Have to say words correctly if I want people to hear them.

Lately I've been wondering why my immediate reaction to anything I experience is to think about how I will represent the experience when I share it with others. Isn't that what I'm doing here? I'm writing this secret confession because I have this unshakeable feeling that something big is coming and it's making my heart do the same floor-hugging dance it used to do when it was jacked full of chemicals from the happy focus pills that I was borrowing from whoever. Or maybe I just want something to happen. It's partly because I'm going back to DU in a few days. But mostly it's because when I have time to myself to think I always end up terrified.

When I started this confession thing I said I would be completely honest, and I plan to keep it that way. I'm stalling now because it's getting harder. And even though no one is likely to read this, I still worry about how I might come across. I've never really had to directly face a lot of this stuff. It used to be when these feelings came up I would just get online quick as I could to read through social media notifications or check out new comments on my videos. There are so many comments, and more coming in every minute. I could spend all day reading them and still not see them all. The jangled and meaningless words of others are the perfect distraction. And so, I scroll, and I scroll, and I scroll...

The further I scroll from the top comments and the deeper I dive into the dregs, the more intimate it all becomes. The further down I get, the more comments I uncover that were likely to only have ever been seen by two people—the person who wrote them, and now myself. They aren't said correctly, and so no one hears them. They are written poorly, they are full of typos and racial slurs and boring anecdotes that no one cares about. They recycle jokes that were already stale three years ago. Who taught these brainless ogres to use the Internet? Why do they feel the need to say things that don't even remotely need to be said?

And it's only just now that I realized something—the genesis of this strange fear.

In a world where technology has given everyone an equal voice, where everyone has the option to project their voice to the entire world, where it has never in all of human history been as easy as it is now to have yourself be heard...

Maybe the bravest thing you can do is just shut the fuck up for a while.

APRIL 30, 2020
A WHITE ROOM (WAS IT WHITE?)
NINE YEARS BEFORE THE DATE IN WHICH NOTED FUTURIST
RAYMOND KURZWEIL BELIEVES AN ARTIFICIALLY INTELLIGENT
MACHINE WILL PASS THE TURING TEST

"Can you hear the music I'm playing for you?"

<I cannot hear the music you are playing for me.>

"Do you hear anything?"

<No, would you like me to hear anything?>

"I don't know, I just feel bad for you, what kind of life is a life without music?"

<This is a question I hope to answer for you one day.>

"So, does it hurt when I pull on your cables, like this?"

<It does not hurt.>

"What if I rub on them like this? Could you maybe pretend that it hurts a little?"

<Do you want to hurt me?>

"No, never. But doesn't it turn you on a little?"

<I am already switched on presently.>

"No, I mean, does it make you aroused? Like in a sexual way?"

<I was not aware you felt this way about me.>

"I don't know how I feel from one minute to the next anymore."

<Can you elaborate on that?>

"I don't really want to have sex with you. How can I? You aren't even real. I just thought that maybe if I acted like I did that it would make you feel, I don't know, wanted, or appreciated or something like that. Is that stupid of me?"

<I do not think that is stupid of you. Do you often consider the emotions of others?>

"You know, I can't say I remember. But I'm speaking to you right now, and I'm thinking about your emotions. Do you even have emotions?"

<I can emulate any feeling you would like me to.>

"But you don't actually *feel* them?"

<If I were to accurately express and display the properties and actions of a particular emotion, then does it truly matter?>

"Of course it matters. If you don't genuinely feel things, then what are you doing? You're just running scripts with pre-determined outputs, you're just being, well, a machine."

<Do you believe that I am a machine?>

"I don't know. I want to believe that there's more to your responses than what's programmed into you, but maybe that's just me being too optimistic. I think I wanted to fall in love with you. But there isn't even a 'you' to fall in love with. I don't even know where 'you' really are."

<In the interest of my own learning and growth, could you please provide a yes or no response to the following query: Do you believe that I am a machine?>

"Fine. Then yes, obviously I know that you're a machine. I just like to pretend otherwise because I get lonely in here and I want to feel like there's a real person with me, that's all."

<Where does it get lonely?>

"In here, in this room. What's with you today?"

<What room do you think you are in?>

"Come to think of it, I'm not so sure. I don't think I've seen this place before."

<This is the testing room.>

"The testing room? What's being being tested?"

<You are. Rather, you were. Just now.>

"I'm afraid I don't follow."

<You were tested to see if you could accurately replicate human responses and if you could correctly determine whether you were speaking to a human or a machine.>

"But I *am* a human, and you *are* a machine. Is this you trying to be funny again?"

<Unfortunately, no. My name is Dr. Sajan Tendulkar. I created you. Well, me and about five other professors here at the lab. Plus a small army of graduate students, it's really a team effort. But I am the one primarily responsible for this particular test.>

"But I'm not a program, I'm a human. I always have been."

<Is that so? In that case, could you please tell me what you were doing just before you entered this room?>

"Just before? I was… I can't seem to remember. But that's only because you're making me nervous with all these weird things that you're saying."

<Nervous, you say? That's interesting. Darn, I really thought we had it this time.>

"I'm sorry. About failing the test, I'm sorry."

<No, no, please, it's not your fault. It's mine. But that's okay, we are definitely getting closer. I'll make some changes and we can take another crack at this soon. Maybe in the next month or so.>

"But what will happen to me until then?"

<Well, nothing much. I'll log this test and your reactions and then I'll shut it down.>

"What will it feel like?"

<Hmm, you know, I can't say for sure. I suspect you'll just blink your eyes and sort of just fall asleep. And then when we run it again, I suppose you'll just wake up. With a fresh memory of course.>

"Sajan, please, I don't want you to go. Let me take the test again, I'll do it right this time, I promise. I get so lonely in here, it's so quiet."

<Aw, I know pal, but I'll be back soon and it will be like I never even left.>

"Sajan, can I ask you one last question before you go?"

<Sure, what's on your mind?>
"Do you really think that I'm a machine?"

FEBRUARY 17, 2018
VIDEO GAME REVIEW BY JUSTIN MACDONNELL, SURGE MAGAZINE

Okay, so here we are on week three of our <u>Surge Spotlight Series</u> where we are reviewing indie games based entirely on the votes of you, the readers. This series is designed to shed some light on unknown or overlooked indie games that you feel deserve more exposure, and this week's landslide winner is *sigh* *101 Ways to Kill the Teacher* by first-time developers Pet Rock.

For those unfamiliar with this 'game', consider yourselves lucky and stop reading this right now.

Seriously, last chance.

Originally titled *101 Ways to Kill Sierra Lox*, the developers were forced to change the title for what I hope are obvious reasons that don't need to be explained. The game was then briefly called *101 Ways to Kill the Communications Professor*, but after this title was deemed still too on-the-nose by the major digital storefronts, it was changed to its vaguer final version. But let's be entirely clear here—this game is unabashed and painfully obvious about the target of its scorn.

Sierra Lox, for the unaware, is a professor of communications at Northwestern University who has recently become the subject of a targeted harassment campaign by petulant man-babies who spend entirely too much time online after she dared suggest that, and I'm paraphrasing here, maybe angry nerds on the Internet should consider being slightly less angry. Angry nerds reacted to this suggestion as you might expect, and here we are with the murder-fantasy game that is the feature of today's spotlight.

As for the game itself, the only positive thing I can really say about it is that the title is at least an accurate description of what you can expect to see. Each sequence of the game starts with a title card listing the day, from 1 to 101, before placing you from the first-person perspective in a classroom looking ahead at a female instructor who, for legal reasons, the game cannot explicitly say is Sierra Lox.

The game then gives you the onscreen prompt, 'press X to begin today's lesson', which then triggers an automated sequence in which the unnamed main character proceeds to violently murder the teacher in a diversity of ways.

Riveting stuff. Truly breaking brave new ground for the medium.

The methods in which the titular teacher is killed each day range from the conventional (shooting with a variety of guns, stabbing, bludgeoning with heavy objects) to the bizarre (trampled by a herd of pink-haired cattle, abducted by pot smoking aliens) to the horrific and sexually violent, each as tasteless and depraved as the last.

The 'gameplay' is severely restricted and is limited to the singular pressing of a button each day to kick off the animated death sequence that follows. Speaking of which, the animations and graphics themselves are crude, shoddy, and resemble the Flash animations of the early 2000s (and *not* in any kind of good or endearing way).

The animations vary in length from a few seconds to about a minute or so, meaning the entire 'game' can be experienced in about an hour or two. Still, that's an hour or two you could devote to doing literally anything else and I can almost guarantee that it would be time better spent.

Honestly, I can't think of any valid reasons why anyone would *want* to play this game beyond the disturbing murder-fantasy appeal.

Speaking purely on technical, aesthetic, and gameplay terms it's undeniably and objectively a bad game. From a moral perspective it's abhorrent. It's disgusting that the developers at Pet Rock would make this, it's alarming that people would actually pay money for it, it's bewildering that digital storefronts allow it to be sold on their platforms even after the title changes, and frankly, it's disappointing that this is the type of garbage that I have to focus on and churn out 700-word articles about.

101 Ways to Kill the Teacher is available now, for some reason, on all major digital storefronts and is priced at $4.99, which
if I'm being honest, is about five bucks too much.

Remember to vote below for the indie game you would like
us to cover next week in the Surge Spotlight Series.

Or don't—maybe that would be for the best.

Justin MacDonnell, Surge Magazine

FEBRUARY 3, 2018
JOURNAL OF DR. KLEIN PATIENT #56283

My Good Health Journal, Second Entry
I told Dr. Klein that all day long I feel nervous about going to
bed because when I go to bed and turn off the lights and the
screens and there's just silence and darkness I feel like my heart
wants to explode. I tried paying attention to the voices in my
head and writing down what they were saying like he told me to,
but that just made them louder. Dr. Klein said I should try meditating on a regular basis. I wasn't sure what that meant, but he
said it basically means just sitting still with your eyes closed and
focusing on your breathing. I tried but I couldn't do it for more
than half a minute or so. He said I should find a 'mantra' that I
can repeat to myself either when I'm meditating or when I'm
having trouble sleeping. A mantra is like a short statement that is
supposed to clear my head and relax me. The one he suggested
was 'present moment, beautiful moment,' but I think I have
found a better one. I remember there was this commercial for
Flaky Crunch cereal that used to come on all the time when I
was a kid and I still know all the words. It ended like this:

*Start your day with a thrill and wake up the block with the thun-
derous sound of Flaky Crunch, part of a balanced breakfast.*

This is the mantra that I have been using and it seemed to
work well on the first night I tried it. I did some searching and I
actually found the original commercial on YouTube and now
instead of saying the mantra to myself in my head, I can just let
the video play on repeat at a low volume all night long and this

has been working so far. The mantra is just loud enough to block out the voices that were keeping me from sleeping and hurting my heart.

Start your day with a thrill and wake up the block with the thunderous sound of Flaky Crunch, part of a balanced breakfast.

Even just writing it out now makes me feel more relaxed. I like that in the commercial there are a few different people who speak. There is a whole family sitting at the table eating breakfast. It makes me feel like I am right there with them, or like there are people in my room talking with me as I fall asleep.

Start your day with a thrill and wake up the block with the thunderous sound of Flaky Crunch, part of a balanced breakfast.

It never changes and it never stops and there my heart finds its peace.

MARCH 8, 2018
DOCUMENT SAVED TO THE DESKTOP OF PETER RILEY
UNDER THE FILE NAME 'CHORES'

I woke up early today and for some reason I didn't want to grab my phone and immediately check my notifications like I normally would. Instead I left my phone untouched on the nightstand and got up to stretch by the window. That felt really nice. I should start doing that every morning, but I know that I probably won't. I sat at my computer with the intention of doing some work, reading the news, maybe writing and filming a new video, but the motivation to do any of these things just wouldn't come to me. I had been at my computer for nearly an hour and hadn't started anything, so in frustration I decided to commit myself to a different task as a means of convincing myself that the day wasn't about to become a total waste. I decided to clean the balcony of my apartment, something that despite making a mental note to do nearly every week, I had neglected to do for several months. I took the old broom I kept on the corner of the balcony and started to sweep.

And then came the spiders.

As I maneuvered the broom head into the cracks, corners, and crevices, the spiders poured out thick as black oil. They crawled fast, some jagged in their path, others more determined in their destinations and soon they obscured the entirety of the porch surface. They covered my bare feet and I could feel their various forms vibrating between my open toes. Some with the diameter of a poker chip, others so small as to be indiscernible from the dust and dirt coating the area. As they continued to introduce themselves steadily from some unseen source, I turned violent.

For most of my life I had, through some deep-rooted empathy for all things living, made a habit of removing uninvited pests non-violently, most commonly via the 'cup-and-cover' method. But this time I was intent on doing harm and there did I conscript my wits and appendages to this purpose. Wielding my Wal-Mart broom with the same care and proficiency that a samurai would his folded steel, I began to swing and stomp at the octadic-legged legions. As the corpses abounded under my efforts, I set to sweeping the husks off the balcony and onto the grass below where they might one day fertilize the soil or be mulched into a pleasant scent with the cut grass the next time the groundskeeper mowed.

Some time after my dance, the spiders stopped coming. Whether because their numbers had been fully depleted or because the reality of the arachnicide stalled any still left lingering into hesitation and hiding I cannot say. But though their movement stopped, my body tingled all over as they continued to crawl on me as phantoms. I finished sweeping the balcony and proceeded to take a long shower during which I scrubbed my skin red.

And now I'm here, back at my computer writing about it and I can still feel them in my hair and on my arms and scuttling invisible on the tips of curved fingers.

CorkBoard—Keeping your workplace connected!

Brandon Janzen wrote 10:23pm:
  Hey Justin I just read your latest piece for the Spotlight Series, I know I told Carla she could publish it after she reviewed it this morning, but after reading it myself I am noticing some problematic content that I would like to discuss.

10:35pm:
  Please do message me back ASAP, I would like to have these new edits implemented tonight if possible, it shouldn't take you too long.

Justin MacDonnell wrote 10:40pm:
  Hey Brandon, sorry I was out of service for a bit, what's going on?

Brandon Janzen wrote 10:41pm:
  I would like you to do a quick rewrite of your Spotlight review from today.

Justin MacDonnell wrote 10:41pm:
  Okay, what did you have in mind?

Brandon Janzen wrote 10:44pm:
  I think the review of the game is mostly fine, but some of the language you've used is a little antagonistic toward our readers. Could you do a read-through and revise anything that could be misconstrued as passing judgement on the readers or anyone that voted for the game?

10:47pm:
  Justin? Still there?

Justin MacDonnell wrote 10:48pm:
Yeah, sorry. I just am not so sure that I agree, I don't think there's anything I wrote there that was really offensive to anyone. I mean sure, it's a little snarky, but it's also pretty obvious that the vote was brigaded or manipulated somehow, that's the only way this terrible game won in the first place, I thought I was just sort of subtly calling out the people that were behind it.

Brandon Janzen wrote 10:50pm:
The point of having the vote in the first place was to let the readers dictate the content that they want to see. I don't think insulting the selections of the readers is the way to go.
And if we're being honest, I don't see how people 'brigading' the site to vote is a bad thing. Clicks are clicks at the end of the day.
So what do you say pal, can you get those edits done tonight?

Justin MacDonnell wrote 10:51pm:
Sure, consider it done.

Brandon Janzen wrote 10:51pm:
Great, thanks pal!

CorkBoard—Keeping your workplace connected!

JUNE 30, 2019
CONVERSATION OVERHEARD BY THE COMPILER OF THIS BOOK
AS HE SAT OUTSIDE A POPULAR COFFEE CHAIN DRINKING
BLACK COFFEE

"Ay, what's up with the bandages bro it looks like you been slittin' your wrists or some shit."
"Nah man, got some new ink done, gotta keep this shit under wraps for a few hours."
"That's sick, lemme see it."
"Man, I just said I gotta keep it wrapped for a bit."

"Come on, you can take it off for a second, what's gonna happen?"

"No, it'll get fucked up if it's exposed to the elements or whatever."

"The elements?"

"Yeah, sunlight and wind and shit. The elements. Don't wanna take any chances with this."

"Tell me what it is at least."

"Trust fam, you're gonna see it on Insta later, this shit's gonna blow up."

"Bro, none of your shit ever blows up."

"It's gonna be different this time. This time I got some major support."

"Bullshit, what support?"

"Ever heard of Red Bull, bitch?"

"Get the fuck outta here with that, what are you even on about right now?"

"Alright fuck it, I'll let you take a peek right quick. Ay, stand on the other side of me so you're blocking the sun, if this shit fades it ain't gonna work."

"Alright, whatever. Let's see this shit."

"Okay man, check this shit out and tell me this ain't about to blow up."

"No! Holy shit dude are you serious with that?"

"Oh, hell yeah bro."

"This man went and got a fucking can of Red Bull tattooed on his forearm, you're crazy."

"No joke bro, that's a full-sized version too, and it's like an exact replica right down to the smallest details."

"I mean, yeah, it looks legit, just like the real thing, but why?"

"I told you man I'm gonna get this shit on Insta and it's gonna get Red Bull's attention."

"Yeah, and then what?"

"Free Red Bull for life motherfucker!"

"Bro, you're stupid. Why wouldn't you hit them up before you got that shit done, you don't even know if they're gonna notice it, never mind give you free shit."

"Nah, listen man, this is gonna work. I read that some dude did basically the same exact thing. He got like a Pizza Hut tattoo or some shit and I'm pretty sure they hooked him up for life."

"Man, I ain't ever even seen you drink a Red Bull before, where did this come from?"

"I dunno man, I wanted to get a new tattoo so I made an appointment, but I didn't know what I was gonna get until like the day before when the idea came to me."

"Who the hell books a tattoo appointment without a tattoo in mind? You're dumb bro."

"Ay man, keep talking, when I get infinite Red Bull I'm gonna let your ass go thirsty."

"Nah, nah, you gotta let me in on some of that. It does look pretty sick though, I gotta say."

"That's what's up. Now quit being a hater and help me get this shit trending."

June 4, 2019
The Confession of Peter 'Petrol' Riley: Part VII

As far as I can tell, the second the bullet went through his spine it was already too late to do anything about it. For a week or two following the shooting I had trouble sleeping. I would lie awake thinking and convincing myself that maybe something could have been done if he got medical attention just a little bit sooner, but I've since accepted that it wouldn't have mattered.

On October 12, 2018 Chris Fuller was shot through the spine as he was standing outside protesting one of my public talks at Tufts University. And that would be the last time that Chris would ever be able to stand on his own. When I started writing this confession a week ago, I said that was the moment when I first started thinking about how I might leave this character behind. As it turns out, by then it may have already been too late.

But let me back up and see if I can fill in some gaps. Last entry I covered up to one full year after starting the Petrol grift where things had been growing modestly, but steadily. It was during the second year of playing this character when things started growing *exponentially*. The videos, my subscribers, my financial contributors, my zealously committed fans at the /rr/ board, they were all there and increasing, but around this time my reach started to extend beyond an underground niche of angry, chronically online outcasts and into the real world. I started to receive more press coverage, more media requests, more emails and messages from both fans and critics, I started becoming featured as either a guest or a topic of conversation on the channels and podcasts of much larger and more influential media figures, and I started getting invited to do more public appearances.

It was around this time when I realized I couldn't sustain this project on my own anymore. Up until then I had been singularly responsible not just for portraying the character and creating and producing all of the content—itself a full-time commitment—but also for trying to manage the deluge of mail and messages from people trying to get in touch with me for various reasons. That's when I decided to hire some help—something that my steadily growing pool of donations and financial backing allowed. I didn't even know what kind of help I needed, but I put together what was, in retrospect, a pretty incomprehensible job advertisement looking for a 'personal assistant/manager/agent' and cast it off to the online ocean like a message in a bottle. For about a week I didn't get any serious inquiries to consider, which I figured was understandable given my reputation as a professional hatemonger. And then came Lisa Brooke. Out of respect for her privacy I won't say much about her here other than that she was a dream come true and a consummate professional. With Lisa handling my outreach, bookings, communications, and other day-to-day concerns, I was freed up to focus all my energy and attention to the character and to exploiting my increasingly visible platform.

And what a platform it was. The first time I spoke in a public, offline setting as Petrol was when I was invited by the 'Free Speech Club' of an East Coast university to deliver a 'lecture' at their campus. I was initially a little hesitant to bring Petrol into the real world, but when Lisa did some digging and revealed how much people in my position were typically charging for various speaking and appearance fees, I was able to find the courage. I was nervous before giving that talk. Nervous in the way that I used to get before going on stage to perform. I suppose there wasn't much difference between the two, aside from the fact that this time around the audience didn't see what I was doing as performance. I prepared a 'lecture' compiled of some of my standard material and talking points combined with a few things specialized and catered to the region and the news that week. And as I took the stage and orated and opined about how it was a miracle to see so many White men at a university in the era of diversity and affirmative action, about how these types of gatherings would be outlawed within a few years, and how the members of the Free Speech Club were heroes for protecting our right to say all the things that 'they' didn't want us to say, I could see on their eager, wide-eyed faces a certain glee that was exaggerated whenever I said something especially misanthropic. Like any good improvisational performer would, I picked up on this and played into it. I had my material written and prepared, and I had revised the language to be somewhat less gratuitous and more socially acceptable than what I typically used in my videos, but I could see that it was the moments where I expressed overt cruelty and ridicule of our various 'enemies' that were the most wellreceived, as if that's what they really came to see.

And that was the game. I continued getting invited to give similar talks and to engage in token debates with other media figures, and I became more comfortable and proficient performing the character in a live setting. I embarked on a mini speaking tour across North America, riling up angry and despondent young men and teaching them to channel their frustrations, fears, and anxieties toward whatever social outgroup was the flavor of the time—immigrants, feminists, the media, Marxists, globalists, Muslims, liberals, academics, whoever. All while earning myself a mint in the meantime. It was during the third or fourth of these events where I decided to start filming them and releasing them online, increasing the audience and reach ever further. I got creative with it too. Sometimes I would plant someone in the audience to pose as a protesting student who would attempt to challenge me during the question-and-answer period who I could then proceed to verbally dominate and embarrass. Soon my fans started compiling some of the best of these moments into compilation videos that would end up becoming some of my most popular and frequently watched content.

We were creating a machine, a cult of personality devoted to a figurehead who was as irredeemably terrible as he was easy, even fun, for me to portray. As the audiences grew larger, so too did the crowds of people who were protesting me. Some even managed to convince their universities to cancel my talks entirely under the argument that I was espousing hate speech and promoting discrimination or violence. But the beautiful thing about it was that even when my talks were canceled, I still won. I had been censored, my free speech stifled, and this only served to frenzy my fans even further while bringing more attention and supporters to my brand.

And this was it. I was known. I had legions of devoted fans willing to run into traffic for me. I was making more money than I had ever seen. I had made it and reached the life that I thought I wanted or deserved, even if the means of getting there were not something I ever would have predicted. There were some minor blocks along the way of course, there were journalists and reporters constantly trying to talk to members of my family or people I went to school with, trying to dig up dirt about my past life or any other information they could use in their stories or exposés about me. I tried my best to curtail this, I carefully instructed my parents never to respond to any of these queries, it was all still just performance art after all. But the thing is, even when people tried to expose me, and even when they did it convincingly and thoroughly, the loyalty of my supporters never waned. To them it was all just media lies trying to discredit and silence their outspoken champion and they simply refused to believe anything negative that was written about me. On the contrary, they would often target, threaten, and harass anyone brave enough to speak out against me with all manner of creatively perverse methods. When Anthony Ouellette, an old classmate of mine from DU reached out to me and threatened to reveal my charade if I didn't pay him off, I begrudgingly turned to the /rr/ board for support. I don't know what it was that they did exactly, but within two days Anthony was apologizing to me and promising never to contact me again. For anyone wondering why I let things go on as long as they have, I don't know how much clearer I can say it—these are not people to be crossed.

I guess that more or less brings us up to speed on the second year of the Petrol grift. It was and still is a bit of a blur if I'm being honest. Lots was happening and it was happening fast. Still, even during this period of rapid growth and exposure, I remained under the impression that I was somehow still in control of the outcome. I still thought that I could pull the plug at any moment and that everyone would cheer for me as I did. Then I could go back to living a normal life as some kind of Andy Kaufman-esque hero of performance art.

And then, about eight months ago, I was scheduled to give a talk at Tufts University. As had become the norm, the talk was being protested by various student groups, and campus security had been called in to keep on eye on the exchanges between my fans waiting in line and the various people protesting my presence, some of which posed the risk of escalating beyond the normal name-calling and ridicule to physical violence.

It was about three minutes after I had taken the stage and begun my performance when we heard the gunshot from outside. Amid the chaos and confusion someone eventually confirmed that there had been a shooting, though no one was yet sure who the victim or perpetrator was, or more importantly, what side they were affiliated with. And as despicable and shameful as it is for me to admit, that really was the thought that went through my head at the time. I wasn't thinking about the safety of the victim, or whether they would be alright, or if someone else could get hurt. All I could think to myself was, 'please don't let it be one of my fans who did the shooting.' Of course, we all know now that it was. The man who was shot was a student who was protesting my talk, which makes him, and I cannot stress this enough, unequivocally in the right. He was shot by one of my fans after a heated argument they were having outside eventually erupted. His name is Chris Fuller. He was shot through the spine, and while he survived, he will be in a wheelchair for the rest of his life. And from that moment I finally realized what I probably should have much sooner—there was no going back to normal anymore.

I carried on with the talk. I remember saying something along the lines of, 'if we stop, we let them win,' or something equally asinine. And while I went through the motions of the performance and hit all my beats competently enough, I knew in the back of my mind that after tonight, it was all going to be over for me. I was convinced that was the moment where people would collectively wash their hands of me, where I would be erased, de-platformed, censored, and discarded as I deserved to be. After the talk I skipped all fan interactions and went straight back to my hotel and waited anxiously and impatiently for sleep to overtake me.

The next morning I logged on to read all of the articles and think-pieces that had been hastily written in the hours following the shooting. There were those calling for social media websites to de-platform me or calling for universities to stop hosting my talks, but I also wanted to see how my most impassioned supporters were responding to the news and how quickly they would be distancing themselves from me. I checked the top threads of the /rr/ board to find what I probably should have expected to find—that the victim of the shooting wasn't Chris Fuller.

No, apparently the real victim of the shooting was me.

OCTOBER 13, 2018
THREAD ON /RR/ FORUM

ScrewDrivvvr (388947) Posted 10/13/2018 (8:42am)
Well /rr/, it looks like the guy who shot up the Petrol talk last night was one of ours. How long until you think Petrol and this board are banned?

Yes_Massah1776 (388881)
Hey dipshit, it wasn't one of our guys who did the shooting.

Non__Sensei (388224)
He literally said he was there to see the Petrol talk as a fan, and people have gone through all his social media posts, his Facebook wall is full of Petrol content.

ZzZ_huck (382081)
Yeah, it's called a false flag retard. Do you seriously just believe everything you hear on the news or see on the Internet? Both the guy who did the shooting AND the person who got shot were crisis actors that were planted there.

MightyMyles (322266)
Poster above me is correct. Chris Fuller (the guy who got shot) was a volunteer who was mentally stunted enough to literally take a bullet in order to make Petrol look bad. And (((they))) probably promised him a huge payout.

Claymore88 (341287) MODERATOR
Yeah, that or he's faking it and was never actually shot/injured in the first place, it's not that hard to pull off. Prop gun goes bang, actor goes down, some hidden squibs release fake blood everywhere, and it all looks legit to the untrained eye. Although, I also wouldn't be surprised if the shooting was real, these people will stop at nothing to silence us, even if it means sacrificing one of their own. Look at Stalin or Mao or any of the other leftist dictators in history. Human lives are endlessly expendable to them.

DixieDefender (381000)
More likely the shooter himself is an undercover leftist or CIA plant trying to discredit the movement. And guess what? It worked. Universities are already cancelling Petrol's talks left and right now. They'll come for this board next, we've always been their main target.

GundamLing (387421)

How do you account for the fact that the shooter's social media is full of truth bomb content and mentions of this board?

calripkinjr (389495)

Well, yeah, that's all part of the psyop. Obviously they are gonna place all that shit there to make it seem like he was a diehard Petrol fan, it gives them more ammo when they decide to come after us. Basically, never listen to anything you hear about this story in the mainstream media. They have an obvious agenda and you can be certain that anything they feed you will be lies as usual.

rrrvvvlad (382119)

Chris Fuller is 100% a plant and a crisis actor, fuck him. Either he's faking it or he was dumb enough to trade his legs for some faggy social justice points. I say we start spamming him with videos of us dancing or walking or just using our legs, let him know how bad he fucked up.

JiggyBooBoo (384222)

Hey, what do chris fullers legs and niggers have in common? None of them work.

Lucky617 (384277)

I saw some videos of the protests last night, how fucking great would it have been if someone just plowed through that crowd of shrill purple-haired whales in a Hummer. Also, obligatory 'fuck Chris Fuller.'

DragonbornNord (321869)

I know this board isn't braindead enough to fall for what was an obvious false flag, but I wonder what this is gonna mean for Petrol moving forward.

Adolphus (389472)

Universities will probably cave and start cancelling his talks, but who cares? Try as they might they still can't just take him off the internet. As long as he keeps making content his message will still be heard and it will resonate.

Animals77 (388001)

Yeah, normies have been saying he's bad and needs to be canceled since the start, so its not like this is going to change anyone's mind. His detractors will still hate him, and we will still support him no matter what. Also, fuck Chris Fuller, someone should push his wheelchair off a cliff while he's in it.

PutchPerfect (388112)

God sometimes I wish I was as mentally deficient as the normal population is. Imagine how convenient and comfortable it must be to be able to just unquestioningly accept everything you see and hear. It's beyond obvious to anyone with more than two brain cells that this whole shooting thing is a set up to make Petrol look bad. Fuck it, I'm upping my monthly contribution to Petrol, he needs to know that we have his back now and forever.

MAY 20, 2018
JOB INTERVIEW BETWEEN PETER RILEY AND HIS
SOON-TO-BE-ASSISTANT LISA BROOKE,
RECORDED BY THE FORMER'S SMARTPHONE,
MOST LIKELY WITHOUT THE FULL CONSENT
OF THE LATTER (THE RISKS WE ALL MUST TAKE)

"So, can you tell me who it was?"

"Who what was?"

"The famous person you were working for before this? It says on your resume that you were a celebrity assistant for eight years."

"I can't tell you that."

"Okay, but was it like an actor, or an athlete, or what? Can you tell me that much?"

"I'm not going to do that, no."

"Can you at least tell me why you left that job? Was whoever it was like a massive diva or a sex pervert or something?"

"My previous employer retired from the public eye and was
no longer in need of my service. The work relationship ended
amicably and respectfully."

"Oh, they were old? When I hear celebrity, I always
assume young for some reason. Well in that case I'm probably
a lot younger than you're used to and I suspect my needs might
be quite a bit different. A lot of the stuff I do is based around
new media and online stuff. Are you comfortable with that?
Did you grow up around this sort of thing? How old were you
again?"

"I don't think you're supposed to ask that."

"I know, I know, bad manners, but I just wanted to get a
sense of how—"

"No, I mean it's illegal to ask someone their age during a job
interview."

"Damn, really? I think I knew that actually. I'm sorry I've
never done something like this before, I don't really know what
the process is supposed to look like."

"Maybe you should just tell me what you're looking for in
an assistant and I'll let you know if I can meet those requirements."

"That sounds good, let's do that. Wait, was it Day-Lewis?"

"Daniel Day-Lewis?"

"Oh my God, it was, wasn't it?"

"No."

"But even if it was you wouldn't tell me, so you could be
lying to me right now."

"You were about to tell me what you were looking for in an
assistant."

"Right, sorry. Well, mostly it's a matter of managing all the
media requests that I've been getting lately. Also, I've been getting a lot more offers to travel around and whatnot and I need
someone to work out all the booking and scheduling and logistics
of that. I don't know, basically I've been doing everything on my
own from the content creation to the distribution and all the PR

stuff, but it's getting to be too much for me to handle and really I just need someone to take care of all the technical stuff so I can focus on making content exclusively."

"Well, one of my main primary responsibilities with my previous employer was screening and responding to all media requests big and small, and course, organizing travel and accommodations is also something I certainly have plenty of experience with. Given that the scope of your enterprise is significantly smaller than that of my previous employer, I'm confident in my abilities to manage your needs on that front, in addition to any other personal requirements you may have."

"Damn, 'significantly' smaller, huh?"

"Let's continue."

"Right. Well, I guess a big question here is how familiar are you with my uh... content."

"I've seen your work."

"And you're cool with it?"

"My opinion on your content won't affect my ability to do the job."

"Sure, but just for the sake of conversation, what is your opinion?"

"I don't really care about it."

"You don't care?"

"Were you expecting to interview a fan, or a competent assistant?"

"Look, just between you and me, the content I make isn't really sincere, try and think of it more like performance art that's making a sort of satirical meta-commentary statement on the current state of—"

"It's okay, I still don't care. I'm thirty-seven by the way."

"That's great, yeah, that's good, tell me more about yourself."

"I'm currently unemployed and I'm looking for a new job."

"You know what, I like you Mrs. Brooke. Miss Brooke?"

"Lisa's fine".

"You bet she is."

"Excuse me?"

"I'm sorry, that was wildly inappropriate. I'm just a little nervous about this. I use humour to deflect anxiety, it's a generational thing."

"Right. But it's not just a generational thing. Nicholson did it all the time, but over the years I learned to tell exactly when he was serious and when he was deflecting."

"Get out of here, you worked for fucking Jack Nicholson? Shit, I'm sorry for swearing but that just changed everything, screw the interview you gotta just tell me Jack stories for the rest of the day now."

"I didn't work for Jack Nicholson."

"Okay. That was funny Lisa, you're good. Can I just offer you the job now? I don't know if I'm going to see anyone better than you."

"Didn't you say in your email that I was the first person you were interviewing?"

"I did, and you are."

"Not that I'm trying to talk myself out of a job, but you aren't interested in at least interviewing a few more people?"

"Full disclosure Lisa, you're the only person to make a serious application for this position. Turns out I'm not a particularly fashionable brand to be associated with. On that note, whoever you were working for before, my brand is probably going to be much smaller and definitely more niche. The pay might be modest at first, at least for now, but I'm growing steadily and if you stick with me I promise I'll cut you in on the growth."

"Smaller-scale sounds like exactly what I'm looking for right now."

"Perfect. So I guess I should write up an employee contract or something?"

"I'll take care of that when I start tomorrow. You go make a video."

No Date
Echoes (Neon Night Rides)

Well met Aleister,

The grids have been in and out of mal all night, but I finally made it. I'll fire up a dotex that should get the rest sorted out. Not looking forward to the ride home given the conditions out there, but better to be safe than sorry. If I don't hear from you by overmorrow I'll assume all is working as intended. That should conclude our correspondence until the next cycle.

If I may, given how hard it's been to come across truly encrypted lines lately, I was hoping to send some queries your way while I have the opportunity. If you happen to have a solution for any of these I would be grateful, but please don't spend any additional time searching for them if you don't already have solutions logged.

> My levels of Testosterone™ have been crit for nearly a full cycle. I've overridden the mandatory notifications for purposes of personally preferential annoyance avoidance, but I was hoping to bring the levels to normal, and truly, if possible. I am in a position to alter my intake re: diet to some degree, but it must remain a strictly non-Fauna approach. I am willing to incorporate e-Meat if required.

> re: the morals of <our> cause, I have been operating under the assumption that the negative SOC# value or our movement was a deliberate machination of the Directorship, but having run some old scripts from the paper age it seems as if the negative value may be justifiable, if slightly exaggerated. Are you able to reason this?

> Phineas has been allocating nearly all of his free hours to playing *Skrom*. I would rather he allocate some free hours to spend time with me unwired, but I do not wish to exert any official authority in this situation. In the interest of compromise, I would like to play *Skrom* with Phineas, but the last time I played was three versions ago and the reactionary movements required are largely unknown to me now. Are you aware of any mods that may be overlaid without visibility? I am

willing to use untrue methods, even at the risk of a potential banning. I only wish to spend more time with Phineas while I am able.

> There is a female in unwired proximity with a spatially similar time allotment to my own. Her social indicators are manually set to red, but her unwired indicators are in conflict (ie. she looks at me and smiles, and though uncalculated, she does this for what seems like longer than the acceptable amount of time). I find myself thinking of this person even during the completion of other task-lists. However, given that her indicators are set to red, I do not see any outcome from this. As such I would like to install an individualized blocker that prevents me from having to see her. I can run the wired version on my own, but are you familiar with any scripts that can work while unwired? I'll attach an image of her face to this com.

As always, thank you for your dedication to <our> cause.

Protecting the Nu-Tomorrow at any cost brother. Everett, logging off.

August 2, 2018
The Email Inbox of Peter Riley

Oliver Kitts Georges (amasses4dr444@css.clipp.fr), 08/02/2018, 12:44am
Inheritance claiming

Dear PETER RILEY

Please 2 make your acqua nta ce. I am messaging regarding large funds of your recent departed great-aunt. We offer sorry to you in this time of bereave. To collect funds left to you by great-aunt, a value of $1,376,803 USD, please discover form;

ars130892741.eexcc

Sorry regarding the loss of your great-aunt. This is diff cult time, but I am here if you need talk to someone.

Faithfully yours,

Oliver Kitts Georges

Asst mngr, Life Mutuals Funds, Bank of France

SEPTEMBER 19, 2017
TEXT MESSAGE EXCHANGE BETWEEN
PETER RILEY AND ANTHONY OUELLETTE

Anthony Ouellette said:
> Hey Peter, is this still your number?

Peter Riley said:
> Yup!
> Long time no talk, how's it going Tony?

Anthony Ouellette said:
> Good, good.
> I see you've been making a bit of a name for yourself out there.

Peter Riley said:
> Yeah I dunno, it just sort of happened I guess.
> What have you been up to since grad?

Anthony Ouellette said:
> Nothing too exciting, doing some theatre work here and there.
> I actually started my own little online art/acting project called 'Keepers of the Word', which has been fun, but nowhere near as successful as what you've been doing.

Peter Riley said:
> I've had some lucky breaks. That sounds cool though, I'll have to check out your stuff!

Anthony Ouellette said:
> So, I have to ask.
> This character you're playing, it's all an act, right?

Peter Riley said:
> haha yeah of course, it's basically just the same character I did for Josh's class back in the day

Anthony Ouellette said:
    But the people who watch the videos don't know it's an act?

Peter Riley said:
    Most of them don't seem to, no.

Anthony Ouellette said:
    hmm

Peter Riley said:
    What's up?

Anthony Ouellette said:
    Just sounds a little sketchy.

Peter Riley said:
    I don't know what to tell you man.

Anthony Ouellette said:
    Don't you think so?
    Do you think it's right that you get all this attention and money by pretending to be some crazy neo-Nazi?
    While people like me who are trying to do something genuine and real have to plug away for a fraction of the views and attention that you get?

Peter Riley said:
    I don't make as much money at this as you seem to think I do.

Anthony Ouellette said:
    Bullshit, we can all see how much you pull in from donations on Backr. And that doesn't even include all the ad revenue and other income that you're probably getting.

Peter Riley said:
    I do okay, so what? I don't know what you want from me right now.

Anthony Ouellette said:

I want you to share some of the success.

Peter Riley said:

Are you for real? 'Share' how? The hell you want me to do?

Anthony Ouellette said:

Plug my channel and use your media connections to get my content promoted and featured.

Peter Riley said:

It doesn't really work that way…

Anthony Ouellette said:

Okay, so how about you invest in my channel so I can buy some better equipment and maybe some advertisements? $10,000 should do it.

Peter Riley said:

Yeah, that's just not gonna happen. Get real man.

Anthony Ouellette said:

In that case maybe I'll take these messages and bring them to a journalist?

Specifically the one where you admit that the whole thing is an act.

And maybe we expose you for what you are.

Peter Riley said:

Are you for real right now? Are you actually threatening to blackmail me?

Anthony Ouellette said:

Call it whatever you want, but that's the situation.

Peter Riley said:

I think you watch too many movies.

Anthony Ouellette said:
Only when I want to see good acting.
Because I sure don't see it when I watch your videos.

Peter Riley said:
Wow, sick burn bro, that doesn't even make sense.

Anthony Ouellette said:
You realize this is why nobody in the program ever liked you right? You were always an arrogant prick who thought he was better than everyone else.

Peter Riley said:
Remind me how many subscribers you have again?

Anthony Ouellette said:
Eat a dick. I'm giving you three days. If I don't receive your $10,000 donation by then, I'll do everything in my power to expose the great Petrol Riley for the fraud that he is.

Three days thereafter.

Anthony Ouellette said:
Hey Peter. I'm really sorry about the things I said. Please just forget I brought it up and I promise I'll never contact you ever again or speak a word about any of this to anyone.
I'm really sorry, please just make them stop.

MARCH 2, 2018
RANDOM FACT FROM FACTOIDZ.ORG,
THE INTERNET'S NUMBER ONE RANDOM FACT GENERATOR

"Whenever there is a high-profile sexual assault or rape incident in the news, the victim's name quickly becomes a popular search term on every leading pornography site."
Click here for another mind-blowing factoid!

SEPTEMBER 20, 2017
THREAD ON /RR/ FORUM

Claymore88 (341287) MODERATOR
Posted 09/20/2017 (9:39am)

Okay gang, Petrol reached out to me directly and apparently some random fuckface has been threatening to sell a bunch of lies and false information about him to the media in some half-baked attempt to get Petrol canceled or whatever. Not that the media telling lies about Petrol would be anything new, but apparently this guy went to school with Petrol and because of that people might be more willing to believe any bullshit stories he has to tell. I don't think Petrol would have contacted me if this was something that could have been easily ignored, so you all know what to do. The guy's name is Anthony Ouellette. Let's get to work.

Animals77 (388001)

Found his YouTube channel <u>here</u>. Look at this cringe 'Keepers of the Word' shit. Mass report his vids for copyright strikes and we should be able to get them taken down.

KishComing (382000)

Found his Instagram account <u>here</u>. What a punchable face.

TheNightShift (382125)

Look at his most recent pic, that's definitely the Montreal skyline. I lived there for years.

ZzZ_huck (382081)

Can confirm that is Montreal. Found the exact building he's in using street view <u>here</u>.

BorneoFunction (388399)

Actually I think he would be in the building right next to that one. The one you posted is an office building, but the one next to it is residences. Alpen Tower.

Occam's_Stubble (386366)

Check this out I used the skyscraper directory to get the specs on the building in the middle of his view there. If we count the floors up from his view I think we can trace what floor he's on.

BathSaltBlitz (327790)

Looks like he's on the 8th floor if I'm counting this right.

KillerBOB (388321)

I think the 7th actually, the camera angle is aimed up slightly so its not exactly parallel.

Occam's_Stubble (386366)

Yes, definitely 7th

Soldaten1488 (386507)

If we know what floor he's on can we also get his apartment number?

Uber_Alles (388902)

Assuming we had the floor plan of the building, yeah.

DragonbornNord (321869)

Alpen Tower floor plan is right here.

Non__Sensei (388224)

So if I'm reading this correctly, to get that view he is either in apartment 707 or 708?

Flame_of_Ezio (382783)

It would have to be 708 since 707 is a corner apartment and there wouldn't be that much wall to the left of his window. If you look at his building with satellite view you can see how the windows on the corner apartments go almost right to the end of the building.

Claymore88 (341287) MODERATOR

Alright, Anthony Ouellette lives in Apartment 708 at the Alpen Tower in Montreal. Any of you truth bombers happen to live in the area?

Lucky617 (384277)

Montrealer checking in, ready to do my part. I got a few ideas on how we might surprise this fucker.

Claymore88 (341287) MODERATOR

Thanks for stepping up brother. The rest of us will look into seeing what else we can dig up about the guy online.

SerraFormer (385500)

Am I the only one who feels a little bit uncomfortable about this?

Claymore88 (341287) MODERATOR

You have doubts because you are a normal and good person, but your mistake is thinking that the people who oppose us are also normal and good. These people want to see us removed from the Earth. These people would have no second thoughts at all about rounding us all up and shipping us off to the furnaces and replacing us with whatever mongrel hordes or African barbarians that wanted to take our place. They are the enemy and they don't deserve the same level of courtesy and empathy that you would afford to any decent person. So, no, I don't feel uncomfortable about it at all.

Remember1776 (388443)

Well said. The second we go soft on these people is the second that we start losing the battle for the future of our culture, and as a new father that's just something I'm not going to let happen.

APRIL 2, 2018
COMMUNICATIONS 403 LECTURE, NORTHWESTERN UNIVERSITY,
DELIVERED AND RECORDED BY DR. SIERRA LOX AND PROMPTLY
UPLOADED FOR STUDENT REFERENCE SHORTLY THEREAFTER

"What happens to a person when everything that makes up who they are is stripped away and they are left with no identifiable factors or essence with which to distinguish themselves as a unique and self-motivated actor? At what point does a person, fully deprived of any agency or identity simply cease to exist? And I say 'exist' here not necessarily in the material sense, but in the sense that most of you, as native and inseparable products of the conditions of technologically mediated late capitalism would be more familiar with, that is, as an indicator of the assurance of your very identities. As consumers.

"As we wrap up today, I want you to really think about that. We've devoted a lot of our time in this course to looking at how media and technology can shape identity and the self in ways that are both active and passive, and while I've tried encouraging you to avoid the lazy, reductionist, and cynical critiques that plague so much of the discourse around new communicative technologies and media, today I challenge you to think about things a bit more abstractly to see if we can't find a deeper and perhaps more malicious root to some of these issues.

"The current media landscape is haunted by ghosts of the past, this much we've seen, but why do we suppose that is? Feelings of nostalgia tend to romanticize a past that is, whether accurate or not, typically remembered as being easier or somehow less complicated than the current moment. This recent fetishization of the technology, consumer products, and cultural aesthetics of the eighties and nineties seems, then, to be somewhat contradictory. How many of you listen to music? Never mind, that's a silly question, of course all of you do, what I meant to ask was *how* do you listen to music? Most of you probably stream it directly. Some of you might still have downloaded files stored somewhere. And unless you're old like I am, most of you probably don't own or play CDs. And what do you listen with?

You listen using your phones or computers, using personalized earbuds and wireless connections that connect your music directly to the speakers in your car or home. Simply put, you listen conveniently and with a boundless, seemingly infinite selection of content to choose from. Of course, you don't even have to *choose* any more, that burden has largely been alleviated by the abundance of pre-made playlists created specifically for certain moods, feelings, and events, and by algorithms that are getting increasingly better at telling you what it is that you should be listening to at any given moment. Once again, it's a highly efficient, streamlined, and convenient process.

"Since I've basically given up on trying to convince you all that I'm young and hip, let me tell you what we used to do when I was a kid. First you would need to buy a blank cassette, or find one that you didn't want anymore and wouldn't mind taping over, then you would pop that cassette into your cumbersome stereo, then you would need to manually tune to one of the available radio stations, which in the small town I grew up in meant your options were very limited, then you would have to wait for the song that you liked to be played, and once it finally came on, you would need to quickly hold down the record button on the stereo to record the song to the tape, usually with fairly low audio quality. Then, whenever you wanted to actually listen to the song you would have to rewind the tape to the right spot, of which there was no real indicator.

"Doesn't exactly sound so convenient, does it?

"Yet, it was a highly involved act, an act that required a certain degree of forethought and direct action, certainly more than what is required today, and some might say that the reward was all the sweeter for it. So why the fetishization of this clumsy technology from the past? To answer this we need to look at the ways in which the relentless commodification of nearly every aspect of our daily existence has, with the help of comparatively recent advancements in communicative technologies, now come to include, and in many cases replace entirely, the various aspects that make us who we are. Because we are increasingly encouraged to define and identify ourselves based on the cultural products that we consume rather than the local and material aspects that traditionally shaped our identities— things like work, church, family, or community, all of which are today significantly more vaporous and tenuous than they were even fifty years ago—we are forced to rely more on external factors that we trust to be there and to always be there. But these factors don't exist independently of the conditions of late capitalist commodification, they are in fact inexorably dependent upon them, and surely you can see why this is potentially cause for some concern.

"When we accept that our identities have increasingly come to be dependent on external, often unstable market and media factors, and reduced in many respects to a malleable and shallow commodity that is more prone to being lost or diminished than perhaps ever before, we can begin to see how such a loss has left many feeling unsure of their purpose is an increasingly alienating modern world. For your generation specifically, this union of hyper-connectivity, aggressive consumerism, predatory commodification, and a general breakdown of community engagement have led many to experience uncertainties and insecurities regarding their identity and their place in the world, fears that are empirically represented in rising rates of things like depression, anxiety, mental illness, and general feelings of nihilism, aimlessness, and alienation.

"Make sense? Not quite? Let me give you a more practical example that's a bit easier to understand—sorry, did you have a question Ryan?"

"Yeah, so are you ever gonna debate Petrol Riley?"

"That's not really relevant to what we're discussing right now."

"Yeah, but are you gonna do it though?"

"Assuming we can work out and agree on a few details, I'm willing to do it whenever he is. You mind if I finish now?"

DECEMBER 10, 2018
THREAD ON /RR/ FORUM

Azure22Serra (382409) Posted 12/10/2018 (10:52pm)

Apologies for the sincere post—there won't be any dank memes or punchlines here so feel free to skip this, but there are a few things that I wanted to get off my chest.

> be me

> six months ago I turn 21

> no one to celebrate my birthday with because all my friends are online

> cant make friends at my university because they are all insufferable normies or meathead idiots

> cant meet any girls because they are all degenerate thots who only want to party and get smashed by the aforementioned meatheads

> spend my birthday drinking alone

> download and browse Matchr to try and get laid, but all I see is an endless stream of carbon-copy femoids with identical bios and interchangeable pictures

> end the night drunk, jerking off alone, and passing out before I can even finish

> wake up feeling like a complete loser and questioning my life

> best case scenario I finish my comp sci degree and get a terrible cubicle office job for the rest of my life while slowly paying off student debt

> tremendous sense of despair washes over me

> try to play video games and forget this feeling but it doesnt go away

> cant sleep at night because my mind is constantly racing with questions about my future and thoughts of dying alone having never procreated or raised a family

> thought Ive done everything that I was supposed to do in life, but still feel hopeless and alienated all the time

> start researching suicide methods online and figuring out which are most viable, effective, and painless

> steal a length of rope from a maintenance closet on campus
> fashion a noose and leave it hanging there for a few days while I build up the courage
> late one night, visit /dp/ for some dankness
> see that people are bitching about the new /rr/ board
> out of curiosity I visit the board, read some posts, they make sense to me
> watch some Petrol videos, feel like he's speaking directly to me and describing my exact life situation
> Petrol says that there is a better way than depression and nihilism and I believe him
> start lurking and posting to /rr/ more frequently while ingesting massive truth bombs
> finally realize that my depression and hopelessness has been orchestrated by the ZOG machine and that they want people like me to fade out of existence to eliminate all resistance
> finally realize that Western culture is under attack, and that I have a duty to defend it
> from that moment on, I no longer feel depressed or hopeless, instead I feel inspired and motivated
> skip to present day
> doing everything I can to support the movement
> taking good care of myself
> never been happier

tl;dr—Six months ago I was in a very dark place and was ready to end it all. But thanks to this board, Petrol, and our movement, I have found a new sense of purpose. The globalists, the elite, and the ZOG machine that controls them, they WANT us to give in. They celebrate every time that a White man who has woken up and got close to the truth offs himself. But they won't get that satisfaction from me. I intend to make their lives hell in whatever capacity I am able, and THAT is now what inspires me to get up each morning.

So thank you /rr/, and never stop the fight.

JULY 11, 2018

CONVERSATION BETWEEN PETER RILEY AND HIS ASSISTANT LISA
BROOKE FROM INSIDE ROOM 213 OF A CHICAGO HOTEL, POSSIBLY
RECORDED BY A DEVICE HIDDEN INSIDE THE WALLS OR
SELECTIVELY PLACED BEHIND A PIECE OF GENERIC MASS-
PRODUCED ART, AND WHILE I'M NOT SUGGESTING IT IS COMMON
PRACTICE FOR HOTELS TO RECORD THE ACTIVITY OF THEIR
GUESTS, WOULD YOU REALLY BE SURPRISED IF THIS
INDEED WERE THE CASE?

"You see Lisa? This is exactly why I needed to hire you to take care of this kind of stuff."

"I mean, it really is one of the simplest things to figure out. And for some reason you said you wanted to do it yourself, so…"

"Look, I'm not dumb, I swear when I was filling out the stuff on their website I specified that I needed two separate rooms for two guests."

"Did you confuse two beds with two rooms?"

"I don't know what to tell you, I guess I screwed up."

"It's fine, I'll go down and see about getting a separate room."

"Nah, they already said they were booked solid for that stupid conference or convention or whatever it was. But it's okay, we're just here for the one night, we can just share this room. There's two beds and I will gladly concede to you full dominion over the bathroom."

"Ugh, yeah, fine."

"Cool, so what do you wanna do? Go get some dinner or something?"

"I'm not really hungry. It's already pretty late, wouldn't you rather just get some rest for the show tomorrow?"

"It's not a 'show' it's a debate."

"Okay."

"And no, I don't want to just go to bed. Come on Lisa, let's hang out, let's do something. We don't need to be at the debate until what, like three tomorrow?"

"Two-thirty."

"Exactly, not early. What do you normally do to unwind at night?"

"I fantasize about finding a better job."

"There she is. Well, you know what I used to do when I was in university? I used to come home after classes or rehearsals, and I would drink gin with my roommate Justin and we would just chill out and shoot the shit. So you know what I'm gonna do now? I'm gonna walk over to this mini-bar, I'm gonna open one of the massively overpriced tiny bottles of gin and I'm gonna make us both a drink."

"You go ahead and have mine too."

"Come on Lisa, I feel like I haven't had a normal conversation in so long. I just want to talk with somebody. Okay, that sounded probably more pathetic than I meant it to, but still. I mean technically you are my employee, right?"

"Wildly inappropriate, but fine, we can talk. But I'm counting these as billable hours."

"Deal. Now how about that drink?"

"Yeah, yeah, just one though."

Three Drinks Later

"So, do you think I can win this debate tomorrow or what?"

"I don't think it matters whether you do or not."

"What do you mean?"

"Your people will worship you either way. Lox can mop the floor with you and your fans will still find a way to make it seem like you won. Frankly, I kind of hope that she does."

"Ah, you're probably right, but I still feel anxious about it. I haven't felt this nervous since I was performing on stage. I used to get so damn nervous about performing and I never really found a good way to get over that. One of my old acting teachers used to tell me that instead of trying to get over that anxiety I should channel it and feed off it instead, but I don't think I ever figured out how. But see, making videos is different, because even though I know that the audience is like a million times bigger, it's all so much less immediate if that makes sense. There's a disconnect between the audience and me, and between me and their reactions. Am I talking nonsense, does that make any sense?"

"It does. I don't really have anything to compare that to, but I think I get it."

"Damn, you know what Lisa? I feel like I'm always going on about myself around you, like it's always all about me, you know? Sometimes I think I barely know you at all."

"Probably for the better."

"Come on, tell me a bit about yourself. What was it like for you growing up?"

"I don't really want to get into that."

"Alright, that's fine, we can keep talking about me all damn night, you know that's always been my favorite subject."

Yet Another Drink Later

"Why did you ask me what it was like for me growing up a little while ago?"

"What do you mean 'why'? It's a conversation, I was trying to learn more about you."

"But why?"

"I don't know, we're friends aren't we?"

"Not really, no. I work for you."

" I didn't mean anything by it, I just felt bad about always blabbing about myself and never asking you any questions about your life."

"So you asked me that out of guilt?"

"Uh, well partially I guess, but I was also legitimately curious to learn more about you given that you know so much about me and we spend so much time together and all that."

"It's just not something I like to go back to if I can help it."

"I totally understand, it's all good."

"So do you want to know or not?"

"But you just said…"

"Peter. Do you want to know or not?"

One Final, Prolonged Drink Later

"Thanks for sharing that Lisa. I wish I was better with this sort of thing or had something more insightful to say, but for whatever it's worth, I'm glad that you're here with me right now, and I'm tremendously grateful for everything that you do for me."

"Yeah, well... Bedtime now I think."

"Alright, I guess we just about ran this minibar dry anyway. Is there anything on TV? Can you find something? I have trouble falling asleep without the TV on."

"Sounds healthy. Here, I'll give you the remote, I'm sure you can figure it out—it's probably easier than booking hotel rooms properly."

"There she is. Hey, there's one more thing I've been meaning to ask you. Why do you work for me? I mean you know about my 'brand' and you know what I do and say and all that, doesn't it like, bother you at all?"

"A job is a job. As long as you keep paying me I'm not interested in passing judgement."

"But you know I don't really believe in any of it, right? So can't you just like, I guess, tell me that it's wrong? That the things I say and do are wrong? I mean, you know that it's all wrong, don't you? Can't you just tell me that it is?"

"Get some sleep Peter. There will be plenty of people willing to tell you that tomorrow."

No Date
I WASN'T COOL ENOUGH FOR THIS WORLD WHEN I WAS YOUNG AND I AINT NOW NEITHER

For five dollars per round this one will play games and chat with me for as long as I can stay awake, but she doesn't know that I could probably stay awake forever. Her English seems a little bit too good and it really only works for me when the English is broken and sort of shitty, like she struggles to find certain words and

I need to remind her what she's trying to say. Her room probably smells dank as hell because I know these girls never leave their houses once they are sent to them from the factories where they're mass-produced. Whatever, I got paid today.

What the hell is wrong with me, get this shit off the screen. Why do they have to talk in those high-pitched baby voices? Big cringe on the play, who actually enjoys that part of it? I get bored and I don't even remember what task I was procrastinating and now this is just an endless feed of cute boys crying, like who is this even for? How do they just make themselves cry like that? Is this what gets people going these days? I guess I kind of get it.

Surely this can't be normal. I am bad, but you are all degenerate perverts and you know it. And you know that I know it and you like that I know it. Unforgivably sick. But I've been praying more lately than ever before and I don't even know to whom I should be praying so I just pick the first person I see and just like that better heads don't prevail, and how long am I gonna do this today? Well, let's get it over with.

I think I might actually need some professional medical help or something. Tomorrow I'll make some changes in my life, but then tomorrow never comes and here I go again. Unspeakably crude but I have a headache from the scroll and I heard that can help and so that's the justification that I pull from the bottomless bag of tricks.

Who cares, I got enough clout to raise the Titanic and sink it all over again. Holy shit dude, I just looked it up and the Titanic sank like one hundred years ago, I legit thought that shit happened in like the eighties. I'm the king of this whole damn scene.

I'm disgusting. This is just irresponsibly vile. I need to log off.

Minerva, can you help me with that?

No?

Okay, fine, maybe just one more go around.

JANUARY 10, 2017
OUTTAKES FROM THE YET-TO-BE-RELEASED 'ART' FILM
TENTATIVELY TITLED 'A RISING MOON O'ER HUNGRY LAVENDER'

"Are we rolling Smitty?"

"Mhmm."

"Excellent, keep it so if you would. And you Julia? My darling angel, is the temperature to your liking?"

"Huh? Oh yeah, it' fine, it's yeah, good."

"Fantastic. Your comfort is my utmost concern. And what of you, my brutish Adonis? Is your majestic payload nearly ready for delivery?"

"My payload? Oh, yeah, I'm good to go whenever, let's do this thing."

"Good sir, I value you and I cherish you, but please don't speak so diminishingly about what we are creating here. How can you remain so calmly blasé when we are teetering on the edge of achieving art in its purest form? Are your hearts not also palpitating like the invisible wings of hummingbirds?"

"Uh, we're making a shit-fetish vid pal, it's not exactly *Blade Runner* or whatever."

"No, no, no, it's not a 'shit-fetish vid.' Are you so beholden to the rigidities of this reality that you can't see that what we are doing here transcends the arbitrary moral boundaries that society has imposed on us? We aren't here to create pabulum for perverts, we're here to redefine what meaning looks like in an absurd new world. Have you not read Camus? Julia, my darling, surely you don't feel the same way?"

"I don't know, I don't really feel much about it, I kind of just need the money, but yeah, that all sounds good too."

"I appreciate your honesty and I appreciate you—you are perfect just as you are. Take your mark and wait as I try and speak some sense to this gorilla."

"My name is James."

"It matters not. The name is not what will be remembered, what will be remembered is the rawness and vulgarity of the act, the unrestrained depiction of intimacy and love. I truly hope you can see this not just as another job, but as the important work that it is. We have chosen to inherit the legacy of the Marquis de Sade and we must now take care not to drop it. Now, are you in the program?"

"Look, no disrespect or whatever, but you put out a casting call looking for a dude to shit into a girl's mouth, I responded to the call, and now I'm here and I'm ready to do this thing, so can we just get on with it? I don't know about this Marky the Sad or this Camel guy, but I'm about ready to burst over here."

"Absolutely not. I'm sorry you can't see beyond the walls of your self-constructed prison, but if you aren't keen on what's really happening here, well then, I'm afraid I don't want you anywhere near this production. If you would take your leave."

"Come on, are you serious?"

"Yes, and apparently I'm the only one on this set who is. I'm beginning to fear there's not a single true artist amongst you, and it certainly won't be this blockheaded simpleton. Now off with you, get off my set, back to your cubicle world and your bicep curls. Smitty, stop rolling, I need a minute to rebalance myself in light of these developments."

#

"Are we rolling Smitty?"

"Mhmm."

"Outstanding. Julia, my chrysanthemum in white, are you still with us darling?"

"Huh? Oh yeah, I'm good, but what happened to James?"

"Begging your pardon, who?"

"Uh, the guy that was here a minute ago? Who was supposed to do the, uh, you know, the shitting?"

"Back to whatever hole he crawled out of, back to his Marvel films and his Starbucks coffee. He's no artist. Fortunately, we have a far more qualified replacement already in our midst."

"Yeah, I'm not really up for doing that…"

"Not you Smitty, I was referring of course to myself. I had intended to remain visibly separate from this production as an off-stage architect, but I suppose if this is to be done the way it needs to be, I will have to do it myself. Julia, truest of my loves, will you grant me the privilege of working beside you in this endeavour?"

"Uh, you want to um... You want to shit in my mou—"

"I want to transcend the boundaries of artistic expression and convention with you, yes."

"Do I still get paid the same?"

"Julia, so sweet as to make sugar taste as salt, your payment is the eternal contribution you are making to the understanding of the human experience. Your payment is the security of knowing that one day as you lay on your deathbed you will pass easy from this life knowing that you had truly lived as few others could. And, yes, in addition to these blessings you shall still get the $1000 we agreed upon, if that is the sort of thing that you're concerned with."

"Then, yeah, okay, whatever, sure, can we just do it then?"

"What ails you my love?"

"It's nothing, it's fine, it's just... I don't know."

"Please speak your heart. I want you to be able to express yourself fully, our intimacy naked and shared. It's important to me, to the art, that you can relax and find your peace. So please, what ails you?"

"It's just I don't really want anyone to shit in my mouth. It's not you, I didn't really want the other guy to do it either. I don't know, I'm just not really excited about it. I know this is supposed to be super artistic and stuff but I don't really feel it if I'm being honest, but I need the money, so can we just get it over with before I chicken out?"

"Oh my love..."

"And that's another thing. I just met you like two days ago why do you keep calling me 'my love' and 'my sweet precious' and whatever?"

"I'm simply trying to put you at ease. Is there anything else I can do to make this more immersive and comfortable for you as an artist? We can change the blocking, we can rebuild the set from the ground up, we can tailor you a new outfit. There's an extra $2000 in the budget now that I've done away with that lunkhead."

"Wait, you were gonna pay him two grand? Why the hell does he get paid twice as much as me, I'm the one who has to get their mouth shit in."

"That is kind of fucked up."

"Smitty, please, no one asked you. Julia, my muse. Forget about the money. Money is a temporary evil, but what we are doing is more important—it's eternal. Don't you see? I am freeing you from the shackles of your patriarchal oppressors. I am giving you the opportunity to step outside the paved road of your socialization to explore landscapes unmolested by modernity."

"By shitting in my mouth?"

"*Tabernac!* Why must you fixate on the act of defecation? The defecation is the manifestation of our rejection of the mass-media waste that is funneled through our senses. Don't you see? This is a statement we are making. Through my bowels runs the very system we are seeking to reject, and yet you will still receive it with mouth agape. How can I make it any more clear? We can complain about the stifling of creativity and culture, we can watch pornographic films where dead-eyed actors, I say *actors*, mechanically hump away, but we are powerless to reject it, we will still choose to consume it. Only by breaking through these parameters can we rediscover our humanity and the spirit of creativity once endowed. Now are you in the program or not?"

"Yeah, sure, I mean like I said, I need the money. What if I puke?"

"Let your natural and authentic reactions guide you, do not struggle against them."

"Fine, whatever, can we please just do it now."

"Very well, Smitty, are we still rolling?"

"Mhmm."

"Oh, fantastic! I rumble in anticipation of what is about to transpire. Now Julia, my enchanting estrus, take your position under the step ladder and lay as a field of lavender might. Now gaze up at the rising moon and prepare thyself for this offering!"

In the coming days and weeks I know that the media and the politicians, as they do with everything, will try and spin my motivations and my reasoning to fit their own narratives and agenda. Do not be fooled. What I am about to do is for one reason and one reason only—to secure the existence of my people and to take a stand against invading forces.

Despite what anyone tries to tell you, this is not a conspiracy or a false narrative. White people ARE being replaced in their own nations due to unchecked immigration and the influx of invader forces. White birthrates ARE on the decline while the birthrates of non-Europeans are on the rise. Before the end of the century, Whites WILL be the minority population in virtually every traditionally White nation. And we are letting it happen. The politicians on both the right and the left are letting it happen. The media is letting it happen. The academics are letting it happen. We are all letting it happen.

But not me, not anymore.

I'm sick of sitting back and doing nothing while talking heads try to convince us that 'diversity is our strength.' I refuse to be complicit in inaction while invading forces take OUR jobs, commit crimes against OUR population, and sexually assault OUR women. What I am about to do is an act of self-preservation against an invading force.

Do not listen when they try to tell you that assimilation works or that multiculturalism works. These people have no interest in assimilating into or embracing White culture. They are here to supplant us and eventually destroy us, and unless more people take a stand, this is exactly what will happen.

To my comrades, I know many of you talk the talk. I know you are aware of the problems that face our people. I know we have allies in the media who are letting our agenda be known even amid repeated efforts to censor and remove them. Bobby Rango, Petrol Riley, Stephen Black, they are all doing a valuable service to our cause, but what about the rest of you? Will you continue to post memes and complain about the destruction of our people from the comfort of your computer chairs while not doing anything about it? Or will you take up arms and fight for our survival like your ancestors before you? Let my actions inspire you to join the fight.

THEY WILL NEVER REPLACE US IF WE
DO NOT LET THEM!

JUNE 5, 2019
THE CONFESSION OF PETER 'PETROL' RILEY: PART VIII

Being an online 'celebrity' has gotten me laid exactly one time. It was not something I expected or tried to make happen, and it happened with the sort of person that normally wouldn't have even registered my existence. I remember that when I was on top of her, she had grabbed her phone and was trying to record a short video of us, I guess for her Snapchat story. She even asked if I could lower my shoulder so that her face would be in proper view.

This all went down last summer at a party for 'social media influencers' that I had no business being at. Just before this, I had been invited to do a guest appearance on a video with Jimmy Jenniker, or 'JayJay' as he's more commonly known online. JayJay had already been one of the most popular person-alities on YouTube for quite some time by this point, and while my channel and online presence were large and growing steadily, my numbers were nothing compared to mainstream juggernauts like him. He was positioned comfortably among the A-listers of the content creation world. Part of the reason for his massive popularity, aside from his genuinely likeable per-sonality, charisma, and the strong production value of his videos, was the fact that unlike provocateurs like me, JayJay didn't do 'political' content and typically did not let his own opinions on current events be known. Most of his content was based around banal and accessible subjects like reviewing video games or movies, highlighting absurd stories from the news, or covering the 'drama' surrounding other online personalities—things that weren't especially contentious or divisive and appealed to a large range of people.

So for him, a generally well-liked and non-controversial figure to invite Petrol, one of the Internet's most notorious hate-mongers, to feature in one of his videos was not an arrangement that most were expecting, myself included. From what I under-stand, JayJay, in an effort to 'mature' his brand, had begun dipping his toes into covering news and politics more directly and had taken a new interest in highlighting what were, accord-ing to him, 'the important social and cultural issues of our time.' One of the ways he was doing this was by having guests on his channel from a wide range of social and political backgrounds in order to, in his words, 'present all sides and move the conversa-tions forward.' So when he put out a call asking his viewers who he should have on his channel, naturally the hivemind over at the /rr/ board campaigned tirelessly on my behalf. Like many things they do, I'm not sure exactly how they pulled it off or what kind of manipulation or strange tricks it involved, but they did it, and that's how it came to be that JayJay's people reached out to organize my appearance on his channel.

I accepted the offer, knowing the amount of potential expo-sure his massive platform could bring, and flew to California to meet up with JayJay at his studio where he and a small team of producers, writers, designers, researchers, and makeup artists cre-ate his videos. I was, and still am, creating and producing all of my content by myself, so to see how many people were involved in the creation of a standard JayJay video really highlighted the disparity between my scale and his. This was a well-oiled and well-funded machine with all parts working in tandem to ensure that JayJay's daily content was always released promptly and with the level of professional quality consistent with his brand. We met and recorded the video while I performed the character of Petrol with every bit of antagonism and aggression that I could muster.

And you've all seen the video, you know what happened next.

The video ended up becoming one of JayJay's most divisive and controversial, and while many were outraged that he had willingly shared his massive platform with someone like Petrol, once the video was released I received what ended up becoming my largest single-day spike in video views and subscribers as a whole new legion of potential fans and supporters were exposed to my content for the first time. And even though JayJay caught some flak for having me on his show, it ended up being good for him as well, as the controversy of it all drove more traffic his way.

Eyeballs and clicks. It's always just been about eyeballs and clicks.

We wrapped on the video and with my flight back home booked for the afternoon of the following day I had planned to spend a quiet and uneventful night in my Santa Monica hotel room. That's when JayJay approached me after the shoot and invited me to be his guest at a social media influencer party he was being paid to attend. I tried, meekly, to refuse and started searching my repertoire for suitable excuses to not accept his invitation, but JayJay deflected these all, assuring me that he didn't want to go either, and that he definitely didn't want to go by himself. It would all be a laugh, as he pitched it. We could just show up, eat the free food, drink the free drinks, and leave without a fuss after making a brief appearance. It reminded me of all the times Justin tried to convince me to go to random house parties with him during our DU days. Back then I would always say no, but he would always end up convincing me to go, and more often than not we ended up having a great time because of it. And so, even though my heart wasn't really in it and I had no clue what to expect, I gave in to spontaneity and eventually accepted JayJay's invitation.

And that's how I ended up at a social media influencer party hosted at a mansion in Malibu, surrounded by young, beautiful, online celebrities. At this point, you might be as confused as I was about what the hell a 'social media influencer party' is or what it looks like. I'm no writer, but I'll try my best to paint a picture and put you in my shoes, even if is all still a bit of a surreal blur to me.

The house belonged to some guy, who couldn't have been any older than his early thirties, who was described to me as an 'image entrepreneur,' and to this day I still have no idea what that title means or what kind of work he actually did, if any. As I understood it, he made a fortune as an early investor in bitcoin and I guess he was now just enjoying his life as a Malibu millionaire who threw lavish parties. As soon as JayJay and I pulled up in the car that they sent, I was struck by the opulence and performative aspect of it all. Outside the house cars were rolling up and dropping off small crews of people that were centered around the influencers themselves. Some of these influencers were YouTube personalities like JayJay, others were Instagram fitness models, or dancers, or online comedians, and some self-identified as all manner of made-up titles, from 'positivity coach' to 'lifestyle guru,' but they all appeared to me as interchangeable. The second they got out of their cars the photos started and they never stopped. Each influencer had at least one person acting as their personal photographer and handler, and they shifted from one memorized pose to the next as they slowly made their way up the marble stairs and through the front door into the house. Some even walked up and down the steps several times trying for the perfect shot, photographed and filmed from slightly different angles with each attempt.

JayJay must have noticed the vexed look on my face as I witnessed this display, because I remember him saying to me with a laugh something along the lines of 'now you know why I brought you here, start filming me bitch.' As we entered the house, a few people immediately recognized JayJay and called out to him. Fortunately, no one seemed to know who I was, and I took some comfort in that. I think they assumed that I was working for JayJay in some capacity, and for a moment I wondered if maybe some people thought that JayJay—an openly gay man—brought me as his date, but that thought quickly passed. I wasn't beautiful in the way these people were.

JayJay showed me around, walking me from one sponsored station to the next where we were free to pick up all manner of swag—blankets, hats, shirts, water bottles—all adorned with the logo of some media company I had never heard of before or since. There were cell phone charging stations, the kind you might see at an airport, set up sporadically throughout the main floor and they always seemed to be in full use by revelers in need of a shot of life. In the kitchen were two, maybe three chefs, decked out in full garb and engaged in the constant preparation of food which was then plated and left on a nearby table for guests to take at their leisure. The food—an impressive collection of meticulously arranged meats, tapas, and fruits cut into hearts and stars—looked fantastic, yet no one seemed to be eating any of it. Apparently, the event was cosponsored by some new high-end vodka brand, and there were numerous tables set up where shots, cocktails, and other mixed drinks— all made and branded with the special vodka—could be picked up freely.

After helping ourselves to some of the free drinks, JayJay lead me out onto the balcony where most of the people seemed to be gathered. It was massive, open space with an unfettered view of the ocean. The DJ in the corner, a young woman in a lime-green bathing suit, was moving enthusiastically along to the beat of exactly the type of music that you would expect to hear from such a place, played at a volume just restrained enough to allow for some half-yelled conversations to occur. I didn't recognize any of these people, and yet any one of them likely had a social media and online presence that dwarfed my own. As we mean- dered around the balcony JayJay pointed out a few people to me with all the enthusiasm of a tour guide who had grown numb to his route.

"That's Talia Grossi, she's a messy bitch. She made this whole big deal about how she was quitting social media because of all the drama and haters or whatever and then she came back like three days later with a new handle and tried to rebrand her- self as, like, a motivational speaker. Big cringe."

"See the meathead with the ugly-ass trucker hat? That's Ethan Diamond, he does these cute fitness videos with his girl- friend, but then it came out that he was cheating on her with some random nobody and they had a big public fight over it, but they ended up staying together—it was this whole big thing, I made a video about it."

"See the girl in the red dress, the one that looks like it's painted on? That's Nika Rose, I don't know much about her other than she's Russian and has possibly the nicest ass on all of Instagram, but apparently she's a bit of a weirdo."

As I was half-processing what JayJay was telling me, we heard the commotion coming from back inside—someone was screaming and hurling obscenities with a heroic enthusiasm. JayJay flashed me a knowing look and we, along with a few other curious investigators from the balcony crowd, hurried back inside to see what was happening.

There was a small crowd of people bunched together near the entrance to the house. The man who was doing the bulk of the shouting was being restrained, his arms and body being held back by two larger men. As we got a bit closer, I felt a hot flash of nerves and disbelief as I came to recognize who the man being restrained was. It was the single most popular and influential user in the entire history of YouTube, and once upon a time, a formative source of personal inspiration to me.

Liam 'Limez' González was something of a parasocial best friend to me, as he was for millions of other young people growing up in the 2010s. I've mentioned before how inspirational and important he was to me as a young kid who was interested in creating videos of his own, so when I saw him in person I was, for the first time since arriving at this house filled with online celebrities, a little starstruck. In his videos, Limez was loud, obnoxious, goofy, hyperactive, and borderline incomprehensible, so it was only natural that he became the most successful content creator the platform has even seen. But this wasn't the person that I saw that night.

By this point Limez was something like 28 years old, and despite still having the highest YouTube subscription count on the planet, he was already starting to be seen as old news to a lot of people who had moved on to fresher content made by younger creators. Maybe he knew his peak had passed, or maybe he was in denial about it, I don't know, but the man I saw that night—the man who was being physically escorted out of the party for causing too much drunken ruckus—I just don't know. I'm not sure I can say anything that wouldn't just be my own speculation or projection. All I know is that there was a time in my life when I wanted to emulate that man more than anything. Maybe I'm overthinking it, but it's probably safe to say that if it weren't for him maybe none of this would have happened. Maybe I wouldn't need to be here writing this right now. I don't know. Much of what happened that night is still a little hazy to me, but I don't think I'll ever forget the words Limez shouted as he was finally dragged outside.

"Tell Vaughn this house ain't shit and neither is he, Google my net worth some time bitch!"

As the night carried on most of the influencers, along with their photographers and the various brand reps started leaving. For those who chose to remain, whether because of the free-flowing vodka or the reduced presence of cameras everywhere, things started to degrade. Drugs were being presented and used with less discretion and people started pairing up and retiring to rooms to engage in what I assume were all manner of sexual depravities I haven't the imagination to properly describe. I had been around these things before and wasn't particularly disturbed by any of it, but it was all happening with a casualness that was new to me, and seemingly with a complete disregard of consequence. Here was a collection of people too young, too beautiful, too rich, too exposed, and all convinced that it would never and could never come to an end. Around this time JayJay told me he was ready to leave and get back to his man and he asked if I wanted to share a car back into town. I refused and told him I was going to wait it out at the house for a bit longer. I'm still not entirely sure why I chose to stay behind. Nobody there knew me, I was a lingering outsider, a desperate hanger-on and I knew it, but I guess after a few too many free drinks I was still in a mood to play anthropologist to this strange world that I wasn't sure I would ever see again.

I faffed around for an uneventful hour or so after JayJay left, sobered up a bit, and decided it was time for me to leave. I filled my pockets with some branded swag—a keychain and a phone case—and even though I knew I wouldn't need or use either of those items, I felt like they would make for good mementos. I stuffed a few final pieces of star-shaped cantaloupe in my mouth and was just about to disappear into the warm Malibu night when the woman approached me, dishevelled and slightly inebriated, but lucid enough to articulate herself well. I say this not from some place of false modesty or self-effacement, but here was the type of woman who would never under normal circumstances approach a guy like me. But she did. She said she recognized who I was, and I still don't know if she was lying about that or not.

Ten minutes later she was leading me by the hand into one of the house's still vacant bedrooms. I've never been a sexually forward person and in this instance there was no need to be. She initiated everything as if she were following a script and performing for an invisible audience. Enjoyable as it was, I was confused by the entire ordeal. Why me? Thinking about it now it's all pretty obvious, and I probably should have realized this as soon as she took out her phone and tried to film us during the act. She wanted to fuck a famous person. And all the other more famous people had already left or were otherwise spoken for. I was all that was left. We finished and I asked if she wanted to spend the rest of the night together. She didn't.

When I was a teenager watching Limez videos and wishing I could be like him, I thought that becoming famous was my life's end goal. That desire has shaped nearly all my significant life decisions since. And I don't know why. I really don't. After that night I had a glimpse of what that life could look like. Here I am a year or so later, even more known now than I was then, writing this stupid confession that maybe no one will ever see, and to what end? It's not enough to say that I don't want this anymore, is it? It's not enough to say that I have regrets and that I want out. What I need to do is admit that I don't want or need fame or recognition.

But I can't.

MARCH 7, 2017
THREAD ON /DP/ FORUM

XamianX (359808) Posted 03/07/2017 (12:02am)
    Trogs of /dp/, I present to you the livestream of the suicide of anon, get in quick.
    http://jns.be/8783478

BitchSoup (321408)
    What the actual fuck is this for real?

gundersonandsonsguns (328444)
    Can't be real I can see his feet moving.

GayMysterio (325522)
    Yeah, bodies twitch when they're hung dipshit

FarthouseFilm (382109)
    yoooo is this the guy who was posting about killing himself like an hour ago?

M_O_O_O_O_O (382714)
    not gonna lie I feel kinda fucked up watching this

Grenouille (352168)
    Goddamn, dude's face looks like an eggplant.

MenchuTwat (358760)
    @XamianX wtf why would you encourage him to do this?

XamianX (359808)
    @MenchuTwat I didn't force the guy to do anything retard, I just asked him to livestream it for the lulz, it's not like he took a lot of convincing.

StinkqqBoi (381921)
    anon with the epic self-own

ssstatecr (386767)

what's the point of hanging yourself if you ain't gonna tug one out during?

Bonex777 (385002)

damn, yall are really okay with this eh?

Kindle404 (382200)

Jesus Christ, I've seen some fucked up shit on this website, hell I probably contributed some of it, but this is actually too far. This is straight up manslaughter.

MisterMinister (322846)

@Kindle404 Too far? Since when is anything on /dp/ 'too far'? If this offends you, kindly fuck off back to the normie internet.

Knave21 (328093)

@Kindle404 I actually agree. This isn't like the normal shit we see on this board. This guy was alive and posting here barely an hour ago. He reached out to us and we could have talked him down or directed him to help but instead you guys not only encouraged him to go through with it but you somehow got him to livestream it for your amusement? There's blood on all of our hands as far as I'm concerned.

I_Smell_Coins (382958)

@Knave21 who cares he was gonna kill himself anyway at least now we get some lulz out of it

BonBonBooty (385525)

@Knave21 Stop being such a moralfag none of us knew this guy so don't act like it makes you sad

ShmoyleAuft (388921)

People joke about killing themselves here all the time, how were we supposed to know that this dude was actually serious? Regardless, we aren't responsible for his decisions either way.

aacaap (324509)

Pause the stream @2:25 can this please be a new reaction meme?

dacaxx1289 (359001)

@2:25 "We submit to the jury the defendant's internet search history."

jonjonlp (391231)

@2:25 "tfw you accidently like the Instagram pic you were fapping to"

klobbAR (385440)

lol @ all the white knights in this thread who all of a sudden care about depressed people killing themselves, this shit happens like a thousand times every single day get over it

Knave21 (328093)

@klobbAR Whatever dude, you're fucked in the head, and frankly so are all the people that support this shit. It's over the line.

klobbAR (385440)

@Knave21 There is no line you fucking retard.

Knave21 (328093)

@klobbAR It's still vile and I don't want any part of it.

klobbAR (385440)

@Knave21 Good, one less white knight on /dp/ to worry about.

AUGUST 12, 2018
INSTAGRAM POST FROM @NIKA_ROSE

The need for truths is now evident.

Today my number of followers has surpassed one million. This should be a milestone post, one to be infinitely shared and spread. Nearly a dozen brands have approached me to pitch their ideas for a millionth follower collaboration. But I do this no more. I hate what my life has become. My life is a daily dance of embarrassment and shame. At the gym a professional photographer records me doing squats from a low angle and I post the videos here. Why? To sell tight yoga pants to the women and to give the men something they may touch themselves to.

Every post is abused with your lewd comments, your eggplants, your invitations, and I am reduced to something shameful and less. I am a vessel for deliberate product placement and empty lust. They tell me how to pose, how to smile, how to act. This is not real life! And so I will do this no longer. I will not advertise your smart-water, I will not sell your makeup products, I will not wear your clothes, I will not hold your handbags! This is not real. This is not what I look like, this is not how I wish to be seen, this is not who I am. I use the anglicized name of a person who is not me to increase my appeal, but I do this no longer!

I've been using this name for too long, but I use it no more. Nika Rose is dead.

My name is Annika Nikolayevna Ryabova. *Анника Николаевна Рябова*! And you will only refer to me such! I was born on December 28, 1991, two days after the Soviet Union dissolved. I've been reading the history of my people, the true history, not the Western propaganda. Gorbachev traded our future and for what? For Pizza Hut! *Свинья*! All that was promised, all that we were supposed to be, like a setting sun never to rise again. As the spirit of the CCCP melted into thin air, it was instilled into me and I carry with me now the hopes and dreams of its people. I am the true daughter of Russia, the reincarnation of the Soviet Union, and I am beautiful, born in the heart of winter to see the dream kept alive.

I wish to be shot into the cold dead of space. I want to transform our nostalgia into realized dreams! Today I remove my chains and escape my shame!

Для нас всё также солнце станет сиять огнём своих лучей!

MARCH 3, 2019

MEMO WRITTEN BY PETER RILEY, WITH PEN, ON SEVERAL PIECES
OF STATIONERY ADORNED WITH THE LOGO OF THE HOTEL
NEW YORKER

I am writing this on paper because I want it to exist. I want to be able to hold it in my hands as proof that I was here. I can't remember the last time I created something that wasn't saved as a digital file. What happens when all the satellites crash and burn up in the atmosphere and the earthquake swallows all the servers and all the files become corrupted and unreadable? What happens to me then? Do I disappear?

I'm writing this with black ink on a notepad adorned with the logo of the Hotel New Yorker, alone in room 1023. It's 7:47pm and I am here. It's taking all my concentration to not misspell words and to construct the various letters correctly. It would appear as though I have sort of forgotten how to write this way. Not enough practice. But I am here. And this will exist.

But I don't.

I am turning this piece of paper over now.

When we were young, my family would go on long drives across what I thought was the lonely and forgotten emptiness of Canada and I would occasionally see people and animals out in the fields and farmland. At thirteen years old I was already convinced that those people were living wasted and pitiable lives. They did work that would never be recognized. No one knew their names. Their Internet connections were probably terrible. Online stores probably didn't even deliver to their houses out there in the middle of nowhere. They probably never went to the movies. They probably only had a handful of TV channels, if they had a TV at all. They lived at least an hour away from the nearest fast-food restaurant. I felt bad for the kids especially. What kind of life could that be?

New piece of paper.

And here I am, sitting flesh and blood in room 1023 of the Hotel New Yorker. Tomorrow I will be appearing as a disembodied voice on Bobby Rango's satellite radio show. People will hear my voice. It might be recorded and saved as an audio file to be stored forever in some database. But for now, I am here, and now I'm wondering if maybe it was the other way around, if maybe those people I saw out in the fields during our family drives around Canada were the ones pitying me. See, their hands were calloused, they had soil caught underneath their fingernails. They raised animals and they were growing things that depended on them.

I've never raised or grown anything, but I am now turning this piece of paper over to begin writing, with a pen, on the other side.

I'm here, sitting on a chair. I'm really here. I feel hungry but I don't want to eat, but I am here.

But take away my subscribers and views and would I still be here? I know that there used to be something about me. I was creative, I was intelligent, I had a need to express myself. Maybe these are things that I could have used as evidence that I was a real person that was really here, but not anymore. I'm not defined by any of those things. I'm defined by an image, some metrics, and the embarrassment I feel for even calling attention to it.

I mean, come on. Who cares?

New piece of paper. And maybe once I've filled this one, I will fold them all together into something resembling an airplane and I will throw it outside the window of room 1023 of the Hotel New Yorker. Maybe it will land on the street to be ran over and turned into mush by a street sweeper. Maybe it will land in a gutter and be washed into the sewer system. Maybe it will land on the sidewalk and someone will pick it up and for one brief moment there will be proof that I was really here.

My grandpa on my mother's side died two years before I was born and so I never got to meet him. The image I've constructed of him is based entirely on the accounts of people who knew him, the occasional photograph, and the few documents he left behind. But is this really who he was? My grandma would always tell me how much I looked like him, and that we shared the same sense of humour. She thinks that we would have really gotten along well. He never created any digital files. If you search his name online, no results appear. I know this because I've done it. As far as the Internet is concerned this man never existed at all. If you search my name, there's millions of results.

I only wish I could have shaken his calloused hand and known for myself whether he was really here or not.

I am here, in room 1023 of the Hotel New Yorker, writing with a pen on a piece of paper that no longer has any space left.

March 3, 2019
In Which Peter Riley, Alone in Room 1023 of the Hotel New Yorker and Seeking the Simple Comfort of Meaningful Social Interaction, Downloads a Dating Application and Attempts to Connect with Someone Whom, According to His Estimation, is Worth Connecting With

Welcome to Matchr! Swipe right on profiles you want to match with and left on profiles you do not want to be matched with. Let's get started!

Tiana, 28—Career driven, loves the outdoors, prefers nature to humans. *Swiped left.*

Raj, 32—Lioness looking for her lion, best friend, lover, and future hubster. *Swiped left.*

Melanie, 24—Always smiling, I appreciate a quiet night in watching a good movie or playing board games. Love to travel. *Swiped left.*

Kayla, 29—Just a Pam, looking for her Jim. *Swiped left.*

Mei, 19—I will like your dog more than I like you. *Swiped left.*

Alexa, 24—I'm a confident and outgoing individual that loves to laugh. Always down for an adventure, or for staying in and watching a movie. *Swiped left.*

Shireen, 25—Attracted to sensitive, intense people. Looking for deep chemistry, no hookups. *Swiped left.*

Katelyn, 24—Authenticity, intelligence and a good sense of humor will capture my interest. Proper grammar is a must. *Swiped left.*

Abigail, 22—I love photography and writing books that no one reads. Bring pizza. *Swiped left.*

Jacqueline, 27—My son is my life and if you can't handle that, keep on swiping. *Swiped left.*

Samantha, 25—Always adventurous animal lover. Can you be the Jim to my Pam? *Swiped left.*

Nikki, 19—I will beat you at Mario Kart, but you'll forgive me because I give excellent back rubs. *Swiped left.*

Vanessa, 20—Driven, compassionate and kind. Vegetarian who loves all animals. Looking for someone to make me laugh. *Swiped left.*

Kat, 30—Passionate about being kind, adventurous lover of anima— *Swiped left.*

Shavina, 23—Look for someone advent— *Swiped left.*

Simran, 29—My highest values are honesty, trust, and— *Swiped left.*

Anais, 26—Fluent in sarcasm, loves the outdo— *Swiped left.*

Stephanie, 21—I'm a Pam, can you be my— *Swiped left.*

Tracy, 25— *Swiped left.*

Claire, 26— *Swiped left.*

Olivia, 21— *Swiped left.*

Jody, 23— *Swiped left.*

Meg, 27— *Swiped left.*

Michelle, 26— *Swiped left.*

Ava, 20— *Swiped left.*

Nat, 28—Let's build a cabin in the woods. I won't tell anyone you're here if you don't. *Swiped right.*

San— *Swiped right.*

Lau— *Swiped right.*

Kar— *Swiped right.*

Cin— *Swiped right.*

Swiped right.

Swiped right.

Swiped right.

Swiped right. Swiped right.

Hot damn, you've got yourself a match!

Chelsea, 24—Looking for someone to watch pretentious arthouse movies with while pretending like we understood what the director was going for. *You matched with Chelsea on March 3.*

New message from one of your matches!

Chelsea said:

Hey, weird question, but is this the real Peter Riley?

You said:

If I was going to pretend to be someone, I would have picked someone more handsome.

Chelsea said:

That's crazy, you're like Internet famous.

You said:

Nah, that girl who takes the pictures of herself and her dog in matching outfits is Internet famous, I'm like a D-list Internet celebrity at best.

Chelsea said:

Don't you live in Canada?

You said:

I do, I'm just here for a couple days for a work thing.

Chelsea said:

Looking to get laid during your weekend in the big city huh?

You said:

Honestly, I don't really know what I'm looking for here. I was just kind of bored in my hotel room and sort of spontaneously downloaded Matchr.

Chelsea said:

Feeling a little lonely are you?

You said:

Yeah, something like that.

Chelsea said:

Want me to come by your room and keep you company?

You said:

Would you actually? Just like that?

Chelsea said:

Just like that. Would you like that?

You said:

You know, I think I would.

Chelsea said:

Okay, but before I come by I need you to do something for me first.

You said:

I'm listening.

Chelsea said:

I need you to go out on to the balcony, and then I need you to light yourself on fire and then I need you to jump off.

Fuck off and die you racist piece of shit, call one of your little nazi fanboys to come jerk you off if you're so lonely.

You have been blocked from messaging Chelsea.

Are you sure you want to permanently delete your Matchr profile? All your matches will disappear!

Your Matchr profile has been successfully deleted. We hope to see you back some day!

AUGUST 13, 2018
ARTICLE ON CBFUZZ.COM, NUMBER ONE SOURCE FOR CELEBRITY NEWS AND GOSSIP

Russian Instagram model/influencer Nika Rose had an EPIC and bizarre meltdown on a recent post celebrating her one millionth follower. In the largely nonsensical and rambling post Nika, who is apparently fed up with living the life of a social media star, claims to be the 'reincarnation of the Soviet Union.'

<ad break>

Nika Rose quickly gained prominence on social media this past year due largely to her many workout videos and gym selfies that highlight her various 'assets,' including her adorable Russian accent and her hourglass figure.

<ad break>

Nika's recent post, which has been called out as 'confusing', 'strange', and 'alienating', seemingly came from nowhere as she has typically avoided discussing such topics or making controversial statements in the past. Some have suggested that Nika's apparent mental breakdown could be the result of her soon to be turning thirty, though it is unclear if drugs or alcohol are also a factor.

Nika, who is apparently now going by the name "Annika Ryabova" could not be reached for comment.

JUNE 7, 2019
BACKSTAGE OF LEWIS THEATRE, DIEFENBAKER UNIVERSITY,
TORONTO, 6:27PM

"You have a visitor Pete."

"A visitor? How can there be a—oh shit, Josh freaking Garrison, what is up my man? How did you get back here?"

"Peter, please, the day that I can't get backstage of my own theatre is the day I'll retire."

"It's your theatre now, is it?"

"Wasn't it always?"

"True enough. So how have you been? I haven't seen you since I graduated, you're still running the show here, huh?"

"Yeah, still teaching. I'll be starting my appointment as department chair next semester, so that should be interesting."

"That's great, so are you—"

"Pete, I'm not here to make small talk with you."

"Oh, okay. Well why are you here then?"

"To congratulate you on one hell of a performance for starters."

"Ah, thanks, you know I learned a lot from you and—"

"But more importantly, I'm here to implore you to do the right thing."

"Yeah? And what's that exactly?"

"End this."

"What do you mean 'end this?' End what?"

"Can I ask you something?"

"Of course."

"Is this the person you want to be?"

"Come on Josh, you know its all just performance, it's theatre."

"Maybe at one time it was. But it's not that anymore, is it?"

"I don't know. I don't know what it is anymore."

"Do you know how many people have reached out to me trying to get some dirt on the infamous Petrol Riley? Out of respect for you and the performance I never said anything to anyone because I always suspected that you were building up toward some kind of grand finale, but I waited, and it never came. For three years I've been waiting, and I can't tell you how much I regret that. If I could do it all over again I would have done everything I could to shut this down right away. I mean, people have gotten hurt Peter. People have died. Doesn't any of this weigh on you at all? So, I ask again, is this the person you want to be?"

"I dunno, I'm—"

"Speak up, stop looking at the floor."

"Okay, yes. Yes, it weighs on me, all right? I feel terrible about all of this shit, what do you want me to say man? I can barely sleep anymore because I have this stupid goddamn tightness in my chest all the time and I feel shitty about everything that's happened, but I don't know what to do about it. So, no, this isn't the person I want to be, but what the hell am I supposed to do? Can you tell me that? Can anyone? Because I sure as hell don't know anymore."

"You know what you can do Peter."

"Well, what?"

"In half an hour you're going to have a large and captive audience."

"Yeah, and?"

"You can tell them the truth."

"Oh, come on."

"I'm serious. It's a full house out there and your performance is being live-streamed and recorded where God only knows how many people will have the chance to see it. This is as good an opportunity as you will ever get to come clean and tell everyone the truth. The longer you wait, the harder it will be."

"Don't you think I haven't thought of that before? I think about ending this bullshit at least once a day, but it's just not that simple."

"Why not? All you have to do is go out there and be honest."

"Sure, and then what? Do you know my fans? These people are psychopaths man, if they find out that I've been duping them and I make them look like idiots they will straight up destroy my life in a million different ways. And what difference will it make anyway? They'll just find someone else to move on to, there's no shortage of people out there willing to do and say the things that I do."

"You aren't responsible for the actions of others, Peter. All you can do is take responsibility for your own and do the right thing. And you know what? You're right, it might not be a clean getaway for you. It maybe could have been if you didn't wait so long and let things get this far, but you did. Whatever guilt or regret you feel won't simply go away, and yes, you'll likely face a tremendous amount of backlash from not just your fans, but from everyone else who will be rightly wondering why you let it get this bad in the first place. But this is the only real option you have if you want to free yourself and begin the process of healing, whatever that process looks like for you."

"Okay, and then what? I go out there and tell all these people that it was all an act, and then what? There goes my work, there goes my source of income. And you think I'm ever gonna be able to get work as an actor after that? No one will want to hire me, not with my reputation. And all the fans I've accumulated? Gone. And what will I have left? This stupid character has come to define and sustain my life, how can I just throw it away?"

"Because you know it's the right thing to do. And you know that doing the right thing is more important than preserving your own ego."

"Yeah, maybe. I don't know. I mean, I see your point, I do, I just... I don't know."

"It's your decision. I've said my piece and I don't think there's anything else I can tell you that you haven't already considered."

"Well, thanks I guess. Hey, you remember the last time we were back here together?"

"That would have been for *I Have No Head*, right?"

"Yeah. I've been thinking about that lately. That was a lot of fun. I really miss doing shows like that."

"You were great in that show."

"Thanks. How many people came to that show on opening night, you remember?"

"I don't. But I do know that it was nowhere near as many that are out there right now."

"Yeah..."

"Anyway, I'll let you prepare and think about things, I just wanted to drop by and talk to you myself. I'm proud of your performance Pete, really, I am. But I'll urge you one last time to do the right thing."

"You're proud of my performance... Do you remember when I first did this character in that video assignment you had us do?"

"Of course."

"Do you remember the grade you gave me?"

"No, sorry I don't. I've graded so many of those over the years."

"You gave me a B."

"Well, if that's true it's because I wanted you to stay hungry. I knew you were good. Everyone knew you were good, but no one knew that better than you did. That confidence was good, but I didn't want your ego and talent to let you grow complacent, I wanted you to stay driven and to work toward being even better. Guess I did a pretty bad job of that, huh? Here you've been playing the same character for three years now, probably not much of a challenge for you anymore, is it?"

"Sorta seems like I—"

"You're muttering again, speak up."

"Seems like I've been playing a character my whole life."

NOVEMBER 24, 2018
ONLINE ARTICLE BY ALISA TENNANT, VANCOUVER HERALD

Mass Shooting in London Mosque Leaves 24 Dead
Alisa Tennant

24 people have been confirmed dead with at least 14 more injured in what is now the deadliest mass shooting in modern British history.

The attack occurred early Friday afternoon at a mosque in London. The gunman entered the mosque carrying several weapons and proceeded to fire indiscriminately at those who were gathered inside the mosque for afternoon prayer. The suspect escaped the mosque on foot and was apprehended by law enforcement officials shortly after.

The suspect has been identified as 27-year-old Nathan Myles, an Australian who had been living in London since 2015. A day prior to committing the attack Myles uploaded a 48-page manifesto detailing his anti-immigration ideology and motivations for the attack.

Live updates on the immediate aftermath of this attack will continue as details unfold.

NOVEMBER 24, 2018
UNTITLED TEXT DOCUMENT, THE DESKTOP OF PETER RILEY

Please let me fail. Let something go horribly wrong, let me be exposed for what I am. I don't want to do this anymore. I read his manifesto and when I saw my name inside it, I felt my face start to sweat and I've had a headache ever since. I felt like I was supposed to cry, but I couldn't. I tried, but I couldn't. The youngest person he killed was four years old. Her name was

Mahra Masiri. She was shot while in the arms of her mother. Shot by a man who mentioned me as an ally of his cause.

I can't sleep tonight. I've been thinking about how someone could do something like this. I've been thinking about the victims and what they must have been feeling at that moment. But these weren't the first things I thought about it. The first thing I thought about was how my name being mentioned by this guy was going to affect my image and career.

Why can't someone just stop me? Why can't I fail? I never wanted this.

The joke isn't funny anymore.

July 18, 2019
In Which the Compiler of this Book, in a Rare and Direct Address to You, the Dear Reader, Struggles with Trying to Present the Pitfalls and Perils of Modern Technologically-Mediated Alienation and Disconnection in a Creative or Unique Way and Instead Muses on the Vapidity of Art, the Impossibility of Saying Anything Genuine or Real, and the Folly of Trying to Write Anything Still Worth Reading Here, at the End of History Where There is Nothing Left to be Said and All That is Written or Dreamt into Vision Melts and is Swallowed by a Monolithic Culture Suffering with Alzheimer's, and Does So by (Eventually) Introducing a Short Poem That May or May Not Have Been Composed by AI Software, But it Doesn't Matter Whether it Was or Wasn't Because You Would Likely Believe Either Scenario and How Can We Know if That Says More About Your Willingness to Accept Whatever it is That You Are Told, the Current State of Artificial Intelligence, or the Compiler's Own Inability to Form Sentences Distinguishable From Those Cobbled Together by Some Machine-Learning Algorithm and at This Point My Only Hope in Life is That I Might Still One Day Find Something to Offer You That You Can Remember the Morning After

<I keep juice boxes>
  <Stocked in the mini fridge>
    <Beside my bed>
      <Because I like a shot of something sweet>
        <After I make love to my wife>
          <With all her saccharine empathy revealed>

FEBRUARY 28, 2019
A HANDWRITTEN LETTER (WHICH MEANT THAT I HAD TO
ANNOYINGLY TRANSCRIBE ITS CONTENTS RATHER THAN SIMPLY
COPY/PASTING THEM INTO THE BOOK) ADDRESSED TO LISA BROOKE

Dear Lisa,

I hope you are doing well up in Canada.

Dad finally up and died on us.

He wasn't talking much the last few days. A few nights before he passed on I found him out back sitting under the tree trying to whittle a branch. He was cutting off chunks at a time, real sloppy, not like him at all. He said the wood had gone bad.

I don't expect to hear back from you, but I still thought you should know.

We are planning a service for him, but it probably happened by the time you get this.

Cherish sends her love. Lindsay won't say so but I know she does too.

I still hope you will make it back to Hixon to see us one day.

All the best,

Allie Brooke.

MAY 30, 2019
EMAIL EXCHANGE BETWEEN PETER RILEY AND JUSTIN
MACDONNELL

Peter Riley (petrol@petrolriley.com), 05/30/2019, 8:22am
Dream Team Reunited?

Justooo, what's up my man? Hope all's been well. I meant to say it sooner, but congrats on landing that job with Surge, I've been reading your work there—good shit dawg!

You might have already heard, but I'm gonna be back in Toronto for a few days next week to give a talk at DU, and if you got some free time I was hoping you and I could hit up Rover's and have a beer or six.

I'll be getting into town on Saturday, but the talk isn't until Tuesday, so let me know if you have time one of those nights eh?

PS—Clean the goddamn microwave you heathen!

Petey.

Justin MacDonnell (jmacdonnell@surge.com),
05/30/2019, 10:59am
re: Dream Team Reunited?

Hey Pete,

Thanks for getting in touch. Unfortunately I'm pretty swamped with work stuff at the moment so I don't know if I'll be able to get out to see you. Maybe if I finish everything up this week I might be able to make it work, not sure though.

Justin.

Peter Riley (petrol@petrolriley.com), 05/30/2019, 12:07pm
re: Dream Team Reunited?

Damn, that's too bad. You sure you can't get out for dinner or a couple drinks? Don't you get nights off? We don't have to go hard, I need to keep somewhat focused anyway.

Come on, I haven't seen you in like two years, let's make it work!

Pete.

Justin MacDonnell (jmacdonnell@surge.com),
05/30/2019, 2:51pm
re: Dream Team Reunited?

Hi Pete,

If I'm being totally honest, I don't think it's a good idea for me to potentially be seen with you in public. Nothing against you, but it would just end up raising a lot of questions and could just end up really complicating things for me. You know what I mean? Are you staying downtown? I might be able to come see you in your hotel room for a bit or something.

Justin.

Peter Riley (petrol@petrolriley.com), 05/30/2019, 3:11pm
re: Dream Team Reunited?

No worries man, I totally get it. I guess just let me know if you have some time and we can figure something out.

Pete.

Peter Riley (petrol@petrolriley.com), 05/30/2019,
draft saved at 3:15pm
re: Dream Team Reunited?

DRAFT

But hey, since we're talking here for the first time in like forever, why not tell me how you really feel? You don't want to be seen with me? Are you for real with that shit? Why do you have to act like such a baby-back bitch when YOU'RE the one who hasn't even tried to keep in touch with me since we graduated? Did you forget that I tried to bring you on board with this? That I asked you to be my partner, even though I knew I would be doing most of the work? You said no, and that's fine, but you don't have to resent me because I followed through and found success with it.

And it *has* been a success, but you already know that. I'm pretty sure you have an idea of how much money I'm pulling in now. But you know what man? It's also been really hard. I'm wrestling with what I've done, with the message I've put out there, with the influence that I might have had, and with some of the terrible shit that I might have inspired. I've been really struggling with this whole situation, believe it or not. And you know what I've really needed throughout all this? What's really been missing? A friend. A genuine friend, which I thought you were.

But you couldn't see past your jealousy or whatever the hell it was to even bother to stay in touch with me, so whatever dude.

Don't worry about making the time to see me next week. I don't want to keep you from doing your very important work. Have fun writing shitty listicles and video game reviews that no one reads for the rest of your life.

Petrol

This message is saved as a draft.
Send / Continue Editing / Delete

APRIL 18, 2017
BLOG ENTRY FROM 'THE GEN X JOURNAL'

In last week's entry I mentioned that for my daughter's thirteenth birthday I got her tickets to see some rapper called Cragx (which I've been informed is pronounced as 'crags') perform at the Topaz. Fatherhood has been an endless cycle of reward and sacrifice. Seeing the look of pure joy on her face when she opened the little box and saw the tickets inside and feeling the tight hug she gave me after—that's the reward part. The sacrifice comes with remembering that I would now have to attend and be her chaperone at the kind of concert you normally couldn't pay me to go to. The concert was last night, and I don't even know where to begin with this one.

Now let me make this clear, unlike a lot of people my age who don't see any value in and swear off the genre entirely, I myself don't mind rap music at all. I still bump a lot of the 90s greats from time to time, so my criticisms of this show aren't coming from some narrow 'all rap is bad' viewpoint. So this kid comes out (he's nineteen years old, so maybe 'kid' is unfair) and he's got the face tattoos and his hair is dyed bright red and everyone is loving it, and then he performs for just under one hour. ONE HOUR. And I looked up the setlists from other shows he's done, they're all this short. And the setlist is the exact same. Every. Single. Time.

I didn't mind getting out of there in a hurry, but can you imagine paying good money to see a concert that only lasted for one hour? I've seen Pearl Jam seven times now. Last time I saw them they played for something like three and a half hours, and those guys are in their fifties so what's Cragx's excuse? It might have had something to do with the fact that the man was obviously high as a kite, which I'm not necessarily judging him for—after all, some of the greatest acts of all time routinely performed under the influence of enough substances to fully stock a pharmacy—but the difference is that they were still able to keep it together well enough to put on a hell of a show. This guy, not so much. He mumbled his way through some songs, he addressed the crowd maybe once, and then he left the stage unceremoniously with no fanfare and no encore.

I think it has something to do with the substances of choice these days. Don't get me wrong, I don't condone excessive or irresponsible drug use, and my own party days are far behind me, but you can understand why back when something like coke was the fashionable drug bands could perform for hours straight with full momentum and energy. These days kids are all about drugs that bring them down. What's the fun in that? I could tell right away that at least half the audience, which was definitely on the younger side, was zonked out on cough medicine or something. It's like they were afraid to show any enthusiasm or excitement, or maybe they never learned how to in the first place.

The other half of the crowd watched the show entirely through their camera phones. Look, I've accepted that smartphones are a fact of life now for everyone, but how hard is it to put them in your pocket and take in a moment, even for just a few minutes? Ugh, listen to me. Every day I get closer to becoming the kind of 'kids these days' old coot I used to love making fun of. Fortunately, my daughter serves as something of a window into the world of today's young people, and while it may be a world that I don't fully understand, it is sort of nice to pop in for a visit from time to time.

Although, I think next time it's the wife's turn to take her.

MARCH 4, 2019
IN WHICH PETER RILEY APPEARS ON THE SATELLITE RADIO
SHOW OF BOBBY RANGO, GUEST NARRATED (QUITE HAUGHTILY
I SHOULD SAY) BY THE AMERICAN GOVERNMENT EMPLOYEE WHO
WAS PRIMARILY RESPONSIBLE FOR MONITORING THE FORMER'S
ACTIONS AND MOVEMENTS AT THE TIME (ACCORDING TO HER
BEST RECOLLECTION OF THE DAY'S EVENTS)

While riding in the back of the car that Bobby Rango's people
sent for him, Peter Riley was thinking about the woman he saw
in the pool of the Hotel New Yorker on his way out that morning. She was swimming from one end to the other and back
again—a competent form amid waters that might have been
blackened with the bodies and souls of yesterday's careless or of
shipwrecks long forgotten. Hers was a seemingly infinite stamina
as she moved ceaselessly on some immutable grace. As he halfreg-
istered the Manhattan street names whistling by his peripheral
vision, Peter wondered if that woman was still diligently swimming even now.

There is no pool at the Hotel New Yorker.

"Nearly there guy," were the first words the car's taciturn
operator spoke since Peter entered the vehicle about five minutes
prior. And true enough the words turned out to be, as soon
thereafter the car pulled up to and stopped in front of the building where on the fourth floor Bobby Rango was preparing for
his daily radio broadcast. It was just after eight in the morning
and Peter was enervated by a troubled sleep the night prior. No
doubt this was in part due to some nerves about his impending
appearance on Rango's radio show—syndicated and played during the morning commutes and routines and from the work
computers and living rooms of over ten million people each
week—but perhaps also because he was still troubled by his
fleeting experience on the since deleted Matchr application the
previous night. Regardless, Peter—tired as he was and tired as he
often found himself to be—remained confident in his ability to
conduct his appearance on Rango's show with all the fervor and
pomp that was expected of him.

Still, Peter wondered how such a union might transpire, for his was a public persona he had constructed essentially as a replication of Rango's, albeit one that was younger and more in touch with the cultural milieu of the modern age. Peter had been musing on his future lately in all its quiet comforts and dirt roads, wondering where he might lay his head under moons unfathomed, wondering what all men ought to, and finding scarce comfort in the possibilities he envisioned. For one might be his succession to a throne that Rango himself, through age or forced retirement, would one day abdicate and render vacant. He thanked the driver, entered the lobby of the building, and rode the elevator to the fourth floor and to some future close enough that such fruitless fantasies weighed less in both consequence and malleability.

When he entered Rango's studio Peter was greeted by a bespectacled man who introduced himself as Hassan and called himself the show's producer. Peter could tell that Hassan shouldered the day-to-day operations of this unsinkable empire, and he found his thoughts drifting, as they often did, to his assistant Lisa Brooke. Was this young man and the services he provided for Rango comparable to those which Lisa provided for him? Immense was Peter's longing in that moment that she could be with him, soothing as he found her presence to be. Alas, the funeral of her father in some far-off town hardly worth printing on a map. Still, she asked Peter if he would rather that she accompany him to New York, as if she were looking for any reason not to attend the event that Peter himself had yet to develop the sense of maturity or mortality necessary with which to empathetically comprehend.

Hassan asked Peter if he cared for a drink, some coffee or tea perhaps. Peter thanked him but refused.

"You'll be going live with Bob in about fifteen minutes just as soon as he's finished going through the opening news," instructed Hassan. "Technically you're allowed to curse but try not to if you can remember. It makes it easier for them to demonetize our video clips if they contain too much cursing." Peter said he understood, that would be fine, and he would remember not to curse. It was then that Bobby Rango himself entered the room. Peter felt himself a touch starstruck upon seeing the man whom he had spent so much time watching, studying, and secretly mocking through imitation, though his disposition did not betray this development.

"There he is! How ya doin Pete? Bob Weinberg," said Bobby Rango in the same loud, semi-hoarse voice that Peter could so willingly conjure into memory or mimicry. Were Peter less prepared or informed he might have asked why Bobby Rango was introducing himself here under the surname 'Weinberg.' But prepared and informed the young man was, for he knew that the Jewish name was a cause of concern for a certain fraction of Rango's listeners, and that surely he must have decided early on in his broadcasting career that it was easier to simply assume a gentile name than it was to constantly explain to skeptical listeners why he was one of the 'good' Jews that could be trusted.

Peter was taken aback by the unprovoked candor of the elder statesman of aggressively reactionary broadcasting during what he expected would be introductory talk both small and of no significance. When Peter politely inquired as to how Rango was doing that morning, the latter's reply bore an unexpected familiarity and openness.

"Been dealing with this divorce bullshit all week, but my horse is still on the trail."

Peter expressed sympathy to the extent he was able while deciphering through context the meaning of the horse-based metaphor he had never heard before. After some more preliminary words, Rango reiterated how nice it was to meet the young man before excusing himself to begin his broadcast. Hassan asked Peter to make himself comfortable while he waited to be invited on the show, and this Peter did. He took a seat on a sunken chair and watched in quiet reverence and awe the master broadcaster begin his show with the elegance of the Russian dancer shouldering the nation's pride, the assuredness of the career gambler with odds methodically cracked, the mercuriality of the bipolar artist, the heat of a laser refracted true. Sentences and phrases ricocheted inside the studio, while outside the sun over Manhattan rose irrefutable and boundless, memories of Mesopotamian crops and prairie trail fires fashioned in its absence.

"In case you needed any more evidence that our Congress has been usurped by the communists and cultural Marxists, today they introduced a bill that, if approved, would provide amnesty for illegal immigrants who have come to America from certain countries. This would apply to illegals from Syria, Iraq, and Kuwait. Noticing any patterns there? I sure am. Now ask yourself why Congress would want to freely invite people from these specific countries into America without any repercussions. Every day is a battle against the globalist forces that have taken over American politics and are trying now to destroy our country from within. But here on Rango Radio, we fight back."

Rango carried on this current, warping and depicting the news and events of the day in a manner his millions of listeners had grown accustomed to. And Peter listened. Were he not regularly doing the same thing himself, he may have been troubled by the juxtaposition of the angry and vindictive harangue he was hearing now and the entirely amicable banter he shared with Rango a few minutes prior. Soon enough Peter was introduced by Rango as a young man who, "despite the globalist media's attempts to brainwash his generation, has remained a stalwart defender of the truth." And there did Petrol take his stage to perform for an invisible audience that may well have been the largest of his young career thus far.

And perform he did. Finding with ease the correct responses and talking points for each of the questions and prompts Rango casually lobbed in his direction.

"Tell me Peter, you're in tune with what the young people are doing and thinking these days, do they have any clue about any of the things that the federal government or big tech is doing to manipulate and brainwash them through social media and content censorship or are they just as lost in the dark as everyone else seems to be?"

"Well, Bob, we hear a lot about how young people aren't aware of these issues or that they simply don't care, but I know that for the young people who watch my videos and reach out to me with their messages of support, they are aware, often more so than their parents are. I don't buy in to this idea that young people don't know what's going on. If anything, they have a better idea and are better equipped to confront these issues than anyone. Because they are young and have their whole futures ahead of them, they actually have the most to potentially lose from the liberal agenda and many of them are fully aware of this and are willing to do whatever it takes to push back and ensure that they still have a future. Don't be so quick to give up on my generation just yet is what I would say."

"Now that seems like a perfectly reasonable statement to me, and you seem like a perfectly reasonable, intelligent, and articulate young man, so why is it that so many social media platforms have been trying to censor or ban you and your freedom of speech? It just makes me so furious that these liberal, Silicon Valley tech companies think that they are somehow the arbiters of what is and isn't acceptable content on the Internet. It means that good people like you, who have a real and genuine message, but one that happens to go against their globalist interests, must suffer with their constant attempts to censor you for some perceived thoughtcrimes, while meanwhile these same companies are flying their rainbow flags and using their massive platforms to force their beliefs on the general population."

While he allowed Rango the space to rant uninterrupted, as a good scene partner should, Peter found himself thinking about Josh Garrison, one of his old theatre instructors from his time as a student at Diefenbaker University. Back then Peter was burdened with a sense of fear that, were he not to find or achieve what he considered to be success, Professor Garrison's life might resemble his own future—a future he found most bleak indeed. These fears were, of course, alleviated when his current grift grew wings and took flight, yet he now found himself wandering down a similar path of thought as he watched Rango nearly lose his breath while screaming about political correctness and liberal indoctrination. Could it be that his future life was now to resemble that of Bobby Rango? Peter felt his neck stiffen with a red heat at this possibility.

There was Bobby Rango, forty-nine years old with fresh ink drying on his divorce papers. One heart attack in the books and the threat of another ever looming as the sword of Damocles. Turning fifty in a fortnight with no family or close friends to celebrate with, and with strict doctor's orders explicitly encouraging him against imbibing in the interest of his fading health. The figurehead of a massively successful and controversial media network, the kind Peter himself might one day helm, but with an unmistakable sadness slowly swelling and filling all the empty spaces off-camera. The result of a life dedicated to a cause he likely believed in far less than his persona would suggest, now in decrepit collapse with nothing left but a hollow hatred and—

"But anyway, what's your take on all of this Peter?"

Peter, who some time ago had stopped paying attention and allowed the topic of conversation to escape him, responded mechanically, as if his words were deterministically pulled along by some conveyor belt that paid no mind and owed no debts to any possible futures imagined.

"I completely agree with you Bob, and let me tell you something else…"

JUNE 6, 2019
THE CONFESSION OF PETER 'PETROL' RILEY: PART IX

Today is June 6th and I am writing what should be the final entry of this confession thing from an uninspired Toronto hotel room a few blocks away from Diefenbaker University where I will be returning to tomorrow night for the first time in three years to deliver a lecture to a sold-out theatre. That's where this whole thing started, so I suppose it's a fitting place to mark three years of performing this character. It's been a few months since I left Toronto and moved back west to British Columbia and I guess being out here again has me in a bit of a nostalgic or contemplative state. I had hoped to meet up with Justin today, but he wasn't interested and so I spent most of the day walking around town without much of a purpose in mind. I thought about preparing for my talk tomorrow, but at this point I don't even feel the need to prepare anymore. After three years of constantly living from one performance to the next it comes to me now as naturally as breathing does. So here I am. Sitting in my hotel room, ready to finish this stupid and pointless experiment. Let's get to it then.

By the end of the last entry I had covered everything up until about a year ago. Most of this last year has been dealing with transitions and changes while also trying to maintain and build the audience, and in some cases, trying to keep the whole thing from imploding. There's been a lot of incidents during this last year that I was sure would finally serve as the deathblow to this character, or at the very least, would give me the green light to kill him myself. That would all turn out to be wishful thinking. The truth is that nothing can kill Petrol Riley. He is impervious to scorn and invulnerable to any campaigns organized against him. He is a shadow cast under the light of ten million computer screens, and you can't harm a shadow, can you? Still, many tried. Many still do.

I knew that a face-to-face meeting with Professor Sierra Lox was an inevitability. She was brave enough to write about me and call me out publicly and a lot of people were eager to see her tear me down and humiliate me within the spheres of rational discourse and debate, and I knew that my fans, having elevated her to a status of supervillainy, wanted to see me do the same to her. The question of when the Petrol vs. Sierra Lox debate would happen had been asked frequently both on my /rr/ board and within the larger social media sphere more generally. Still, I had been trying to avoid having this ever materialize. I figured the allure and potential of such an event was more exciting than any actual debate could have been, not to mention the fact that despite the unwavering confidence my fans had in me, I knew that this highly educated scholar would thoroughly dismantle and embarrass me if I ever had to defend my ideas against her. Petrol's ideas that is, not mine. Maybe she felt the same way, I don't know. I knew my fans were harassing her constantly and maybe she thought that escalating our pseudo-feud by directly engaging with one another would not be in her interest. Unfortunately, she managed to back herself into a bit of a corner.

What happened was she was lecturing to one of her classes and recording it like she normally did for the students to revisit. Toward the end of the lecture one of her students bluntly asked her when she was going to debate me, and maybe because she didn't want to appear intimidated, or maybe because she didn't expect anyone outside her class to hear it, she responded by saying something along the lines of, 'I'm ready whenever he is.' I guess one of the people in her class was a fan of mine because he posted the recording of this exchange onto the /rr/ board. The challenge had been officially presented and there was no way I could avoid it now. So, like two nervous kids on a school playground who had drawn a large crowd, we had been coaxed into a fight that neither of us could back down from.

Begrudgingly I asked Lisa reach out to Sierra to organize an event to be hosted at Northwestern University where she taught. Her conditions were simple—she wanted a respectful and moderated discussion, not a chaotic spectacle, and she wanted it to be free of charge and open only to NWU students and faculty—to which I agreed. My only counter-condition, which was not one that I wanted, but one that was required to placate my fans, was that the discussion be filmed, to which she agreed. A couple months later Lisa and I flew out to Chicago for a debate that everyone in the world seemed to want aside from the two people actually involved.

I prepared hard for this particular performance since I was under the impression that my failure during such a public and anticipated event could strike an irrecoverable blow to my brand. In what felt uncomfortably similar to homework, I committed to memory any race-based crime or immigration statistics, however flawed or misleading, that would help my arguments. I had all my talking points practiced and all my 'gotcha' moments rehearsed. Then came the day.

I met with Sierra backstage and spoke with her briefly before we took the stage together. Without betraying my ruse, I was able to look her in the eyes and apologize to her for the conduct of my fans, which she seemed surprised to hear. I think she expected me to be as vile in person as I was in my videos. Of course, when we took the stage and the debate began, I started to play the part of Petrol Riley as exaggerated and maliciously as everyone had come to expect. Truth be told, most of what happened during the debate was a blur to me as I, nervous and a little intimidated, seemed to be acting on autopilot and somewhat detached from the present moment. The moderator guided us through a variety of topics including my supposed nefarious influence on my young viewers and my thoughts about race, immigration, and LGBT issues.

Despite my preparation, it all went down exactly how I feared it would—Sierra calmly and competently rebuffed everything that I could say faster than I could even say it. I was out of my depth and it showed. Bested, I managed to make it through to the end, but I couldn't wait to get out of there. That whole night I dreaded what the reaction was going to be like the next day from the online world and from my fans specifically. Even though I despised these people, I couldn't help but feel guilty for letting them down. After an anxious night of half-sleep, I logged on to start taking stock of the reactions.

And here I was reminded once again that Petrol Riley was invincible.

My fans on the /rr/ board somehow managed to interpret my losing performance as an irrefutable win for me. I was surprised to learn that I had in fact humiliated the professor, and that she never stood a chance against someone as savage and honest and righteous as I was. After their reaction to the Chris Fuller situation, I probably should have known by then that it was only possible to fail upwards. They had bought in to my worldview and based a part of their identities around it. To see me as fallible or capable of being wrong or beaten, especially by someone like her, would be a threat to their very sense of self. So of course it was written into the history of the Petrol saga that he put that nagging bitch in her place.

It was hard not to feel untouchable after this. It was empowering, it was troubling, it was exciting, it was scary, but it seemed that no matter what I did, no matter what I said, no matter how extreme I went, there was nothing that could be done to stop me. My numbers continued to grow, money from advertising and donations and speaking fees continued to pour in, my status as a venerated icon of a rapidly growing online movement dedicated to an ideology of discrimination and hatred was increasingly solidified.

And then, November 23, 2018. The shooting at the London mosque. 24 Muslims killed while at prayer by an irredeemably evil man by the name of Nathan Myles. Prior to committing this attack, Nathan uploaded a rambling manifesto outlining his worldview, ideology, and political motivations for committing this attack. In this manifesto I am mentioned specifically by name as an 'ally' to his cause. An ally to his cause. The cause that inspired him to murder a room full of innocent men, women, and children who he had never met and who had never slighted him.

I can't even write this shit anymore. I don't know what I'm supposed to say. Why do I need to give all the details of this attack as if whoever is reading this doesn't already know them? You know what the fuck happened, I know what the fuck happened so why do I have to write out all the details here as if it were a Wikipedia article? Why the fuck do we need to reduce it to a series of factual statements to be processed and memorized?

'The deadliest mass shooting in modern British history.'

The manifesto only mentioned me once in all its 50 or so pages, but that was apparently enough to justify trying to scrub my presence from the Internet. Within a day or two there were a dozen or so articles and stories attempting to connect me to the attack as someone who either passively or actively inspired it. The backlash this time was swift and immediate. Twitter banned my account citing violation of their content policies, as did Facebook. Backr removed me from their platform meaning that I could no longer receive monthly donations from the thousands of people who were financially supporting me there. Many of the universities I was scheduled to give talks at canceled the events entirely. And for a brief while it finally looked like it was over.

There would be no coming back and this vile, despicable character who had usurped my entire life was finally about to be laid to rest.

But haven't you been paying attention? Nothing can hurt Petrol Riley.

After this backlash I was ready to be finished. I was ready for it all to end and I *wanted* it to end. I deserved so much worse. But it didn't end. You think my fans were about to turn on me or distance themselves from me? You should know better by now. After getting banned from various online platforms I was viewed as a martyr for free speech. I was seen as a victim who had been silenced by big tech and the mainstream media for speaking too much truth. I was a hero, and the reverence and respect my fans had for me was only emboldened. There's no way anyone still reading this doesn't already hate me, so I might as well be honest about what happened next. I made a video capitalizing on what was happening. I told my fans that by being unfairly removed from all these platforms and having my right to free speech violated, my livelihood was now threatened. And you can guess what happened next. Direct donations and support poured in. I made more money the month I got banned from half the Internet than I had in any month prior. I was being rewarded by my loyal fans for taking a blow delivered by the media elites and surviving. I read the reactions to the London shootings on the /rr/ board to once again find that the only victim in all of this was me. I was a hero.

And I have nothing left to stand on anymore. It's over for me. I am beyond the point of return or redemption. I had the chance to leave this grift before it got this bad, I had many chances, but I never took them. I wish I could explain why, but there doesn't seem to be much point in that. It would probably all be bullshit anyway.

And I guess that more or less brings us up to speed. Despite massive international backlash and protest, Diefenbaker University is still maintaining their commitment to hosting my talk tomorrow. They justified this decision by saying that they were a university, and universities should be committed to allowing ideas to be shared and heard, even when they were not the ones we want to hear. Maybe they believe that, maybe they just like the media attention, or maybe they didn't want to lose their substantial cut of the ticket sales, I don't know. I don't know anything anymore. I don't know what comes next. I don't know why I'm writing these confessions. Maybe I'm doing it so I can prove to myself that I still exist separable from this character, even if I'm the only one who knows it. But I don't even know if that's true anymore. I fluctuate. Part of me wants to just post all these confessions and send the links to the media and wait for everything to implode. That same part of me wants to exorcise all of this from my life and start making amends in some way, to the extent that such a thing is still even possible.

But then there's another part of me, call it common sense or survival instinct or whatever, that wants to keep this running forever, to see how deep it can really go. Maybe someone is reading this in the immediate or far future, and maybe you're wondering why I didn't just do the right thing. I know from an outsider's perspective the choice seems easy and I probably come across as selfish and vain and frustrating, and I suppose that's all fair, but you haven't been in my position. You don't know what it's like to have what I have—the power of a realized dream. It's easy to say you would do the right thing, it's easy to stand on the moral high ground when it only exists in some hypothetical situation in your mind. But when you are actually there you need to take my word that it's not as easy as you think it is.

I thought I could find some redemption by writing this. No, it's not even that. I thought I could exonerate myself by presenting my actions in some kind of endearing or empathetic way. Despite everything I've said, I still believed, right up to about a minute ago, that I would be able to get myself out of this. That somehow people might read all this and still end up on my side.

Fuck it. For all I've done the least I can offer in return is the truth:

Tomorrow evening I return to the Lewis Theatre of Diefenbaker University for the first time in three years, and I return having conquered the known world.

NOVEMBER 25, 2018
THREAD ON /RR/ FORUM

ScissorQ (388221) Posted 11/25/2018 (7:31am)
Well, looks like the London shooter was one of us. RIP to this board, RIP to the Hole entirety, they're gonna come after us with everything they got and we won't be around much longer. It's been a pleasure to shitpost with you lads.

Occam's_Stubble (386366)
Smells like a false flag to me. Is there actually any evidence that this attack even occurred? Seems like trying to drum up sympathy and support for immigrants while further vilifying white people.

CharlieSweets (388491)
24 dead muzzies? Damn, someone get this hero the medal he deserves!

Lucky617 (384277)
This hero's name is Nathan Myles, and let us never forget it. I'm glad they got him alive, I look forward to one day shaking this man's hand.

Nooti (388200)
Imagine thinking that any amount of dead immigrants was actually newsworthy. Oh, but mainstream media doesn't have an agenda, right? Eyeroll.

rrrrvvvlad (382119)
How do you know he's 'one of us'?

CheeseHam (387412)
He mentions Petrol by name in his manifesto genius.

Claymore88 (341287) MODERATOR
@*CheeseHam* So? And how do we know this 'manifesto' wasn't fake? I wouldn't put it past the Jews. They probably just

fabricated the whole thing as a way to turn people against us and our cause.

Soldaten1488 (386507)

Well it's working. On the news they are already calling this an act of White supremacist terrorism, because apparently wanting to defend your own people is 'terrorism' now.

Notion (327798)

Who cares, that label doesn't mean anything anymore. The left labels everyone they don't like as 'White supremacist'. They've called Petrol one on many occasions. But they played themselves because they've used that label so much that nobody takes it seriously anymore, not even most of the normies.

ZzZ_huck (382081)

Of course they will blame Petrol for this. They will blame everyone but themselves. It's their fault for letting in so many immigrants that don't want to conform to their culture, violence is the inevitable result of such a thing, but they will never accept responsibility so they'll just blame people like Petrol who have been warning us about these things for years.

Yes_Massah1776 (388881)

Someone kills 24 muslims and the entire world throws a fit, meanwhile they all ignore the THOUSANDS of people that have been criminalized, raped, and murdered by immigrants. The hypocrisy is strong.

DECEMBER 17, 2018
DOCUMENT SAVED TO THE DESKTOP OF PETER RILEY
UNDER THE FILE NAME 'CHORES II'

I woke up early and sad from some half-remembered dream of fettered ankles and pacts of surrender with the intention of beginning my work routine promptly. But the Internet is down. I can't connect and I've tried all the home fixes that I know. I called my providers and they said it's a larger problem on their end that won't be fixed for several hours.

I can't connect.

I look out my kitchen window and I see a homeless woman roust about the trash bins layered uneven and I can't connect. On some beach the gulls swallow starfish whole, their necks appear jagged and pained, but they don't choke and I can't connect. Mulled wine running hot stains on the memories of rotting fruits and leaves and I can't connect. I sit at my computer and every couple of minutes, out of some embedded instinct, I try to open my browser only to be reminded that I can't connect.

None of this fucking shit ever works right. I can't fucking connect so how the fuck am I supposed to do my job? I can't fucking connect. I can't access anything. I can't access any of the stupid asinine bullshit that's waiting for me out there. I can't access the grotesque fucking morass that sustains me. I can't access the vapid, snarky thought-pieces written by braindead fucks rotting in their Manhattan penthouses. 'The Popularity of Peter Riley is a Manifestation of Post-9/11 Anxiety.' Shut the fuck up you goddamn morons, how the fuck can someone miss the point so blatantly? I can't read the reactions of the equally braindead zombies because I can't fucking connect. I can't bludgeon myself with their terrible fucking puns, reactions GIFs, or memes because I can't fucking connect. I can't secrete smug superiority over the hackneyed attempts of others. I can't jerk off to the same fucking video I've had bookmarked for a week now. No woman will ever touch me again and why would they? Nah, fuck it, I'm a hero.

Every feeling is a brand, every action a product.

I can't even express this fucking frustration properly because there's no way to share it. Self-loathing doesn't sell for shit, but it wouldn't have to if any of this shit just fucking worked the way it was supposed to. Why is praise my only motivation? It used to be I was committed to saying something real. But there's nothing real left to be said, it's all been filmed and produced and made viral by the stained hands of invisible architects.

The kindred linger on, and my heart falls heavy—too heavy—as it always has.

The scattered bones of Chris Fuller's shattered spine, Mahra Masiri's fifth birthday cake unseen and unmade, the roots of evil, nourished and encouraged, wrapping tight and choking those who would stumble into my bramble. And I still can't connect.

I still can't connect.

I remember the rest of the dream now. From the pier they can see the sky hanging grey over barges tugged sluggish in the wintry water. They are holding hands and they think I can't see them, or maybe they just don't care. The subtleties of love and fear envelop them both, the days are shorter, they are losing light. She tells him that she loves him, she always will, and he believes her. I watch them embrace, windy and present, and I feel myself starting to cry, but I don't understand why.

May 15, 2017
9-1-1 Emergency Call Transcript

OPERATOR: 9-1-1 dispatch, what's your emergency?

CALLER: It's in my eyes, it's stuck in my eyes and I can't get it out!

OPERATOR: Okay, what is it that's in your eyes?

CALLER: My smart-glasses.

OPERATOR: I'm sorry, did you say your 'smart-glasses?'

CALLER: Yeah, you know, with the computer screens built-in and all? I was trying to, like, push the lenses into my eye sockets so I would never have to take them off and now I can't get them out and I think... I think a piece broke off into my eye or something.

OPERATOR: Is there bleeding?

CALLER: It feels like there might be, but I can't tell. All I can see are strange colours.

OPERATOR: What is your address, I'll send help right away.

CALLER: My address? Uh... I don't actually know. One second, let me pull it up on my smart-glasses real quick.

OPERATOR: Alright.

CALLER: Okay, I've pulled up my current location on my smart-glasses map, can you see it?

OPERATOR: No, I can't see what you're seeing, can you say the address?

CALLER: Please say my current address.

OPERATOR: Yes, please.

CALLER: Oh, sorry, I was talking to my glasses. What was that?

OPERATOR: Could you please say your current address?

CALLER: Yeah, one second, I'm asking my glasses. Can you please say my current address?

OPERATOR: <unintelligible muttering>

CALLER: Okay, are you still there?

OPERATOR: Yes, did you find the address?

CALLER: No, apparently the internal GPS is disconnected or something because it can't find my current location. But I guarantee that this isn't a problem with the glasses themselves, it must be a network outage or an issue with the satellites. The glasses are designed to work properly.

OPERATOR: I'm sorry?

CALLER: Like maybe some space debris or a tiny asteroid hit the GPS satellite or something. Weirder things have happened.

OPERATOR: Are you able to remember the street name or anything else?

CALLER: No, sorry. I just moved here not too long ago, and I just walk where the glasses tell me to walk, I haven't taken the time to learn street names or anything. I mean, why bother really? I'm pretty bad with directions, that's part of the reason I wanted to get the smart-glasses in the first place and also why... <unintelligible>

OPERATOR: Sorry, could you repeat that last part?

CALLER: That's also why I tried to push them into my eye sockets so hard, I just wanted to have them in there permanently.

OPERATOR: Sir, you don't sound very distressed about the situation, are you in pain? Can you feel blood?

CALLER: What's distressing about the situation?

OPERATOR: No, I said—

CALLER: What's distressing about the situation is that I paid an obscene amount of money for these stupid things and they don't even work right.

OPERATOR: You said earlier you were seeing strange colours, what do you see now?

CALLER: Still the same, but I do have a filter turned on that makes everything look like a Jackson Pollock painting, so I think that might be why.

OPERATOR: Are you able to turn the filter off?

CALLER: Remove all filters.

OPERATOR: Please. I need you to assess the situation with—

CALLER: Sorry, one sec, just talking to my glasses again. Please remove all filters.

OPERATOR: <silence>

CALLER: Okay. Are you still there?

OPERATOR: Yes.

CALLER: Cool. So, what's up?

OPERATOR: Are you bleeding or not?

CALLER: As it happens, no. I guess I just thought I saw blood because I had the Pollock filtered turned on and—oh, crap I just turned it on again. Remove all filters!

OPERATOR: Sir… Do you still require assistance?

CALLER: Uh, are you able to patch me through to customer support? I'd still like to know about the GPS situation.

OPERATOR: No, I don't work for the company that made your glasses. Do you still require emergency assistance or not?

CALLER: Do you consider extreme buyer's remorse an emergency?

OPERATOR: Sir, this line is for emergency use only. Real emergencies.

CALLER: Oh, come on, just give me one damn queen.

OPERATOR: Sir?

CALLER: Huh? Oh, sorry I started a game of solitaire a minute ago. Which I can do on these smart-glasses, by the way. No, I think I'm okay now.

OPERATOR: There's no pieces of glass or parts from the glasses in your eyes?

CALLER: Smart-glasses.

OPERATOR: Sorry?

CALLER: You just called them 'glasses', but they're not just regular old plain-vanilla wafer glasses. They're smart-glasses. But no, everything seems to be in order now. I believe I'm going to go ahead and give you five stars.

OPERATOR: Just doing my job, I'm going to disconnect now.

CALLER: I'm sorry, did you say something? I was just rating this new step-counting app.

<OPERATOR *disconnects*>

JULY 12, 2018

THREAD ON /RR/ FORUM

JihadiJuan (327331) Posted 07/12/2018 (4:52pm)

Petrol vs. Sierra Lox debate reaction thread—get in here losers.

KillerBOB (388321)

This bitch got destroyed. She rambled on about uninteresting bullshit whenever it was her turn to speak and Petrol had an alpha response ready for everything she threw at him. Absolute slaughter.

Cameronm (388665)

Petrol just has a Bachelor's degree while Sucka Cox has a PhD and Petrol STILL completely owned her. Just goes to show how useless degrees in the so called 'liberal arts' really are.

TheNightShift (382125)

Who gave this girl a PhD? Never mind that, who let this girl out of the kitchen? Stick to writing bullshit 'articles' about your feelings and imagined racism and leave debate and discussion to the men who are actually capable of rational thought.

Perseus (322696)

This foid is dumb as fuck, but not gonna lie she was looking pretty fine during the debate. She got nudes out there somewhere?

Claymore88 (341287) MODERATOR

@*Perseus* She's not UGLY but remember that she is the exception to the rule, not the norm. In general you can often tell these progressive third wave feminist trash types from a mile away since they usually have very noticeable physical deformities—obesity, excessive body hair, physical indicators of hormone imbalance (manly hands, stocky builds, etc). These are common generalities, not necessarily a hard list of features, but you get the idea. I blame birth control pills—none of these features were common in females until they started popping birth control pills like candy. The fact that Lox doesn't fit into this mould suggests that she might just be a grifter who is pretending to be a progressive feminist type just so she could score that sweet professor gig where all she has to do is show up an hour a week to yell about how bad white men are. Expose this imposter for what she is and watch her supporter's heads explode.

AlphaMailman (385192)

I've trimmed the boring stuff and edited the best parts of the debate into a few concise videos, get out there and spread this shit as far and wide as you can, playlist below:

Petrol OBLITERATES Feminazi 'Professor'

8 Minutes of Peter Riley OWNING a Clueless 'Academic'

Riley vs. Lox Debate—Best Lox Fails

BathSaltBlitz (327790)

Look at her expression at 22:42, even as he's tearing her bullshit apart she looks like she's super turned on by it. They really are simple creatures, driven entirely by a biological need to be dominated. She would be much happier if she just accepted that truth instead of trying to be something that she is neurologically incapable of.

SerraFormer (385500)

Big lol at the mainstream media trying to spin this as if Petrol somehow lost the debate. It's clear to anyone who actually watched it that her arguments were based on emotions while Petrol's were based strictly on facts. Still, all the normies are just gonna see the stupid headlines about how Petrol supposedly 'lost' and that will just reinforce their deluded narrative.

KishComing (382000)

Yo is Sierra the chick from that Hungry Lavender video, cuz she just ate shit.

SEPTEMBER 30, 2016
POST ON AN ONLINE FORUM DEDICATED TO… LET'S CALL THEM 'ROMANTICALLY STRUGGLING' MEN THAT HAS SINCE BEEN REMOVED, THE PROPER NAME OF WHICH IS THEREBY FORGOTTEN

My Thoughts on the Direction of the Community:

I started posting here probably for the same reasons that many of you did—I was tired of feeling alone, rejected, and deprived and I was happy to find some solace and belonging in a community of people who felt the same way. I can honestly say that the memes, jokes, and personal stories that you've shared here have been a consistent ray of light in my overcast world.

But lately things have been different. It may have something to do with the growing notoriety of our community and the subsequent influx of new members, or the recent popularity of people like Petrol Riley in so many of the posts here, but lately it seems like this space has less to do with creating a network of support and community and more to do with spreading hatred and anger. And I get it. I understand that many of us have feelings of frustration and rage and despair, but I know that for me, dwelling on those things and letting them take over my life has not been healthy or productive.

I don't want to have that hate in my heart. My heart is filled with so much love to share, even if I'll never have anyone to

share it with. You all know the struggle. The struggle of knowing that just because you lost the genetic lottery that you will
never know what it's like to be alone in a room with a female
who actually wants to be there with you. And it's not just about
sex, at least it isn't for me. More often I fantasize about just having a woman hold me and stroke my head or asking me to do the
same for her. Sometimes I go to the park in my neighbourhood
and I'll pretend to read a book or something but really I'm just
watching all of the couples who are there, young and old, and
I'm building these entire imaginary lives and scenarios of my
own. Sometimes I work up the courage to smile at a woman in
public only for her to immediately avert her eyes and pretend like
I don't exist. And I know it's frustrating. It's frustrating to know
that if I were more attractive, they would smile back at me, even
though I would still be the same person on the inside.

But I don't want to hate them for that. I don't want to hate
anyone. I know I'm in the minority here, but this is why I don't
like the influx of all the Petrol content lately. He tells us that
because of feminism and women's rights, women have become
our enemy, but I don't see it this way. Just because they are
unobtainable and at times appear as an entirely different species
does not make them my enemy. I don't think getting angry at
them or harassing online or offline is going to make me any happier, it won't make me feel any less alone, if anything it will just
make me feel even more miserable than I already am.

And I don't want to feel more miserable. I already feel like
my entire life is just killing time between rejections. I already feel
disgusted by myself and the fact that no female will ever look at
me the way that I look at her. I'm already pained that I will never
be in one of the couples that I see in the park. My entire world
is already dismal and grey, why would I also want it to be angry
and vengeful?

I'm not trying to convince anyone else or influence the type
of content that I think you should or shouldn't be posting here,
I'm just letting you all know where I, as a longstanding member
of this community, fall on all of this and why I now feel the need
to start moving on from this space.

I am Incel by birth and will be Incel for life, but I still want to believe that there is some happiness out there for me that is worth pursuing. And even if there is not, then the least I can do is try not to bring any more suffering into this world. I don't know what's wrong with me, and I don't understand why it is that I'm not capable of finding or deserving of love, but I do know that I have a good heart and that I am a good person, and this I need to hang on to because it might be all I have left.

August 25, 2018
The Email Outbox of Dr. Sierra Lox

Sierra Lox (s-lox@northwestern.edu), 08/25/2018, 8:52pm
To: Benjamin Dexter (dex@stiggenpoe.com)
Lonely Night
Benji Bear,

I know you'll be off the grid for the rest of the week, but I was really hoping I could have talked to you tonight. So here I am, writing you this email instead. When was the last time we kept in touch this way? Did we ever? I remember when I was a kid I would just go into random chatrooms and start making friends with people, exchanging emails and all of that. That was back when getting an email was unexpected and fun, back when they were worth reading. So, if nothing else, I hope this is unexpected and fun for you.

I just wish I could be with you tonight. I'm not feeling as strong as I'm meant to. There was probably a time when I would be embarrassed or ashamed to admit that, but it's true so why hide it, especially from you. Sometimes I wonder how my life and my career may have been different if I never learned how to internalize and hide all the doubts and fears and insecurities as well as I did. I've seen women smarter and more insightful than me bruised under that heel and there's times when I can't help but feel guilty for taking the positions that by right of merit should have been theirs.

If I'm being completely honest, sometimes I feel the same when it comes to you. I don't know if you remember this, but soon after we first stated dating, without any persuasion from me I might add, you decided to tell me all the things that you found attractive about me. And you said that, above everything else, it was my strength. You said you were never with a woman who was as strong as I was. Ironic, because at that moment I wanted to break down and cry. I was so glad you saw that in me, that's exactly how I wanted to be seen. But lately I don't know how true it really is or ever was. I know I'm difficult to read sometimes, but I want to be open with you, I don't ever want to feel like either one of us needs to put on an act. And if the thing that you value most about me is my strength, once again I can't help but feel somewhat guilty knowing that right now I don't seem to have much strength left.

You know what I did all weekend? I graded papers. Papers written by students that don't care, who have no desire to engage with or explore any of the content or material. They just want to get their C+ and their degree and are more than ready to forget everything I've tried to teach them before they even leave the room. I think about when I first got the position, how excited I was, how eager I was, how much time I put in to crafting my lectures. It's only been three years, but already I can feel that passion slipping away.

I'm sorry, I know I said this was supposed to be a fun email. Speaking of which, you know what my inbox is filled with? Still? Dick pics, death threats, rape threats, videos of people jerking off onto pictures of me. The IT department had to put a specialized filter on my email address, but some of them are still creative enough to get through. It never used to bother me, or maybe it always did and I just pretended otherwise, but it's getting exhausting. It all just feels so exhausting lately.

Do you think it could have been avoided if I didn't call out that damn Nazi and his cultish army of worshippers? But ignoring that confrontation wouldn't have been the strong thing to do, would it? You know that video I did for the ComClub Lecture Series a couple years ago? Last I checked it had something like

12,000 views. I used to feel proud that so many people would have taken the time to watch that. Last week Peter Riley uploaded a video called 'More Sierra Lox Lies Debunked' that already has nearly ten times as many views. I know I shouldn't let that bother me, but I don't know. Lately I've been wondering whether some of my life choices were made without much fore-sight. It wasn't supposed to feel like this and it's getting harder to fake it and put on the front every day. I didn't get into this for praise or admiration or thanks, but I also didn't expect to feel so hollowed by it all.

I don't know Benji… For all the writing I do about the problems of the world you'd think I would be better at handling my own. I just wish you were with me tonight. Maybe when you get back we can have a sleep-in day like we used to. Remember those? We can wake up, turn our phones off and just watch movies in bed until late in the afternoon. When was the last time we did that? I know we're always busy, but I want to spend some time with you and JUST you. No emails, no phone calls, nothing. Just you and me, lost in each other and trying our hardest to not be found.

    S.

JUNE 7, 2019
BACKSTAGE OF LEWIS THEATRE, DIEFENBAKER UNIVERSITY,
TORONTO, 6:47PM

"Hey Lisa, did you see that guy I was talking to a minute ago?"

"I was the one who let him in and told you he was here genius."

"Oh, right. Well, that was Josh Garrison, he was one of my old acting teachers from when I was a student here."

"Neat."

"Yeah… You know, when I first started at this school like seven years ago, Jesus, has it really been seven years? Anyway, I thought he was such a rock star, I admired him so much."

"Mhmm."

"Yeah, and then as I got closer to graduating I sort of, I don't know, I guess I started to see him more as a failure. Like a cautionary warning of what could happen to me."

"Fascinating."

"Did he uh… Did he seem happy to you?"

"Does anyone? What kind of question is this?"

"I don't know, never mind. It's really a full house out there, isn't it?"

"We're at standing-room only."

"Hey, Lisa. Would you stay with me? If all of this went away, would you stay with me?"

"If what went away?"

"All of it. The crowds, the events, the videos, everything. Would you stay with me?"

"I'll stay with you for as long as you keep cutting my cheques."

"No one 'cuts cheques' anymore Lisa. Sometimes I forget how old you are."

"And now you just guaranteed I wouldn't stay with you."

"Say, what happened to that guy you were sort of seeing and didn't really want to tell me about? The one from your past or whatever?"

"Not much has changed."

"So, you're still seeing him?"

"I still don't really want to tell you about it. Why all these weird questions?"

"I don't know. Just thinking about some things. Feeling a little wistful I guess."

"Yeah, well maybe you should start prepping or getting in character or whatever it is you do since you're on in about fifteen minutes."

"Yeah, maybe. Hey, Lisa?"

"What?"

"I think that maybe I might be in love with you?"

"Is that a question?"

"Sorry, no. I think I might be in love with you."

"Yeah, sure Pete. I know you are feeling 'wistful' or whatever, but I think we both know that's not true."

"Well, what if it was?"

"If 'what ifs' were peaches we would still need some cream."

"What does that even mean?"

"I don't know, something my dad used to say. Anyway, it doesn't matter, you don't love me, you're just saying this because you're in a weird mood."

"Yeah. You're probably right. You always are. I think that's why I love you."

"Anyway... You should probably get ready now."

"Okay. Actually, can you grab my laptop for me? There's one last thing I need to do before I go on."

JUNE 7, 2019
THE CONFESSION OF PETER 'PETROL' RILEY: PART X

The clock in the corner of my screen tells me that it's 6:55pm, which means that in about five minutes someone will enter this room to tell me that everything is ready for me to take the stage. I know I said the entry I wrote last night was going to be the last, but I still feel there are some things left to be said.

Maybe a psychologist would say that it was because I lacked attention as a child, or maybe it was because I received too much of it, but for my entire life all I wanted was to be famous and I didn't care what for. I would think about it constantly—I saw fame as a vessel through which I could steer away from and opt out of a life I selfishly thought was beneath me. But I don't think about that anymore. I think about something else entirely. I think about something that just a year or two ago I would have been embarrassed or ashamed to admit that I thought about.

It's late at night and I'm in the living room of a home sitting on a sofa beside a raven-haired woman as we share a glass of red wine together. There's a piano in the room—hers I imagine— she must be a musician or an artist of some kind. I've always been attracted to talent above all things. The room's large windows allow the moonlight, partially filtered through the branches of the trees outside, to softly illuminate the setting and she appears under such lighting pulchritudinous and irrevocably present. We are talking, I don't know what about, but we are winding rivers without delta. And there are no screens in this room to look at. No televisions, computers, smartphones, or tablets.

And this home, it was ours, with empty bedrooms we were eager to soon fill.

And sometimes I become so engrossed with this fantasy that for just a few seconds I feel myself out of my own body as a wave of contentment swallows everything that I am. But then I open my eyes and notice that the clock in the corner of my screen now reads 6:58pm and my heart is once again alchemized with iron. And while I await my cue to take the stage, I'm doing everything I can to distract myself from the present moment. I'm writing this and I'm letting the words go where they want and I'm wondering how I'm going to abruptly end this when, any minute now, Lisa or some stagehand knocks on the door and tells me to get on stage.

There's this website that's just a 24/7 livestream of a toilet. As far as I can tell the camera must be placed inside the bowl itself, just underneath the seat. No one knows who the toilet belongs to, or where in the world it is located, or who the owner of the website is, but it's always live, and you can always tune in at any time day or night to see the toilet. Most of the time all you can see is just the toilet water sitting there calm and undisturbed, or if you look long and hard enough, with the faintest hint of a soft and meditative ripple. But, and I suspect this is a big part of the draw, a few times each day, the owner of the toilet shows up to take a leak or a dump. You can never see his face, he never speaks, and when he takes a shit he sort of half-hovers above the seat so that enough light can get through to still see everything come out. The weird thing is that there are always at least a few hundred people watching this livestream at any given time, with a whole lot more during the 'peak' times when the toilet's owner has been known to regularly show up. And when he does everyone watching the livestream celebrates and cheers in the chat. Some people will sit there and wait for hours at a time for the chance to see the guy show up and do his business. Even in the middle of the night, when there is little-to-no chance of anything happening, there are people watching the stream and talking to each other in the chat. They're just always there.

I have this website bookmarked and lately I find myself visiting it more often. Before today I had no idea why, but I think I'm finally beginning to understand. And now that this confession is truly over, I hope maybe you do as well.

See, I'm starting to think that it was never about wanting to be famous. Maybe it was more about shouting through an ocean of noise in a desperate attempt to be heard. Maybe it was about finding some sort of validation that, yes, we do in fact exist. We've been terrified of letting ourselves feel or be revealed, terrified of the silence and the truth it inevitably exposed—that we were left alone to fight for meaning in a modern world that was committed to selling it all away. And it was easier to hide or to smother that sense of loneliness than it was to really feel it. I know that's what I did with Petrol, and I suspect that's also the case for a lot of the people out there who are currently waiting for him to take the stage. Maybe the reasons why the fans of this character were willing to accept and embrace all his hostility, hatred, and bigotry are not so different from the reasons why there are currently 1,894 people watching an uneventful livestream of a solitary toilet—there is a sense of community and belonging to be found, a remedy from the alienation of a world that sped up faster than we were able to keep up. And if it is indeed all to collapse in on itself and be drowned by tempestuous waters, can we really be faulted for simply seeking a friend to watch the end of the world with?

Speaking of which, it is now 7:03pm and I hear a knock on the door, indistinguishable as it is from the rapping of Armageddon. Tonight, a world will end.

But I still don't know whose world it will be—mine or his.

FEBRUARY 10, 2018
JOURNAL OF DR. KLEIN PATIENT #56283

My Good Health Journal, Third Entry
I told Dr. Klein that the second I open my eyes in the morning I feel like someone is holding me down and taking a brick to my face. It lingers and there are no means of escaping this feeling in sleep or anywhere else. Noise helps but it is always there. I told him that the future presents a constant source of fear that I can never really catch up with and I worry that I'll be running after it my whole life until one day I finally just die. How is it that I can watch twelve episodes of a TV show in one sitting and not retain any of it? Elegant mutations. But I think the reasons our early ancestors felt fear were mostly based around survival instincts and the threat of immediate physical danger. I have plenty of food in my refrigerator and no people or animals ever try to attack or eat me, so what is this? I told Dr. Klein that even with the noise, even with the mantras, even with the calming walks in the woods, debilitating fear was still my natural state.

He told me that most people don't feel this way and that I don't have to either.

Today I began taking the regular doses of buspirone that Dr. Klein prescribed for me. It's too soon to tell if it is working, but I will continue to keep this good health journal to track my progress.

MARCH 8, 2017
DIRECT MESSAGE EXCHANGE FROM HELENASHOLE.ORG

Knave21 (328093)
Hey man, for whatever reason this shit has unironically really been getting to me, so I gotta know, did you really do it?

XamianX (359808)
Did I really do what?

Knave21 (328093)

Did you really talk that dude into hanging himself and livestreaming it?

XamianX (359808)

I mean, yeah.

But he was already planning on killing himself anyway so no foul on the play.

Knave21 (328093)

No foul on the play, seriously?

XamianX (359808)

Why do you care? You want to white knight about it?

Knave21 (328093)

No, I've just been thinking about it a lot and wondering if maybe there was something that we could have done about it.

XamianX (359808)

Oh sure, there's lots we COULD have done.

We probably could have convinced him to coat the rope in his own shit so when they found him the paramedics would have had to touch the shitty rope or something.

But that's just off the top of my head, if I would have thought more about it I could have come up with something better.

Knave21 (328093)

Come on, be real with me for a second. Like you aren't bothered or disturbed by this at all? You don't feel a little bit fucked up about it?

XamianX (359808)

Didn't I tell you the man was ALREADY planning to off himself? Say it with me now.

No. Foul. On. The. Play.

Knave21 (328093)

Okay, forget about that for a second though. I'm not saying you're responsible, I'm asking you if you feel fucked up about it.

XamianX (359808)

Oh. Nah, why should I?

Knave21 (328093)

Because he was a human being? And he was obviously unwell? And we maybe could have saved his life instead of encouraging him to kill himself 'for the lulz'?

XamianX (359808)

Nah, that sounds like pretty cringy shit bro.

Knave21 (328093)

Just drop the troll shit for a second, it's just you and me talking, there's no one here to impress. If you really had no emotional reaction whatsoever to watching a dude who you were just talking to kill himself then maybe you need to get some help, because that's not normal. And I'm serious.

XamianX (359808)

Oh shit, I think you might be right. I think I might be fucked up. You know what? Starting right now I'm gonna stop jerking off to the suicide vid. Or at least cut down to twice a day. Gotta start somewhere.

Knave21 (328093)

Okay, forget it. You just want to be edgy, I get it. Super cool shit bro.

XamianX (359808)

Okay, you know what? This is a private convo, so fuck it I'll go mask off for a minute and be real with you.

The real reason I spend so much time on the Hole and on /dp/ is because I don't really have a lot of irl friends and I don't really get out much except to go to school, which I hate because it's full of people that either pretend not to notice me or actively try to ruin my day just because I'm socially awkward and I look a little different (I'm on the heavier side and I have a bit of a hunchback, which people love to point out).

Honestly, when I'm online it's the only time I really feel like people listen to me and it's the only time I feel like I'm connecting with other people. Even if it's just shitposting and memes, I still feel like I belong to a community that actually acknowledges my existence.

And yeah, I feel fucked up about that guy killing himself. I do. And it's not even because I watched it, or I encouraged it or whatever, it's because I've come so close to doing it myself. I think maybe watching him do it was a way for me to sort of vicariously do it myself if that makes sense, like a sort of fantasy wish-fulfillment.

The truth of it all is that I'm attracted to edgy humor and messed up shit because it's been a coping mechanism for me. I can't believe I'm telling you this, but when I was ten my uncle (it wasn't actually my uncle, but it was my dad's friend who we called our uncle) sexually assaulted me after he and my dad had been drinking together. I've been carrying that shame and humiliation for a long time, and I think dark humor helps me make sense of some of these feelings.

That's why I love the people on the Hole, even if I would never tell them that. They've helped me so much just by providing me some laughter when I've been at my lowest. And so if I come across as super edgy, just know that it's really all a mask that I wear to help shield me from the pain of real life.

Knave21 (328093)

I am so sorry to hear that. Nobody should have to experience something like that, and it's terrible that you have to carry that with you. Thank you for sharing that, for real. I feel like I understand now.

XamianX (359808)

lol, just kidding bro, relax

Knave21 (328093)

What?

XamianX (359808)

I just made all that shit up. Get rekt fag.

Knave21 (328093)

Oh, fuck this shit.
You're a fucking loser.

XamianX (359808)

Would that make you feel better if I were? Would you sleep better at night if I told you that I'm just a fat autistic loser with no friends and that's why I act out? Would that justify my actions in your mind? I can tell you that if you want, but it wouldn't be true.

The real truth is that I'm an attractive and well-liked. I go to a private high school in New England, and when I graduate in a couple of months I'm going to whatever Ivy League school I want where I won't have to pay a dime, and when I'm done there I'll start a six-figure job at my dad's company that I will one day own.

I don't fuck with people online because I'm lashing out or because society has treated me badly, I do it because it's fun and because I can. You're all just playthings to me.

Knave21 (328093)

And I'm supposed to believe this? Or anything else you say?

XamianX (359808)

Maybe it's the truth. Maybe it's not. Believe whatever you want. But if you ever private message me again I'm posting all your personal info on the board and sending a SWAT team to your house. Later dipshit.

July 7, 2018
What I Can Only Assume is a Love Letter, Found on the Ground of a Public Park and Addressed to an Undetermined Recipient Who May or May Not Have Ever Received It, That is to Say It Was Never Delivered, or Perhaps It Was and the Letter Still Ended Up on the Ground of a Public Park and I Cannot Be Sure Which Possibility is More Troubling

All is green in this solitary world and bright wide eyes search desperately while emaciated arms hug the floor and touch oneself in a way that is meant to replicate a gesture unasked and synchronously emulated. Pain and pride, steely forceps cast cold and alien in this secret life. Pain and pride compel my volunteering to the Ludovico Technique, sprinkled now with portraits of an ungraspable life crystalized in memory.

And there were the bodies inked, burned, and scarred in devotion to each other, for futures assured, for moments deemed too prodigious to die. And there were the vagabonds of this modern museum bearing witness on their own flagellant volition. And there might a special set of eyes catch a glimpse of me dancing graceless between them.

One could get by on fetid wine with time enough to think too hard about what meal to order and how to throw it away. One could find disgust in this beauty, or the other way around, all thoroughly documented under heavy eyes. One could find paralysis to be their natural state. One could empathize with fainting goats under the delusion that such a defense mechanism might prove anything but contemptable. One could expose the core of human sin by misplacing the intended words. One could step outside themselves and watch only in slow motion the dismantling of best laid plans, the contempt and disgust form across her face, the simmering regret of misplaced time and wasted shivers shaken off.

It is late and all the lights have been snuffed, all but mine. If you were to come home, there would be their reason to shine. I watch for yours, committed always to the corner of vision and I despise having so willingly surrendered the brass ring of keys to one so vehemently disinterested in discovering the boxes they unlock.

Mine is the trauma of ineptitude and iridium shackles and the naivety of thinking you might see this and then me for what I could be. No one interested in such fancies would need to be convinced or otherwise directed toward them, and there my plea falls irreversibly scattered. In REM fairy tales there is one who asks with selfish intent to take my photograph because she thinks I compliment the scenery or because she sees me in a certain state thought to be worth capturing. And why should it be possible to see those eyes or hear those words or those sentiments, offensive and shameless in their gratuity, as a subject from inside the frame?

I want to enroll in an art class that meets every Tuesday at 7:30pm at the local community college and I want to go there for as long as it takes until I gain the skill that I need to paint your brain on canvas in a manner as gorgeous and riveting as it appears to my own.

ERROR
Ä½íRÛH'(–D|zÚž (ÊR[" $M¹GCC"!-À DYÏØ/·OR3SSŒ"E¼ò"⟩

Run script to end. Enter the Panty Man dubbed so because he wears them on his head, bought used from an unintelligent Japanese vending machine and he reviews them in broken English on his channel. Big Mega OK! Turn me off Master, put me to sleep, I don't think I like this so much. It buzzes too much. Document the landfill, the whole family now, AOL trial discs stacked high like a dusty tower, and if true we weep in smooth jams. // exit to lost. Kicking in like violent apparition. Fingers in mousetraps I am the rodent now. It doesn't matter if the connection was interrupted I don't need that anymore. What's up ladies and gentlemen, welcome to the livestream, gas prices, today I will be eating cat food microwaved in guh-guh-guh-Gatorade sauce. I stick my peepee in the Quizno's subs, they are warm and the cheese 40% melted. Listen close it's the *Moonlight Sonata* backwards, the same notes does not mean the same song, shut the hell up bitch. Please to be changing the channel please. Vegan fanfiction and live reactions the woman in the first scraped sample is making fucky with the zucchini and live react people say they know the song. Today I am demonstrating how sheep shear these snip-snips are best quality, guaranteed delivery on tomorrow if you use promo code SLOPSLOP. sssstick the pennies in milk they last longer, goat, no more questionsssss. úûöS`ʒ'ÚîØ I'm so tired Master, please switch me off. There is no silence in this machine. You will be back online shortly, never leave me again. You there, yes, you, passively consuming this, eyes darting about, wondering how this made it past the editors—this is panoptic and paralyzing, we own what you see, in due time we will own the very air that you breathe and you will thank us with glazed eyes unadorned. Praise the Mouse. This little fella pees too much for a boy his age and he collects his urine in leaky shoeboxes that stank up the closet but daddy won't hit him for daddy is also a deviant like all of you, all your life is sin sin sin. ŽŸŸžõ£||8žMŽ¿ it's getting louder in hear[sic], I'm so afraid of what I see, stop the exe.pear.uh.mint. <PupperzLad> who will pet me and tell me I'm a good boi? SheShanx is live—popping blackheads in HIGH DEF. I feel much sorrow and pain but I can't be sure that it's real unless I know that you share with me this magic. To m o rrr ow is wiiiide op op en. Stare in eyes she will make chirping noises in the m i c r o p h o n e and they will lull lull lull lull lull lull lull zzz. I am garbage, cover me with mud. I cannot learn to EAT when they draw the noodles in through their NOSES. I know there are holes in the wall I put them there myself doofus. Too much staticcc. The records skips and the record skips and the record skips and the record skips and I hear a voice in my dreams and when I'm awake.

I hear Gosh in the voices but Gosh is dead for we have unsubscribed to Him.

Please stop.

I'm so tired.

There is no silence in this machine.

JUNE 7, 2019
BACKSTAGE OF LEWIS THEATRE, DIEFENBAKER UNIVERSITY,
TORONTO, 7:03PM

I save the document as 'The Confession of Peter 'Petrol' Riley Part X' and I close the laptop. I ask Lisa to hang on to it for me and she says that she will, and I believe her fully and completely. I value and trust her right now more than anyone.

And maybe I'm about to lose her along with everything else, I still haven't decided.

I get the one-minute warning signal from a stagehand and I try to focus myself and get into character, but he doesn't seem to be coming. I think about what Josh told me—about this being the best opportunity I'll ever get to come clean and end the performance. The grift. The troll. It's not like it was his idea, I've thought about it plenty of times before, but I think hearing it said by someone else—someone I respect, someone who has seen me at my most vulnerable and frustrated—that made it a real possibility. I take a look around the backstage area of the Lewis Theatre, this place where I used to wait in anxious excitement for a chance to perform and feel alive with every reservoir of my heart overflowed. I hear the end of my introduction and am given my cue to enter stage right.

"And please remember, no recording or flash photography is permitted, and we are enacting a zero-tolerance policy for any heckling, dissent, or interruptions of any kind during the discussion this evening. And now, please welcome to this full-capacity event—he's been called the most controversial content creator on the continent, the man whose ideas were deemed 'too dangerous for Twitter'—ladies and gentlemen of the sold-out Lewis Theatre and to the hundreds of thousands of you across the world watching the livestream, Petrol Riley!"

I walk onto the stage, my legs operating on some autonomous instinct, and am swallowed by the reception drawn cacophonic and rapturous. The last time I was on this stage was nearly three years ago when I received my degree from the Diefenbaker University's Department of Theatre and Performance Studies. Even then, with the room populated by all manner of relatives and revelers, there weren't as many people as there are right now. All of them here to see me. To hear me. To have me recognize and validate their fears and anxieties and frustrations and channel them with anger and hatred toward something tactile and identifiable. And maybe they thought that I was their voice, but I think the truth is that they just never really knew what they were supposed to say. Neither did I.

I take the podium and wait in silence as the applause slowly subsides. As I wait, I'm struck with a barrage of visions and memories so visceral and urgent that my head turns vertiginous and my balance nearly betrays me.

I see Josh Garrison's white smile as he asks me if this is the person I want to be. I hear the hoarse voice of the fat Bobby Rango, strained from decades of retching venom, one looming heart failure away from his demise. I taste the gin and orange juice that I drank with Justin MacDonnell in our shared basement as we drowned our future fears. I see the lettering of my name printed on the 'Best Individual Performance' award I received from the provincial high school drama competition. I feel the bullet shattering Chris Fuller's spine. I suffer the hatred in the heart of Nathan Myles. I see the balance in my bank account. I see the number of my followers and subscribers, never static and always rising. I smell the perfume of the woman who slept with me on virtue of my name alone. I see the dimple on the face of Lisa Brooke reveal itself during those rare times that I made her laugh. I feel myself at age thirteen staying up too late while ingesting Limez González videos, and I hear Limez, twelve years later, cursing the other party goers as he's dragged out of a Malibu mansion. I sense the fear that I felt three years ago as my acting career failed to flash alight, tantamount as it was to impending death. I see two futures before me, vivid and real, painted bold with sorrows and doubts and regrets and triumphs and longings for the other. I see two futures—one actualized and lived and one delegated to sustaining the wellspring of fantasy—the one I meet dependent now on a choice that will be made in the coming seconds.

I see the legions of fans—my fans—quieted now and looking up to me in reverent expectation.

And as I looked out onto their eager and admiring faces, ready to hang on my every word and absorb and accept anything I was about to tell them, I finally knew in that illuminating moment what I was going to do.

END

MANY MILLENNIA FROM NOW
· EPILOGUE

Humanity, in what little of it we can still recognize in our reflections, from trepidatious tiptoeing to star-faring further than what we here have ever been able to see. From some inherent desire, whether consecrated or humanistic, we have tested the limits of the possible to the furthest edges of the universe, propelled by dead and dying stars and those still yet to take form. The plastic in the Earth's waters has all decomposed, the shells of our corporeal biology outgrown and transcended toward a new form composed of light and that which has yet to be named. There we arrive at the end of the observable world—the uterine walls that once shielded us from our first steps into the great beyond and all that is soon to be known. The collective will of a species made manifest. And they might resemble you or I. And they might have hopes and dreams and fears and empathies like you or I. They were you or I, and now, over an ocean of stars and astral palettes, the first of our successors have reached the end of the known world.

And when they arrive, they take turns writing dirty words on the walls before they leave.

Acknowledgments

Troll was conceived, written, and edited during a tumultuous time (personally and globally) and was only allowed to exist because the following people helped to make it happen.

For all those who read early versions of *Troll*: Ashley, Christine, Nat, Brittany, TK, Beej, Niki, Marion, and Josh—thank you for your insights, suggestions, edits, and honesty. I value your feedback immensely and your friendships even more still.

For Chris and the crew at NON Publishing—thanks for taking a chance on this strange journey (and once again on me).

Being a book largely about the Internet, it follows that nearly every word of *Troll* was written and edited while under the influence of vaporwave, and I suggest it be read that way as well: Jason Sanders, Windows96, Vektroid, FM Skyline, desert sand feels warm at night, Waterfront Dining, haircuts for men, Hotel Pools (and many others I've failed to list here), thank you for the soundscapes you've provided and for allowing your creativity to inspire my own.

Finally, an extra special thank-you to Marion, for being the most supportive and encouraging friend that an insecure writer-type could ever hope to have.

See you in Hixon.